S0-BEG-998

LIFE ON MARS

-A NOVEL-

ROBERT KLOSE

Black Rose Writing | Texas

2019 by Robert Klose

All rights reserved. No part of this book may be reproduced, stored in a retrieval system or transmitted in any form or by any means without the prior written permission of the publishers, except by a reviewer who may quote brief passages in a review to be printed in a newspaper, magazine or journal.

The author grants the final approval for this literary material.

First printing

This is a work of fiction. Names, characters, businesses, places, events, and incidents are either the products of the author's imagination or used in a fictitious manner. Any resemblance to actual persons, living or dead, or actual events is purely coincidental.

ISBN: 978-1-68433-304-2
PUBLISHED BY BLACK ROSE WRITING
www.blackrosewriting.com

Printed in the United States of America
Suggested Retail Price (SRP) $17.95

Life on Mars is printed in Calluna

PRAISE FOR ROBERT KLOSE

For *Adopting Alyosha*

"...[M]ight be considered requisite reading for anyone planning to do what Klose did...instructive..."
—Dave Eggers, *The New York Times Book Review*

"A combination journal, travelogue and, above all, love story, this is a wonderful read, even for those uninvolved in adoption."
—*Publisher's Weekly*

"The climax of the story...reads like a cold-war thriller."
—David Conrads, The Christian Science Monitor

For *The Three-Legged Woman and Other Excursions in Teaching*

"Professor Robert Klose has produced a delightful book that will warm the hearts of all educators. The writing is crisp and entertaining and provides a refreshing personal perspective on the sadly unappreciated teaching profession."
—Eric Scerri, author of *The Periodic Table: Its Story and Its Significance*

For *Long Live Grover Cleveland*

"The author, a college professor, does a very nice job of keeping the tone light and of using his characters to generate the laughs. There's even a nifty twist ending. Good fun for fans of campus satire."
—David Pitt, *Booklist*

"Long Live Grover Cleveland has a good, entertaining story line that many people can enjoy—especially if they went to a small college in the '70s. Robert Klose writes in a similar style to what you might see in Dave Barry—light and whimsical."
—*LibraryThing*

"Long Live Grover Cleveland is a delicious farce."
—Deb Baker, *The Mindful Reader*

"Long Live Grover Cleveland—quickly sweeps you into a story about academia that's an exploration of the extremes of personalities you'll find on college campuses and a story of relationships in a light, irreverent tone."
—*Bangor Daily News*

Well-written, Long Live Grover Cleveland is an entertaining look at academic life, filled with both subtle and laugh out loud observations on the egos and insecurities that fuel it. ...An enjoyable read...particularly for anyone who has experienced college life in any form.
—Lynne Hinkey, *Underground Book Reviews*

For Mary Gardner
The finest mind I have ever known

Acknowledgments

I am grateful to the following for taking the time to read my manuscript and render thoughtful comments: William Bart, Robert Favarato, Eric Furry, Richard May, Cathie Pelletier, Paul Puccio, Deborah Rogers, James Spruce

LIFE ON MARS

*It is even harder for the average ape to believe
that he has descended from man.*

- H.L. Mencken

ONE
BEGINNING

Life on Earth was different before the Treatment. But before the Treatment, there was the Reinterpretation. And before the Reinterpretation, my best friend Poye and me were just two normal Maine boys, part angel, part impossible. We didn't know it at the time, but an incident in the summer of our twelfth year would change our lives forever.

"Poye!" I sang beneath his bedroom window. I glanced about like a frightened bird, worrying that somebody would hear me. "Poye! Let's go!"

I launched a pebble and, just my luck, it cracked the window. "Goddamn," through gritted teeth. Poye was my best friend, but also my slowest. I stood there in the dark, under the tulip tree, and continued to wait, dancing from foot to foot like I had to pee bad, but I was just nervous. My mom didn't want me roaming at night.

Finally, a light flashed, and Poye showed his face in the cracked glass. He put a finger to his lips and then proceeded to run that same finger along the crack, examining it with stars in his eyes, like it was a rare butterfly. "Poye!" I rasped through cupped hands. "Come on. It's hot, and the pond is waiting."

Poye pulled the window up and crawled out backward, on his belly, his bare legs kicking for a toehold on the roof shingles. "I-I'm gonna fall," he worried.

"If you fall I'll catch you," I said, not knowing how I could do such a thing, since Poye was chunky.

"The shingles are scraping my legs," he fretted.

"Then hurry."

Poye made it to the edge of the roof and shimmied down the copper drainpipe. He jumped off halfway, hitting the ground with a thud. "I scraped my hands!" he said, throwing them out for emphasis. "Look!"

"Girl!" I said, slapping his hands away. "Let's go." We ran off together into the night.

There hadn't been a hotter day in Sledge, Maine, since anybody could remember. The old-timers liked to talk about winters when the snow piled up to the second-floor windows and cars disappeared under the drifts, but they never talked about heat because it was such a rare thing. "A fluke," they were saying now, telling exaggerations about car tires melting and the tar on the streets becoming soupy. Mr. Beaulieu had bought a live, snapping lobster down at the pound and before he got home fifteen minutes later, it was as limp as a washcloth. "Heat exhaustion in a lobster," he said. "You ever hear such a thing?" People didn't even walk their dogs on the hot pavement. Mrs. Osnoe tried to, but her pug, Tippy, yowled in pain as it lifted its little paws in a kind of dance before she swept him up in her arms and took him inside. The next time she walked him he was wearing booties.

Which is why Poye and me decided to light out for Debec Pond. We had to do something. Nobody had air conditioning, so when you opened a window to admit a breeze, it was like a furnace.

After fifteen minutes of hustling through the woods, we were there. "Come on, Poye," I urged. We hunched low and snuck down the slope through a thicket of wild honeysuckle that tore at our clothes. We got to the big flat diving rock and raised our faces to a full moon throwing a blanket of light over the water. I kicked my sneakers off and dipped a toe. "It feels good, Poye. Let's strip."

We shed our clothes and slipped into the pond, our pale bodies shining in the moonlight. We both went under and then came up, our heads bobbing, our hair slicked down like helmets. Poye sighed with delight. "I think I'm gonna cry, Nest."

"What are you talking about?"

"I'm just so happy, Nest. I want to stay here forever. I'll bet if other people knew where we were they'd be jealous that we found a way to cool off."

I smiled. "Yeah," I said. "I know what you mean. J-Jeezum," I chattered. "My nuts are like prunes. Why is the water so cold? You'd think the heat wave would make it hot."

"Because it's spring-fed from below."

"I like you, Poye. You know things."

We swam around a bit, then crawled onto the diving rock, where we stretched out on our backs, our hands knotted behind our heads. "The moon's washed things out," said Poye.

"What?"

"The moon," he repeated. "You can't see a lot of stars. They're washed out by the light of the moon."

"Yeah," was all I could think to say. And then I fixed my eyes on a big, creamy yellow point of light that was hanging over the tops of the pines on the other side of the pond. "Except for that one."

"It's beautiful," said Poye. "But it's not a star. It's a planet. You can tell because planets don't twinkle. I think it's Venus."

The thing was, neither of us could keep our eyes off it. It was like a magnet. A magnet of light. "I-I think it's getting bigger," I said.

"No," said Poye. "It's just an optical illusion. Probably because of the heat. It makes strange waves in the air that turn into mirages, like when you're in a car and it looks like there's water on the road up ahead, but when you get there it's gone."

I considered this. "You're smart, Poye." I watched as he sat up and crawled to the edge of the rock. He bent down and peered at his reflection in the water. "Nest," he said.

"Yeah?"

"I'm wicked ugly."

"Well, so was Abe Lincoln, but he made out okay."

"Until somebody shot him."

"Can't you talk about positive things, Poye? You always got to turn our conversations dark." I noticed a hand-sized bruise on the side of his body. "What happened there?" I said, pointing.

Poye craned his neck around. "Oh, that was just Joe."

Joe Christiani was the official school bully, a pig-eyed, freckle-faced blob who was about two and a half times the size of your average sixth grader. He was also a liar and a thief. My mom said Joe would steal the Lord's supper and come back for breakfast. He once took my skateboard from the dooryard without a second thought, like he was entitled to it. He decided on day one of middle school that he didn't like Poye, and the rest was history. "He still bothering you?"

"It's not so bad," said Poye in his even, unexcitable way.

"You want me to take care of him?"

Poye looked at me and smiled. I was scrawny, but there weren't too many things I was afraid of. I could think of ways to get at Joe without him knowing who had done it.

"No, it's okay," said Poye as he stretched out next to me again. "I just have to think things through." We were good and dry now, the heat settling back over our bodies like a heavy blanket. And then, "Nest?"

"Yeah."

"You're right. That planet's getting bigger."

"Maybe it's a plane," I said. We both rose to a crouch.

So there we were, naked on a rock, staring up at a growing light like two wolves about to bay at the moon. Of the billions of boys in the world, we two were the ones who were about to make a special kind of history.

"Nest," began Poye without taking his eyes from that light, "you ever wonder..."

"You gonna ask me one of your you-ever-wonder questions now?"

"Well, you ever wonder if there's life in space?"

"Sure I do. Everybody does."

Poye closed his eyes to think, and then he said, "Some people say that we're all alone and it would be a miracle if there was life on another planet. But I look at it the opposite. When you consider how big the universe is, I think it would be a miracle if there wasn't life out there."

I sighed. "Did I ever tell you I wish I had your brains, Poye?"

"A million times," he said, still with his eyes closed. "But you're just as smart as I am. You gotta read books, though." He opened his eyes. "Nest!" he hollered. "Jump! Go!"

Like a shot, we were in the water. When we bobbed up, there was this umbrella of light capping us. I tried to look up at it, but it blinded something awful. "Go under, Poye!"

"I-I can't, Nest," he said. "I'm frozen stiff. I can't move a muscle."

I couldn't, either. My toes were just touching bottom, and there they stayed. I clamped my lids shut with all my might. "Close your eyes, Poye! Just c-close your eyes!"

Even through closed lids, I could see the light. It was all around us. But it wasn't hot or anything. "Poye! Don't look! Keep your eyes closed!" And I did what Father Alger at Sacred Heart Church said to do in times of crisis. I prayed. "Hail Mary, full of grace... Poye, pray with me!"

"I-I forgot the prayer, Nest."

"Then I'll pray for both of us. ...the Lord is with Thee..."

"Nest! Hold my hand!"

"...blessed art thou among sinners...I mean, women. I can't, Poye. I can't move a pinky." I wanted to stay strong for Poye. "It can't last forever," I said.

"Just start counting."

"One..."

"Keep going!"

"Two..."

Wait for instructions

"What?"

"Three!"

And then the world was dark again. Like somebody flicked a switch. Except for the full moon, which still smiled down. Poye and me looked at each other. We could move again. "Wh-what was that?" he begged. "I'm wicked scared." And then, "Nest, I peed in the pond."

"What did you say to me about instructions?"

Poye pulled back. "What are you talking about, Nest? What instructions?"

"Nothing," I said. And then, "It had to be the Holy Ghost. You remember what they told us in church, when the apostles had those flames dance on their heads at Pentecost, and they got all kinds of powers?"

Poye's face went wide. "Yeah, I remember, Nest, but I don't feel like I have powers."

"Maybe we just have to think about things for a while before we understand. Before my dad died, he told me that everything becomes clear in time."

Poye nodded. "Your dad was smart. So you must be smart too."

"You're the smart one, Poye," I offered. "You're just too dumb to know it." We crawled back out of the pond and stood on the diving rock. My knees were knocking. A cloud passed in front of the moon and the sky became studded with stars. I could hear Poye's teeth chattering, so I decided to calm him by talking normally. "Look at that red star there, Poye," I said, pointing. "I think it's Mars. I'd go to Mars if I had the chance. Wouldn't you?" Of course, at that moment I was thinking of my bed. I didn't give a damn about Mars.

"Yeah," said Poye, still catching his breath. "We'd go together."

I let this thought hang in the air for a bit. We finally calmed down. "Let's get dressed. It's time to go home. I'm not gonna swim in a pond you pissed in."

We wandered back the way we had come, neither of us saying a word. I gave Poye a boost back up the drainpipe, and then I lit off for home. The trailer was dark, so I knew mom was stone asleep. I lay awake that night, but I left the curtains open, so I could see that light if it came back. So that if it wanted me, it could find me.

I didn't understand then what had happened. But, as my dad told me, everything became clear in time. Especially as the day of the Treatment approached. In the meantime, I waited for instructions.

Two
Poye

It's hard to understand Poye as a man, and the role he would play in the Treatment, unless you know a little bit about how he came to be Poye in the first place, so let me fill you in.

Actually, Poye's given name was "Foye," but his mother pronounced F's as P's, and so "Poye" stuck. You can imagine the handicap of having such a moniker. Kindergarten and first grade went smoothly enough, as kids at those ages have larger fish to fry, like learning to tie their shoes and pee in the bowl and not on the floor. But by third grade, they've gained enough confidence in basic life skills that they find themselves with time on their little hands to look around for opportunities to make mischief. Once they became aware of the name "Poye Trubb" they decided that Poye was somehow different and began to bother him. At first, the taunts were little more than a nuisance, like when in third grade his classmates filled his gym shoes with potato chips. But by sixth grade, they were filling his shoes with dog shit. The teachers were aware of these shenanigans, and they were sympathetic, but not to the point where they took any kind of action for the sake of one unfortunate soul.

And so Poye bore up. He was, after all, the first of four siblings, and first children tend to suck things up and quietly persist. Unfortunately, things did not improve in high school. In addition to having the uninviting name Poye Trubb, he was pudgy, with hunched shoulders. None of this escaped the porcine alpha bully Joe Christiani, who smacked Poye around as a matter of course — all the while commanding him, "Fight back! Fight back!" — and for no good reason (as if a good reason could exist).

But Poye bore up. Because he was a first child and had something that would come to be near and dear to my heart: Perspective. Poye saw himself as a solitary individual walking a narrow road that, in several years' time, would come to an end, freeing him at last. Joe Christiani was the one who had no Perspective, and what happens when one has no Perspective? Well, that's simple too. Little things become big things. Nothings become somethings. Things lose track of their proper places. The result is that things don't go well in the end.

And so Joe was guilty of mistaking the little thing that Poye was for a big thing that needed to be taken care of. I remember one incident in particular.

One day, in the middle school locker room, when Poye and I were changing up, a crowd gathered around a little stray mutt that had wandered in. It was a mangy, unloved thing with patches of hair missing. Joe picked it up, drew it back over his head like a football, and yelled, "Go out for a pass!" A bunch of boys ran back, waving wildly. "Here!" they sang. "Here! To me!" Just as Joe was about to launch the frightened, yelping creature, Poye swooped in and fetched the animal from his hand, so that when Joe lunged forward, he threw nothing but air. Everyone laughed. Joe was humiliated. Hate boiled in his eyes.

Joe cornered Poye and me. Poye was cradling the terrified puppy. Like all bullies, Joe had his cheering section — four toadies: two with skinny wrists, one with a mask of freckles, and the fourth a kid nicknamed "Bucky" for his horribly snaggled teeth. (When he talked it sounded like "Fa-fa-fa.") Poye looked bewildered as Joe and his boys circled in. "Are you afraid?" Joe taunted.

Poye, still cradling the whimpering puppy, paused to give this some thought, as if it were a question worth pondering. He didn't look scared, even though he could see that Joe and the others were closing on him and there wasn't a thing he could do to stop them. But something motivated him to ask a question. He swallowed hard, pulled himself together, glanced at me, and then raised his pitiful eyes to Joe. "Are you going to hurt me?"

This query stopped Joe and his claque dead in their tracks. The sycophants looked to their leader for direction. Joe hated himself for hesitating, and he hated Poye for making him hesitate. In a move to save face, he ordered his toadies to grab hold of the two of us. The two skinny-wristed ones pulled my arms behind my back while Bucky and Freckles grabbed the puppy from Poye, gave it to Joe, and pulled Poye's arms back in the same way. "Let go!" I growled, kicking at the air. Joe smiled his pig-eyed smile with deep satisfaction. But Poye didn't even peep. I watched as a strange scene began to unfold. Joe opened Poye's locker and, with his free hand, removed all his gym stuff. But he didn't rip it out and throw it on the floor, as you might expect. Instead, he began to hum as he carefully laid everything out in a neat pile on a bench, very businesslike. And then the hum became a whistle as he nodded to Bucky and Freckles. "There you go," said Joe as he laid his own paw on Poye's arm as well. "Now lift your foot. That's it. Step up."

I watched, my eyes wide, as Poye did as he was told. He put a foot forward and stepped into his locker. Then the other three pushed him, wedging him in but good. As Joe handed Poye the dog, the little thing snapped and bit Joe's finger. "Goddamn!" he roared as the animal clawed its way up Poye's shirt. "Close the door!" he commanded as he sucked the wound.

The last thing I saw as the toadies complied was my friend's eyes, full of sadness, as they disappeared in the darkness. Joe, still sucking his wound, put his own combination lock on the handle and spun the little wheel. "There," he said like he had just finished a good day's work. "Let's go."

They released me, and I stood there in my rage, but what could I do? Joe and his toadies left the building. I went up to the locker and squinted through the little vent. "Poye? You okay?"

"It's dark in here, Nest. I can't move. And the dog is scratching me something awful."

"Why'd you cooperate like that? It's like you wanted to go in there."

"I just wanted to get away from him, and I knew he couldn't follow me into the locker. But it's so cramped in here."

"I'll get the custodian. He's got bolt cutters." I lit off and came back running with old Mr. Bednarz, who moaned, "Oi, oi, oi," as he worked the cutters and finally snapped the lock and opened the door. The dog jumped out and ran off. Poye looked immeasurably sad as he squeezed back out, rubbing his arms.

"I shoulda kicked him in the nuts," I said by way of commiseration as we left the school and headed for home.

"It would have only made things worse," said Poye as he continued to rub his arms and drag himself along.

"Dog bite you?"

"No," said Poye. "Just scratches."

"Well, it bit Joe. He deserved it."

Poye heaved a deep breath. "I am so unhappy in school," he sighed, his voice sinking. "But I don't have the guts to leave."

I clucked my tongue. "You can't just leave, Poye. Stick it out. I'll help you.

And some of the teachers are okay."

It was true. Somewhere along the line Poye found a sympathetic teacher, Mr. Mindy, who taught biology. Like many people who have suffered personal loss — Mr. Mindy's wife and little boy had died in a car crash — he was tuned in to the pain of others. He took note of Poye and began to give him little jobs to do in the biology lab, for which Poye was grateful. In fact, he was so grateful that he resolved to earn Mr. Mindy's praise by doing nothing less than perfect work. But one day, Poye dropped a jar of sulfur, and it shattered on the floor. He cried. Mr. Mindy came over, put his arm around Poye's shoulder, and said something that Poye would never forget: "Don't worry. If this is the worst thing that happens, I think you're going to have a pretty good day."

And that's when Poye had another encounter with Perspective. He didn't call it that when he told me this story, but years later when I became an authority on the subject, I made the connection. Poye had not dropped plutonium. He had dropped sulfur. The glass could be cleaned up. The sulfur could be cleaned up. Neither was dangerous. Neither would contaminate the planet. Neither would lead to the extinction of a species. Poye never forgot Mr. Mindy or the wisdom he had imparted. Further, from this, he was able to discover a truth that demonstrated how well he had learned the lesson of Perspective: *After I am out of high school I will never again be forced into a closed space with people I don't choose to be with.*

Poye would never say a word to his parents about the incident in the locker room. His father would have simply told him to "bear up" — something that Poye was already good at. As for Joe, he would have to endure a series of painful rabies shots in his ample belly. The moral here is that Joe had made a big thing out of the little thing that Poye was and it didn't go well.

As the end of our high school years approached, Poye told me he had no plans to attend graduation. "I don't see the point, Nest," he said as we headed home one day. "I'd feel like a hypocrite, pretending like these four years were the most wonderful years of my life."

I understood what Poye was saying. He always did have trouble pretending, and it was hard to picture him up there on the stage with everyone grinning like a bunch of baboons. But I didn't want to be there without him, so I pressed. "Sometimes we have to do things for other people, Poye," I reasoned. "Maybe graduation isn't just for us. Maybe it's for our parents too."

Poye threw me a doubtful look. "My parents don't care," he said. "They fed me and gave me a place to sleep. But they never told me that they loved me. When I was little and fell, the best they could do was say, 'Get up.' Your mom was always there for you."

Well, Poye was right about that. My mom exhaled the word "love" with every breath. She constantly hugged and primped me and combed my hair. Every morning, when I went off to school, she acted like she might never see me again.

"Poye, if you don't go, I won't go," I said, even though I knew it would put a knife in mom's heart.

Poye threw me a serious look. "I can't let you hurt your mom, Nest. You had a pretty good high school experience and have a reason to celebrate. I'll tell you what — you go for both of us and that will make me happy."

So that's what I did.

It's a shame Poye didn't attend graduation because he missed the satisfaction of seeing Joe Christiani get bitten by another dog on his way into the auditorium. If Poye had had a vindictive nature, he would have considered this a just reward for the years of heartache he had suffered at Joe's hands. Instead, he never gave Joe another thought.

For a good long while, at least.

THREE
PERSPECTIVE

The thing that interrupted my friendship with Poye was geography. When people live in the same place, it's easy to stay friends because you see each other all the time. But when you move away, you make new friends in new places. That's what happened after graduation. My mother was shocked when I got into Wytopitlock College, the only place that would take me. "It's unbelievable," she told everyone in the trailer park. "My Nestor. In college." I guess I understood her joy because, for one, nobody in my family had ever gone to college. I wasn't sure some of them could even spell "college." For two, my grades were pretty miserable because I had spent most of my time in high school screwing around.

Poye got into Yale, but that was expected because, even though he didn't have much common sense, he was book-smart. Even with Joe Christiani on his heels, he had gotten all A's in high school, like an act of defiance, or strength, to show that even when he was being chased down by the school bully, he could ace his courses without breaking a sweat.

We went down to Debec Pond on the last summer day before leaving for college. Only this time it was broad daylight and not so hot. Poye wasn't so chunky anymore. He had stretched out but still had those hunched shoulders, which made him look like a question mark. His short hair and thick glasses gave him an owlish appearance, like he was always considering a deep thought. I was skinny as a whip and had let my own hair grow long, with my mother's blessing. "Do what you want with it while you have it," she said, "because your father was bald as a cue ball."

We sat next to each other on that same diving rock where we used to skinny dip, our knees drawn up to our chests. "So what're you gonna study?" I asked while staring out over the water, feeling lost.

"Biology," said Poye. "I always liked bugs and things. And Mr. Mindy was my favorite teacher. He inspired me."

"You'll be good at that. You're smart."

"But you're the strong one, Nest," he offered. "You kept us calm when that light came. Remember?"

I had never told anyone about that light at the pond. As far as I knew, neither had Poye. Over the years we tried to explain it to each other in all sorts of ways. Ball lightning, or fireworks, or someone playing a prank with a searchlight. "I was wrong, Poye," I said. "We're eighteen now, and it's time to admit that it had nothing to do with the Holy Ghost or Pentecost. It was what you call an unexplained phenomenon."

"I suppose."

"Give it time," I said. "It'll become clear." The truth was that I didn't care to think about it anymore. I felt like I had outgrown the memory, and I was no longer waiting for instructions.

"That's what your dad said," Poye reminded me.

"Yeah."

"So what are you going to major in?"

I shrugged, picked up a stone, and flung it plop into the water. "No idea," I said. "Someone told me that if you don't know what to study you should study philosophy."

"Philosophy," said Poye, softly, like he was tasting the word.

"I guess."

And that was that. Poye went off to Yale, and I went to Wytopitlock College in the Maine woods, not ten miles down the road. We did our best to stay in touch — meeting up during Christmas break and every summer during our college years — and Poye did major in biology, and I did major in philosophy, and I did make new friends. Over time Poye, like that light over Debec Pond, threatened to become a memory that I would outgrow. And yet, on dark nights, even in the dead of winter when the air was so cold it felt hot, I looked up and couldn't shake the feeling that one of those stars knew who I was. Who we were. That's when I wished Poye was with me because he would understand without my having to say a word.

• • • • •

If the four years of high school passed quickly, the four years of college went like a rocket. If my mother was shocked when I got into college, she all but fainted when I graduated. The truth is that I had become interested in school and got good grades. My philosophy professors said I had a bright future. By the time I was a senior I had even developed a research interest. Yes, Perspective — the idea that everything develops context if you can make the world around it big enough. Look at it like this. If you got some poems published in the Wytopitlock Student Literary Review, you would think you were really something. But if you moved to a bigger place, say Boston, no one would give a hoot about your poems.

After Wytopitlock I went off to get my master's degree at the University of Maine. But degrees are like scabs: once you start picking them, you gotta keep going. So I got another degree, a doctorate, from the University of New Hampshire. And that one let me write my own ticket. By the fall after my graduation, I had come full circle and got hired as an assistant professor of philosophy at Wytopitlock College. I was on my way. And in a very short time, I became the world's foremost expert on Perspective. I dealt with Perspective in the arts and sciences. I wrote articles and papers, and even books, on the subject, including *Say Perspective Three Times Fast* and *Perspective for Idiots.* But most importantly I became very well known to the Elders of Spong, who had been monitoring me — and Poye — ever since that night at the pond. That umbrella of light had been their calling card and a preamble to their promised instructions.

FOUR
DARWIN

Before I tell you how Poye and I reconnected — and in a very different, reinterpreted America — I need to say something about evolution, for two reasons. One: Poye would eventually teach evolution, which would get him into trouble. Two: for the Spong, evolution was the whole ball of wax. Please bear with me.

When I look back at my career as a writer and lecturer on the subject of Perspective, I am astounded at the hullabaloo the mere mention of evolution caused. I could say "rape," "murder," "child abuse," "torture," "lobotomy," "incest" or "jock itch" with impunity and people would do little more than yawn. But if I said "evolution" they went ballistic. Some called Darwin *The Antichrist.* Ouch.

Poor Darwin. He couldn't find peace even in death. But even as a child he was hectored by his own flesh and blood. His father once remarked, "You care for nothing but shooting, dogs, and rat-catching, and you will be a disgrace to yourself and all your family." One can imagine how lonely the young Darwin was. He was hounded into medical school but left. Then he was hounded into divinity school but barely finished. He finally set sail on the *HMS Beagle* and spent his days at sea puking over the gunnels. What a life.

But although he was uncertain about his future, and lacked parental encouragement, he had the big tamale — Perspective. Of all the souls on earth at the time — 1.2 billion by my guess — Darwin was preeminent among the few who got the big picture. He said that we humans had not been planted on earth like daisies, but were the product of natural laws acting around us. In short, he took a step back, surveyed the general landscape, and saw humans as subject to the same laws as cockroaches and box turtles. In other words, humans were, like all creatures, basically snuffling for food and sex.

This idea of evolution — the greatest idea in all of science history —

earned Darwin great applause but also great opprobrium. He was vilified for daring to suggest that man was not a custom model but rather a stock collection of cells and genes and fluids like any other living thing, and that he had descended from lower orders of animals. And that's how the word "evolution" came to excite the passions. In fact, an attendee at one of my lectures had looked up at me in astonishment when I uttered the word "evolution," sprung to his feet, and commanded, "Let's get him!" I am ashamed to say that I ran from the stage and out of the building. Due to such unanticipated aggressions, I judiciously avoided mentioning the word ever again. I did not have the courage of Poye Trubb, who became hopelessly entangled with evolution but would make no apologies, even when people threatened to do him great harm.

Even though Darwin and evolution would cause Poye no end of grief, the irony was that Poye himself was exquisite evidence of survival of the fittest. Despite all his adversities — unsympathetic parents, Joe Christiani, and an unlovely appearance — he somehow adapted to survive where many of his detractors failed.

And so Poye Trubb moved on into his future. He didn't want to be like his dad, who had told him, "Go along to get along." Instead he wanted to be like Mr. Mindy, who, besides imparting the wisdom of the spilled sulfur, had told him other things, such as, "You can't eat an omelet without ketchup," "A watched pot can be pretty boring," and "Beggars can't be astronauts." At the time, Poye didn't understand any of this. It was years before he realized these were Mr. Mindy's attempts to be funny. Which leads me to another truth about Poye: I never saw him laugh. Not even a titter. Or a chuckle. And then, one day — I think it was during the summer after our junior year in college — he told me a story.

"Nest, do you remember Mr. Mindy?"

"Sure. The sulfur."

"That's right. Well, he was so kind to me and all, but I never really understood a lot of the things he said to me, even though I knew he was saying them to cheer me up. Things like, 'People who live in glass houses should keep their clothes on.' Nest, there must have been something wrong with me. But I think I'm cured."

"What the hell are you talking about?"

Poye smiled the sweetest smile. "It was like a dam broke. All of a sudden, I understood. I was sitting in my evolution class at the university when I finally got it: Mr. Mindy had been kidding me. For the first time in my life I laughed, I really laughed, like an idiot, right in Professor Todelaw's class. He's my favorite professor, absolutely brilliant, and there I was, laughing as he talked about natural selection and the evolution of the horse. I just couldn't stop. Professor Todelaw's face turned red, and he demanded that I shut up. He made chopping motions with his arm. I finally pulled myself together and stumbled out of the lecture hall, doubled over, while the whole class looked at me. I was so sick from laughing that I bent over a railing and puked my guts out. My God, Nest. It felt so good."

"Well, that's a great story, Poye," I said. "But I feel cheated."

"What do you mean?"

"You would have been so much more fun to be with if you had laughed when we were growing up."

Poye's expression fell. "I guess I didn't have all that much to laugh about," he shrugged.

"Excuses," I said with a wave. I really was annoyed with him. "Well, better late than never. So what happens now?"

Poye's answer was immediate. "I want to teach biology, just like Professor Todelaw. I want to be as smart as he is. I want to help people understand Darwin and evolution."

Poye should have been careful about what he wished for. The Spong had already marked him as an object of study. It was also around this time that the country was deep into the Reinterpretation, and the changes wouldn't help Poye in the least. In fact, they would make life very, very difficult for him.

Poye didn't do anything special with his life after he graduated Yale. At least not right away. Who would have guessed that I would be the one to make something of myself while Poye, with all his smarts, wallowed? And yet, surprising things sometimes come to those who least expect them, and it was this very wallowing that brought something into Poye's life that would change his entire trajectory.

FIVE
LOVE

There is a very good reason not to be cynical about love. From Gilgamesh to the Christ narrative to Bambi, love is what makes stories go. Poye's story would prove to be no exception.

If you were to look at Poye Trubb's life, you would say that I was wrong. That every story is not about love. Because there was no evidence of love in Poye's life. Like Darwin, he had been an unloved child. Poye's father had been distant if not cruel. It was no secret that Rand Trubb left the house early in the morning before his kids were up, and returned home after they had gone to bed. This left Poye's long-suffering mom to shift for both of them. Sweating at home doing piece work as a seamstress, she was always too tired to shed much affection on her spawn. Whenever my mom spotted Poye's dad coming home so late, she would rouse me from sleep just to squeeze the life out of me. "You are loved, loved, loved," she said like a broken record. "Don't you ever forget that."

And so, yes, compared to me, at least, Poye had been an unloved child. Nor had any females taken notice of him in high school. Or college either, so far as I knew. The truth is, there wasn't much to notice. A chemist, if he were to assay Poye, would conclude that he was pH7: average height, average weight, light but not blond hair, gray eyes, and a Buster Keaton expression. He didn´t look like a man but like the pattern from which a man might be fashioned. By the time he graduated college, he no longer walked with a hunch, although he did tend to shuffle. But, true to my theory, Poye's story came to involve love as well. And I was there when it happened.

After I got my doctorate, and my plum job at Wytopitlock College, I reconnected with Poye. We were both twenty-six, eight years out of high school. For some reason — perhaps a simple lack of *oompf* — Poye had faltered after getting his Yale degree and didn't do anything with it. He was living in a studio apartment in an old clapboard building in a run-down section of Bangor and working part-time at a recyclables depot, counting cans and bottles. When I walked in and saw his mean surroundings — a cot, a flea-bitten easy chair, and a hotplate for cooking — I was filled with pity for my old friend. I noticed that he was wearing a cross pendant around his neck, just like me, both of us good, obedient citizens of the newfangled Theocratic Union of American States. "Hosanna," he said as he extended his hand. "Welcome to paradise."

"Thoreau would approve."

"Do you?" he asked without missing a beat.

"You've never needed my approval, Poye."

He shook his head. "You're wrong, Nest. Don't you remember? You were always the one I wanted to please."

"If that's true, then please me now by letting me buy you a meal."

Poye glanced dolefully at his grease-encrusted hotplate. "Okay," he said, and we went out into the cold winter evening.

My inviting Poye to dinner turned out to be the most propitious thing I ever did for him. It would change the course of his life in a way neither of us could ever have imagined.

We left Poye's apartment and headed down Main Street. The frigid wind cut like a knife and flurries dusted the air. Poye buried his face in the collar of his tired peacoat as we trudged along, looking for an inviting place to eat. We came to a buzzing neon sign — *Briody's Tavern* — and heard a woman's voice like the howling of a banshee. This elicited Poye's scientific curiosity. I had never known him to visit a bar, but the pull was now magnetic. "Nest, let's go in here." I glanced at the place — its litter-strewn entrance reeked of vomit— and wrinkled my nose. "This is my speed, Poye," I said, "but isn't it a bit much for you?"

"The sign says they have sandwiches."

Well, we weren't going to get any warmer standing there, so we went in.

Do you know the old saw about opposites attracting? Well, it's often true. In Poye Trubb's case the woman who came into his life was as opposite to him as possible (although it's not difficult to be the opposite of a man with neither personality nor looks). It wasn't long before I learned a great deal about her, simply by sitting at the bar. Her name was Clara Knock, queen of the barmaids at Briody's. She was a fiery, big-boned, square-jawed woman of Irish stock, with brick-red hair and expressive hands, which she waved about when she spoke, theatrically, like a magician about to conjure an orange out of thin air. Her characteristic pose was to stand with her fists on her hips, as if challenging all comers, "You wanna fight? Come on!" She had a reputation for gathering men the way a reaper gathers corn. Her appetite in this regard was phenomenal, the way it was for most everything in her life: drink, laughter, food, tobacco, and song.

Through the smoke and dim light, he saw her, perched on a high stool, holding up a mug of beer and calling out for more, her breasts wiggling like two massive bowls of Jello under her loose, frilly top. Clara locked eyes with Poye, gestured toward him with her beer, and downed the whole thing while a covey of drunken, mostly middle-aged men cheered her on and groped her thighs as she swatted them away with her free hand. She chortled triumphantly, like a Valkyrie, and hopped down from the stool. She waved Poye over, but he turned his head away, mortified, and began to head for the door while I looked on from my bar stool. Of all the other men in the room, he was the only one not clawing for Clara's attention. This apparently electrified her interest in him. She muscled her way through the crowd and latched onto Poye's arm, catching him just before he was able to escape. "Another man for me!" she sang, and the crowd roared. Of course, Poye had no way of knowing that for the insatiable Clara, any man was the man for her. His face flared red. "Hosanna," he greeted her, and Clara frowned. "Don't you 'Hosanna' me," she scolded. "Leave the Theocratic Union out on the street."

Poye had never had a girlfriend and, so far as I knew, he had never been touched by a woman before, although, when we were teens, he had confided to me that he assumed that girls were soft and smooth. I'm sure he hadn't anticipated the vice-like grip that now compressed his flesh to the bone, making him wince. This woman's gravity was inescapable. Poye was helpless, but he didn't seem to be in any particular distress. I sat on my bar stool, nursing my beer, and looked on with fascination as Poye dissolved in Clara's attention. Every so often she absented herself to wait on a customer, but she always returned to Poye, who finally introduced me. Clara paid me only passing heed, remarking "Nice" in an offhand manner as if she were assessing a lamp she had no intention of buying.

As the night drew to a close and Briody's started putting up the chairs, Clara told Poye he would be coming home with her. He turned to me and said, "But my friend here..."

"I can walk back to your apartment," I offered. "I'll crash there."

But Clara had it all figured out. "I got a sofa," she said, and the three of us hustled out into the night, which had grown even colder, the air thick with snow.

Clara's apartment couldn't have been more convenient — directly over Briody's. With me taking up the rear, she dragged Poye up the creaky wooden steps of a dark stairwell redolent with the odors of beer and urine. But her apartment was a cozy counterpoint to this dismal vestibule: it was neat and clean, and filled with oddments. She had a lithograph of a man holding a rattlesnake, a clock with a dead butterfly on the second hand, a sea glass-encrusted table lamp, and assorted bric-a-brac, but also real furniture and, against the far wall, a small Formica table next to a window which looked out onto the street below. Completing the picture was a battered upright piano. Clara pulled bedding and a pillow from a linen closet and threw them onto the sofa. "Sleep there," she told me. Then she dragged the wide-eyed Poye into her bedroom and closed the door.

As I lay on the sofa with my hands knotted behind my head, I could hear the goings-on in the bedroom: bedsprings squealing and the slapping of flesh. It brought an image to mind of a battleship on the bounding main. Clara seemed to be playing Poye's body in crescendos of delight, but — if I was any judge of breath sounds — repeatedly, and skillfully, denying him climax, until, finally, she granted Poye release — a sensation, I was sure, as joyfully cathartic as the pent-up laughter that had exploded forth in Professor Todelaw's class. *My God, Poye*, I thought. *What are you getting yourself into?*

The next morning Clara arose just as I was opening my eyes. I heard the apartment door close behind her. It was then that I ventured to check in on my friend. And there he lay, with a shit-eating grin on his face. Still in my underwear, I sat down on the edge of the bed. "Have fun?"

Poye rolled his head toward me, still grinning. "Does it bother you that she doesn't wear a pendant?" I asked.

Poye's expression turned dreamy. "I didn't give it a thought."

"It's an arrestable offense," I said.

Poye glanced down at the floor, where his cross pendant lay coiled on top of his socks. He looked back at me. "So what should I do?"

"Be careful?" I suggested. "You don't even have a real job yet. I'd hate to see you ruin your chances."

Poye paused to think about this. "Nest," he said, "I've always listened to you and taken your advice and you've never steered me wrong. But I woke up the other day and realized I was twenty-six. Twenty-six! If I don't know how to listen to myself by now, I'm not sure I can learn."

I thought Poye's reasoning was sound, and so I kept my mouth shut, even though I knew that his becoming involved with Clara was risky stuff. My sense was that Clara had grander, more permanent designs on him, risking his Perspective, which, as I have explained, is the only thing that can save one's neck. Once Perspective is lost you're on your own. As an expert on the subject, this seemed self-evident to me. But Poye, in hooking up with the warlike Clara, was like a nearsighted man who has lost his glasses: everything looks blurry and the opportunity for all sorts of mayhem arises, simply because he can no longer see clearly. And this, of course, is what Perspective is all about: seeing clearly.

Before he met Clara, Poye was adrift. He had no direction, no guiding principles, no plans. It was like a piece of his brain was missing, and Clara filled that missing space. In short, she changed his life. Poye moved out of his sorry hovel and in with this wild woman and her bric-a-brac — tokens, Poye later told me, from men who had fallen in love with her.

I visited Poye and Clara often and soon saw that Clara was up to her elbows in Poye's hormones, radiating sex the way a stove radiates heat. And then, after sessions of love-making that lasted hours, Clara would spring to her feet and begin to cook: big, heaping goulashes, stews, pastas, and casseroles, laughing riotously with a cigarette wedged in the corner of her mouth and throwing her red hair back, having the time of her life, as if Poye's sexual pliancy were some sort of fuel, egging her on. She stuffed food into Poye as if fattening a lamb for slaughter and, with a hand thrust upon her hip and the cigarette smoldering, she watched him eat and moan with delight. Even her food aroused him. During my visits I shared the table with them as witness to this, swallowing — along with the delicious meals — any inclination to pass comment. *My God*, I thought as I chewed and swallowed, *everything she does is infused with sex.*

In light of Clara's rampant animal passions, you might be tempted to think that she was a crass woman with no control over her urges. But you would be wrong. She was intelligent and self-aware. She knew what she had, and she knew how to use it. The only mystery here is why her association with Poye was more than a dalliance. Poye was twenty-six, had a degree in biology, was marginally employed, and had no game plan. Clara was forty-five and had complete, confident control over her life. With candor and abandon, she told us she had left high school at sixteen when she realized she had done all she could: she had bedded all of the male teachers, including the seventy-six-year-old principal, Mr. Darling, who had suffered a heart attack and died with a smile on his face. Since then she had been on the move, waiting tables, tending bar, and never lacking for a man. She played men the way a virtuoso plays the violin — intimately, complexly, and never missing a note. They came at her full charge, and she deftly *jujitsued* them onto the nearest sofa, bed, futon or tabletop, extracting promises of mazuma or trade before anointing them with her sex. In a word, she had Perspective. And she had it in spades. Her judgment was finely tuned and flawless. She saw that Poye was different, and that's what intrigued her: he was the first man who hadn't come stumbling after her. And Poye, for his part, was not the least threatened by Clara's propensity to seize meat on the hoof, whenever and wherever she found it.

Clara Lee Knock was to Poye Trubb what Nora Barnacle had been to James Joyce — a propellant. She disturbed Poye so deeply, made him so restless, kept him so constantly on edge, that the only way for Poye to manifest the energy of his arousal and to alleviate this distraction, was to throw himself into some great creative endeavor. But what? He voiced his indecisiveness one night to Clara as she wrestled with him on what I had come to consider *my* sofa, while I sat at the table eating leftover ratatouille. She held him in a half nelson that almost made him pass out. She was determined, she said, to beat the milquetoast out of him. "Think!" she commanded as she gave his head a twist and Poye moaned in a queer mixture of delight and agony. "Use your assets. You have a college degree. Put it to work for you."

She barked these commands with such authority that Poye had to obey. He picked up a newspaper the next morning and spotted an ad seeking an adjunct biology instructor at, of all places, Wytopitlock College. Clara's response: "So what are you waiting for? Go!" She tossed him a set of keys. "Take my car," she said. "It's the Rambler wagon parked out front. But keep an eye on the gas. The gauge is broke. There's a dipstick under the seat."

I followed Poye out the door. As we entered the street below Clara's window, we could hear her cackling as she clattered pots and pans — her culinary encore to yet another riotous night of love-making.

SIX
FAITH

Before I tell you how Poye met with success (sorry for the spoiler), let me say something about what the place once known as the United States of America had started to become not long after we graduated high school, as the Reinterpretation got underway.

First of all, one needs to accept the truism that there's no telling how people will behave when they are made to feel afraid. For example, I read that way back in the 1950s people in the place once known as the United States of America were afraid they would be attacked with nuclear weapons by the place once known as the Union of Soviet Socialist Republics. They dug holes in the ground and filled them with food, water, guns, and toilet paper. They had things called air raid drills: when sirens sounded, they scurried into doorways, as if a doorway could protect them from a nuclear fireball. The school children were taught to duck under their desks, as if ducking under a desk could protect them from an atomic shock wave. It all seems ridiculous now, but it gives me the willies just thinking about it.

Although people came to look back and say how ridiculous it all seemed, it actually got worse. When the place once known as the Union of Soviet Socialist Republics eventually collapsed, people in the place once known as the United States of America felt a void. They were not comfortable with having nothing to be afraid of and therefore decided that everything was a threat. The list is long: immigrants, homosexuals, rich people, poor people, bosses, workers, the elderly, children, the pharmaceutical industry, farmers, airbag manufacturers, soft drinks, dodgeball, peanut products and — gulp — college professors. And that's just the short list. Eventually it was decided to reduce the number of threats to one everybody could agree on. The question was, which would it be? Thus it was that a consensus was reached that the "us" should be people who described themselves as "religious" — more specifically, Christian — and the "them" were everybody else. It couldn't be simpler than that.

Now that an enemy had been identified, all sorts of interesting things happened. The first battles were mere preambles: staving off any attempt to remove the word "God" from the Pledge of Allegiance (an oath schoolchildren were forced to recite before they were allowed to learn) and keeping *In God We Trust* on the currency. Once those traditions had been shored up, the godful pressed onward. They succeeded in inserting a new law, or amendment, into the constitution of the place once known as the United States of America, to wit: it was officially a Christian nation, in honor of the ancient Jewish philosopher Jesus Christ. This caused a great scene because the country was a mongrel nation of races and ethnicities where almost every language on earth was spoken, and where the skin colors ranged from black as the ace of spades to lily white. It was a place where you could get kosher bagels, fiery kimchi, pierogis, sushi, fish tacos, wiener schnitzel, and pizza to die for. But it had also been a place where you could pray to your god of choice and no one would bother you. Or you could choose not to pray to any god at all and no one would bother you. But this all came to an end once the people of the U.S.A. needed a new enemy. Once the U.S.A. was officially anointed a Christian nation, funny things began to happen.

First of all, the name of the country was changed to the Theocratic Union of American States. Then a cross (the Christian symbol of the ancient Jewish philosopher Jesus Christ) was added to the money. Then the Statue of Freedom on the Capitol of the T.U.A.S. was removed and replaced with — you got it — a cross. Citizens were obligated to wear identifying pendants: a cross for "Christian," a star for "Jewish," a crescent moon for "Muslim," an O for "other," or a sad face for "godless." Last, only Christians could be candidates for political office. Once people were made to feel afraid again, all of these things became possible. In fact, it was easy.

The thing was, no matter what line of work you were in, you were affected by these changes. For example, if you worked in a factory making potato chips, your day started with the Pledge of Allegiance (to the Theocratic Union of American States) and a prayer asking Jesus for potatoes with "good chipping qualities." If you were a police officer chasing down a criminal, you were required to shout, "Stop in the name of the Lord!" And if you were a politician, each and every utterance had to end with, "God bless you and God bless the Theocratic Union of American States." If you didn't say this, there would be a scene. (Talk about a loss of Perspective.) Even everyday speech was affected, with citizens now expected to greet one another with the salutation, "Hosanna!"

As a result of this, a lot of other countries developed their own new fear — of the Theocratic Union of American States. Tourism suffered because would-be visitors objected to having crosses, stars, moons, zeros and sad faces stamped in their passports. Beyond this, upon entering the country, they had to raise their right hand and swear to uphold religious principles as encoded in the mishmash of stories called *The Bible* they received as a token of welcome. Many citizens who did not want to adhere to the new way of doing things attempted to escape to Canada and Mexico, whose borders were guarded by T.U.A.S. containment troops. This gave birth to a lively smuggling operation run by opportunists called lobos. In the dead of night, they led the escapees across the border, but success was not always the outcome, and many lives were lost in the north woods and southern deserts.

Sad.

Perhaps the most insidious result of the new way of doing business was the effect it had on science, technology, and education, which is where Poye Trubb would eventually come in.

Overnight, scientific bodies such as the National Academy of Sciences, the Smithsonian Institution, and the Department of Environmental Protection found themselves being "reinterpreted." For a long time, the biggest concern of science had been an unwelcome change of climate known as "global warming," which was causing the polar ice caps to melt and the seas to rise, flooding coastal cities. (The city of Miami was the first to go.) Another big concern was the terrible disease called cancer that affected men and women and children and people of every race and ethnicity. And then there were industries that poured all sorts of cancer-causing and earth-warming chemicals into the air and water. Progress against these things had been made, slowly but surely. Until the Reinterpretation.

One day the scientists at the National Academy of Sciences, the Smithsonian Institution, the Department of Environmental Protection, and other scientific organizations came to work and found a new set of marching orders. They were instructed to change direction and not put faith in scientific data. Instead, they were to realign their thinking to correspond with the sentiments of the American people. In a word, they were to put their faith in faith. That Jesus would not allow global warming to harm us. That cancer could be better treated with prayer. And that the environment had a God-given ability to self-correct any insult inflicted upon it. Anyone who did not wish to adhere to this new way of thinking was welcome to find employment elsewhere.

Of course, most if not all of these dedicated scientists chose not to adhere. En masse, they sought out lobos to take them to Canada and Mexico, or they attempted to cross on their own. Some succeeded and took up new lives on the other side of these frontiers, but, as I said, many others lost their ways and died in the border wildernesses, their carcasses ravaged by wild animals, while others drowned in their attempts to swim or canoe to freedom.

Once again, sad.

The new government of the Theocratic Union of American States knew, instinctively, that if these changes were to be made permanent, the schools had to be reinterpreted as well, so that young people could carry the new thinking forward. And so the President's Council on Right Thinking was created — spawned of the Education Reform Act. Among its tenets was that global climate change had no basis in fact; that human disease could be best treated with an appeal to God; and that the environment, in general, was not being given enough credit for its resilience and its ability to adapt to human activity. But the most telling paragraph was one that dealt with what was perceived to be the greatest threat to the new theocracy. It was on page 66 of the Education Reform Act, to wit:

It cannot be emphasized strongly enough that the beliefs, ethics, and sensibilities of students of faith must be held in the highest regard. No student should feel alienated because he or she holds a belief not in concert with scientific conjecture about the origins and relationships of living organisms. To this end, the instructor will not threaten the religious convictions of any student by suggesting origins of life that do not concord with the record of the Christian Bible.

In other words, evolution. This idea became the solvent that threatened to unglue the entire Theocratic Union of American States.

And it was into this mire that Poye Trubb would soon step by virtue of his finding a job.

Seven
Resolve

I bided my time outside a conference room on the campus of Wytopitlock College while Poye sat behind closed doors in his bid to secure the position of biology adjunct — the lowest rung on the hiring ladder. Adjuncts were paid peanuts. They lived and taught in the hope of renewal of their positions at the end of each semester, as there was no promise of permanency, no matter how well they performed. But hey, any port in a storm. Poye had nothing to lose, and there was always the chance that an adjunct instructor might hang on long enough to replace a tenured professor once the latter retired or died.

After twenty minutes in the isolation booth, Poye emerged. I got up and waited for the verdict. His expression was hang-dog, and he was kneading his fingers. "Well?" I prompted. "Congratulations? Condolences?"

"I got the job."

"Great!" And then I shifted gears. "Then why so glum, chum? I think happiness is the appropriate response."

"I don't know how to feel," Poye said, his face blank. "I've never succeeded at anything before."

"Were there a lot of other candidates?"

"One, but he got hopelessly lost and phoned saying he couldn't find the college."

Poye told me he felt uneasy. He had thought that being a teacher meant that he had free rein in the classroom to communicate the material as clearly and effectively as he could, using whatever creative means were at his disposal. But the dean, Eulalie Wilmot, had disabused him of this assumption at the outset.

"Nest, she just sat there on the other side of the desk, with the other members of the selection committee, boring into me with those black eyes of hers."

I listened quietly as we drove home in Clara's '65 Rambler. I knew Eulalie Wilmot and her arid, austere ways. She was a drawn, cadaverous figure, her salt-and-pepper hair bobby-pinned back to showcase a broad pie face that was singularly difficult to read.

"What did she tell you?"

"Well, she started out by frowning when she said my name, like it was something distasteful. She made smacking sounds when she talked, and she kept shifting her eyes about. And then she said, 'We are looking to hire someone to do a job. The question is, can you do this job?' That's when I glanced at the three men on the committee. They were sitting there, staring with empty eyes, like sphinxes. I looked back at the dean and said, 'Yes, I'm sure I can do the job.' And then I thought of Clara and said, 'You can count on me.'"

"That was a good thing to say, Poye," I told him. "It showed that you were confident. What did old Wilmot say to that?"

"She said 'Good.' Then I sat there for a few minutes as they whispered among themselves. Then the dean turned back to me and said, 'We have decided to give you this opportunity.'"

"Well, you're on your way. We're colleagues now. And Clara will appreciate the good news."

When we arrived back at the apartment, Clara was in a blue terry bathrobe plastered with gaudy yellow sunflowers, pounding a show tune out of her piano. Every so often she paused to seize a goblet containing the blood she had drained from the rump roast baking in the oven. We watched as she drank heartily, wiped her mouth on her wrist, and pounded anew. "You know," she said, "I think I'd like to be a concert pianist."

"I got the job."

Clara stopped pounding, swiveled around to Poye, and got to her feet. She threw her hands upon her hips and nodded. "Well, there," she said. "Nothing ventured, nothing gained. Congratulations."

Poye looked anything but elated. He still didn't know what to think. He had never had a real job, and this was a new feeling. He held out a manila folder to Clara, who took it, opened it, and read his contract. She noted the cross stamp in the upper right-hand corner of the document. "I see they gave you the seal of approval," she said.

"Yes," acknowledged Poye. "That was the first thing they asked. If I was a Christian. I don't know why I said yes. I was never baptized, and no one in my family ever went to church."

Clara looked him over. "Are you Jewish?" she asked.

Poye peeped, "No."

"Muslim?"

"No."

"Atheist?"

"I don't know."

Clara whooped. "Then, by default, you must be Christian. You were not being dishonest. Here, come to bed." Turning to me, "And you, I expect you to keep an eye on my man."

"I will," I said. "I won't let him get into trouble."

Clara recoiled. "Well, what fun would that be?"

The smell of Clara's fruity perfume mingled with the meaty aroma of the well-seasoned rump roast sizzling in the oven. The combination aroused me deeply, but what could I do? Poye was her man. He found himself in bed with Clara posthaste, and I blushed when she left the door to the bedroom half-open. I retreated to the kitchen table and sat with my back to the activities, but their raucous love-making left little to the imagination. Even if he had wanted to resist, Poye was no match for Clara's carnal energies as she washed over him in tsunamic waves of passion.

When they were done Clara leapt out of bed as if she had just finished splitting a cord of wood — flush with a sense of a job well done and ready to move on to her next labor. Poye, for his part, rolled onto the floor and crawled away from the bed on all fours until he arrived at my feet at the table, where he pushed himself up, butt-first, the way a toddler would. While he recovered, Clara marched over to the oven, lit a cigarette, took a serving fork, and impaled the roast, hoisting it like a game trophy. Within minutes she had set a cornucopia on the table — the roast covered with artichoke sauce — and was washing down her meal with generous draughts of blood, which she gulped without removing the cigarette from the corner of her mouth. "So tell me everything," she said.

Poye shrugged as he stared at his plate. As for me, I had no trouble tucking into the scrumptious meal. "There isn't all that much to tell," said Poye. "Once they established that I was Christian they told me I would be responsible for teaching a lecture and two laboratory sections of a very basic biology course called *A Miraculous World.*

"So far so good," said Clara as she sliced into a massive baked potato smothered in sour cream. "Why you looking so down, then?"

Poye pondered this as if wondering if he were really down. He looked at Clara and tried to explain. "It's just that the text doesn't present things the way I was taught. For example, there's no mention of evolution."

"So?" remarked Clara as she chewed.

"Well," said Poye, "evolution is the glue that holds everything together. At least that's what Professor Todelaw told us. Without it, nothing in biology makes much sense." Poye neglected to mention that Professor Todelaw had lost his job over that sentiment.

Clara stopped chewing. "So teach evolution. You can do things your way, right?"

That's where I cut in. "It's not that simple, Clara," I said, but gently, as she was already eyeing me skeptically. "At least, not since the Reinterpretation. Everything has changed, and the idea of academic freedom is no exception. Now there are political lines to be toed."

Poye picked up his fork and nudged his slice of roast. "The committee that interviewed me said expressly that I was not to mention the E word except to refer to it as a discredited idea."

Evolution had never been part of Clara's purview, so she struggled to get a grasp of why this issue seemed to be so thorny. But she did understand people because it was clear that she could see how beset Poye was. She also showed her pragmatic nature. "Look," she said as she poured a rich dollop of artichoke sauce onto Poye's untouched meat. "You got your foot in the door today. Lie low, go along, and keep your mouth shut until you've been there a while. Then you can start to have things your way. You don't have any allies yet. But you will."

I looked at Clara in wonder. She was, of course, correct in her perception of how the academy worked, although I had no idea how she came by this understanding. I turned to Poye. "What Clara's talking about is something called tenure."

Clara's eyes brightened. "Tell me about it, Nestor."

"If Poye keeps his nose clean, teaches his course, does a little useful research or writing, and becomes well-liked, he has a good chance of moving onto what they call a tenure track, which, if things go well, leads to full tenure. This means that it wouldn't be easy to fire him. Unless he did something egregious like murder the dean or burn down the school."

"Or teach evolution," Poye peeped, glancing from me to Clara.

"It's worth it," concluded Clara. "Hold your nose until you get this tenure. Then do what you want."

Poye looked at Clara with stars in his eyes, as if wishing he had her confidence. Maybe that's why he stayed with her. That and the phenomenal, recreational, otherworldly sex.

"I suppose," he said.

Clara reached out and clapped Poye upside the head. "No 'I suppose,'" she scolded. "If it's the last thing I do, I'm going to slap the 'I suppose' out of you."

And, Poye would later confide, that's when he knew that he loved her.

EIGHT
SPONG

The long-awaited — and long-forgotten — instructions finally arrived. I was looking in on my own apartment when a pizza delivery man came to the door at seven A.M. "I didn't order pizza," I said. "And certainly not this time of day." But he simply handed me the box and walked away without even asking for payment. When I opened it I saw a perfectly ordinary pepperoni pizza, with one of those little plastic tripod thingamajigs that keeps the top of the box off the cheese. I picked up the thingamajig and — *bam!* — had my first glimpse of the Spong.

My immediate reaction was revulsion. There were four of them, and they were big — head and shoulders above the biggest man. They looked vaguely like trees, but in place of branches they had tentacles, eight of them, and each tentacle was tipped by a white, unblinking eye that had a pupil about the size of a golf ball. In the place which you might call a forehead, there was a sort of orifice. I couldn't tell them apart, so I gave each of them a number. Spong 1 was on the far left and was the first to speak to me, its voice pouring out of the orifice, sort of like an echo from a cave. It asked if I was afraid.

"Intellectually," I said, "I know I should be."

"But you are repulsed by Spong's appearance," said Spong 3. "Don't lie. Spong can sense it. Spong would like you to know that Spong is equally repulsed by you. Not only by your appearance but by the very idea of you."

Ouch. I felt my ire rise but decided to hang fire. "Look," I said, "let's not get personal. We hardly know each other. Can we stick to the issues?" And then, after a moment's pause, "What are the issues, by the way?"

"The issues are grave," said Spong 3.

"I'm all ears," I said. "I'm sure we can discuss things man to man."

"We are not men," they said in unison. "We are Spong."

That's when they began their discourse, commencing with a little flattery. They said that of the seven billion humans on earth, I was the only one who seemed to "get it." For this reason, I would be spared the Treatment. Further, I was allowed — no, commanded — to write down this story, and Poye Trubb would be an essential part of the story because, at Debec Pond on that beastly hot summer night when we were kids, he had been caught up in their so-called "traction beam" as well. In the interim, the Spong had used their powerful sensing devices to listen in on a lecture I had given at the International Symposium on Perspective in Helsinki. I had pleased them because of my Spong-caliber insight that Perspective is synonymous with order and understanding. This led them to review every electronic transmission on earth since Samuel Morse had tapped out *What Hath God Wrought?* The upshot was that they were disappointed. And that's an understatement. The Spong, for all their intellect and wisdom, had not anticipated humans. They thought that, billions of years ago, they had simply seeded a garden in a climatically pleasant and out-of-the-way corner of the galactic countryside. They were appalled when they learned about slavery, the sinking of the Lusitania, the Battle of the Bulge, Hiroshima, child labor, politicians taking bribes, road rage, the contamination of the air and waterways, the National Rifle Association, the cutting down of rain forests, and the designation of ketchup as a vegetable in the elementary schools. Finally, the Spong said that they had been keeping track of me and Poye ever since that night at the pond. And now they were selecting me to take notes about the lack of Perspective that was characteristic of the unanticipated humans who had so contaminated the garden they had seeded. They added, cryptically, that something had to be done. I was to be, in effect, Earth's final biographer. And Poye was to be my focus, the Spong's "case in point," the representative example of erring, unworthy humankind whom I would document for their archives.

And then the Spong anointed me. All I remember from that moment is a halo around my field of vision, sparkling colors like jewels in the sky, and a buzzing in my ears. This was the formal beginning of my solitary journey as Earth's final biographer. "We believe that Poye is bound for great tribulation," said Spong 2. "Mark his every move. Be his constant companion. Keep a faithful record."

"The only problem," I said, "is that I have a job. It's not like I can just take time off."

The Spong, in concert, answered: "Take time off."

"I can't," I said. "I need the money."

"What is money?" asked Spong 2.

I rolled my eyes. "It makes the world go around," I said. I reached into my pocket and produced a few crumpled bills. "Here."

The Spong ran all thirty-two of their eyeballs over the bills. Spong 1 waved a tentacle and — *poof!* — a thick stack of crisp new fifties lay at my feet. "Does this help?"

I scooped up the wad and riffled it before my eyes. "I'll put in for leave," I said. "It will be no problem so long as you can maintain my cash flow."

"That will be no problem," said Spong 4. "Help us, and in time everything will become clear."

"I'll do my best," I said, noting that the Spong had quoted my dear old dad.

Spong 1: "And do not misplace the triservoskapticon," it said, indicating the little white plastic thingamajig with one of its tentacles. "It's your only means of summoning us."

I fingered the device, which for editorial efficiency I decided to call the "servo." I placed it in my pocket. When I looked up, the Spong had vanished.

I had my orders. The only wild card was Clara, who hadn't yet shown any impatience with my constant presence. Maybe it was because she saw me as a witness to all the good things she was trying to inspire in Poye.

And so, still tingling all over from my interaction with the Spong, I returned to my friend, Wytopitlock College's newest adjunct — the academic equivalent of cleaning the latrines in boot camp. If not for Clara acting as his superego, Poye wouldn't have thought about the potential of his job leading to something bigger, better, and more enduring. Clara had grown curious about the academy, and she intended to learn as much as she could. When I arrived at the apartment in the late morning, she was just about to leave. Poye was sitting at the table, spooning chicken soup to his mouth. He looked up at me and smiled.

"I'm glad you're here, Nestor," said Clara. "You're coming with me."

I glanced at Poye, who shrugged. And then I left with Clara. We got into the Rambler and headed for the University of Maine, eight miles up the road. "I'm just curious, Clara," I said. "Why are we going to the university?"

"So I can get a crash course in how a college works."

I didn't ask Clara why, if she wanted to know how a university operated, she didn't just ask me. I think I was just quietly content that she so matter-of-factly accepted me as part of a triumvirate which included her and Poye. This would make it easier for me to act as Poye's — and Earth's — biographer.

And then, out of the blue, she peeped, "You don't approve of me, do you?"

"Is this why you asked me to come along?"

"Why do you ask? Do you think I want to screw you too? Ha!"

I ignored the comment about fornication. "To your original question," I said, "I think you're the best thing that ever happened to Poye. You're the best chance of happiness he's ever had."

My comment rendered Clara uncharacteristically mute. I think she may even have misted up. Finally, she told me, "I always want you to feel welcome in my apartment. A man needs a woman, but he also needs a close male friend. There are things a man will only tell another man."

"And you want me to report his confidences to you?"

Clara let out a breath and swatted the air. "Don't flatter yourself. Poye's a window. I can see right through him. I just think you're good for him."

This was incredibly candid of Clara, not to mention generous. Nevertheless, I offered, "I don't want to get in your way."

"Believe me, if you get in the way I'll let you know. I'll throw you out on your ass." After a few moments of silence, she edged, "I have the feeling that you're watching us, taking notes. What, are you writing a book or something? I have a lot of stories to tell."

"Well," I began off-handedly, "if you want the truth, I'm working at the behest of a group of aliens who have taken an interest in me and Poye. They seem to believe that Poye will be at the center of some great drama and they want me to write it all down. They also seem to have plans for our planet, and I don't think the plans are happy ones."

Clara rocked back and forth over the steering wheel. "If that's your way of telling me to shut up, I don't like it. Just tell me to shut up."

"And then what would you do to me?"

"You don't want to know."

We soon arrived at our destination. I knew that Clara couldn't begin her exploration of the university's culture in any normal way — by asking questions — because of her showy appearance and brash manner. Once on campus, she bounded out of the Rambler, the breeze blowing her hair about her face. She threw her hands on her hips, took a gander at the joint and, jutting out her jaw, asked aloud, "Now, where shall I start?"

During the two hours she was away I explored my old haunt and visited a few old acquaintances. By the time we rendezvoused Clara told me she had bedded a dean and had learned "a great deal" from him. Having accomplished her mission, we drove back to the apartment. Clara was triumphant and ready to read Poye the riot act. She ordered me to the table and fed me an Italian sandwich brimming with pesto and asiago cheese while we waited for Poye's advent. Within a very short while he arrived home. Clara got up from the table and raised her hands.

"Well, how was your first day, Mr. Professor?" she asked with a note of irony as Poye dragged himself through the door, looking as if he had just dug a ditch. "Oh, okay," he managed as he sat down on the sofa, loosened his tie, and exhaled what sounded like his last mortal breath. "I forgot to lead the students in the Pledge of Allegiance and was reprimanded."

Clara plopped down next to him and grabbed a hank of his hair, giving it a stiff tug. Poye seemed to enjoy this feeling — just on the edge of pain. "Tell me about the rest of it."

Poye went on to describe his students. "They're not very well prepared," he said. "When I asked them how old they thought the earth was, they were almost unanimous that it was about six thousand years old. Which is what the textbook says."

Clara hummed. "You said almost unanimous. What about the others?"

Poye shrugged. "They had no idea."

Clara rolled out her lower lip. "So it seems like you have a lot to work with."

Poye looked at Clara and rolled his eyes, but she clapped him on the forehead. "Don't you roll your eyes at me," she commanded. "I'm trying to be sensitive and understanding, but I don't have to be."

Poye realized that she was right. "Sorry, love," he peeped. It was the first time I heard him use an endearment with Clara. "It's just that the way ahead looks so bleak. I mean, how will I be able to maneuver around the evidence of evolution and molecular biology and still teach a legitimate course that respects some semblance of the truth?" Having said this, Poye began to knead his hands, but Clara, having already exhausted her supply of sensitivity and understanding, returned to native form. She slapped his wrist. "Don't knead those hands in front of me," she scolded. "Put your head up. Be a man."

Poye did as Clara ordered. He put his head up. But how did one be a man?

"Listen," she said, squeezing Poye's cheeks and pulling his face close. "I took time out from my busy day to do some background research."

"Research?" echoed Poye.

Clara detected a note of doubt in Poye's voice. She released his face and threw him a headlong glance, but didn't lose momentum by chastising him. "Yes. Here's the reality. You're an adjunct. Get used to it. For now. If they say dance, then dance. If they say sing, then sing. Dollop out the slop they want you to dollop out. Let them believe people were planted here like petunias. You don't have to say this in so many words, but if this is what they want you to teach, so be it. You're not supposed to tell them what to believe anyway."

Poye raised a finger. "But Professor Todelaw said it was the teacher's job to dictate good taste."

"And where is Professor Todelaw today? I don't see him helping you out. Don't interrupt me. Your time will come. You be a good boy for now. You'll be a successful teacher and will make friends among your colleagues."

"Are you saying I should go along to get along?"

Clara scowled at him. "Yes. For the moment. Right now you're on a merry-go-round where your job is to stay on your horse. But at some point you'll want to reach for the brass ring. You'll have a chance for a tenure job — isn't that what they call it, Nestor? — and you'll be able to do all sorts of things. Then you can speak your mind without fear of being fired." Then, as a coda, she added, "Patience."

I was amazed at Clara's perspicacity and wisdom. In fact, I was aroused by it and tucked deeper into my Italian sandwich to distract myself. But how does one keep the heat from rising to one's face? And then I remembered my mission. I retrieved a yellow legal pad in a vinyl folder I had bought earlier in the day and began my scribbling. I had a lot of catching up to do.

Poye was grateful. He cast loving eyes at Clara, who was staring dead at him to ensure that her message had gotten through. It had. She was there to make sure of it. But it seemed clear to me that she also wanted to ensure her own future prosperity and security. I was convinced that a woman with her sexual energy had no intention of limiting her interactions to Poye, but she still needed some reliable comfort in her life. Someone to count on. Someone incapable of judging her. Poye was the man.

It was at this juncture that I took Clara aside in a quiet moment and asked a bold question: would it be possible for me to live with the two of them as a sort of honest broker and scribe, detailing the path of a young college professor and the woman in his life who provided his inspiration? I must have phrased things just right because Clara agreed without preamble or hesitation. I think it was the idea that my project would include her as a centerpiece of any success Poye might enjoy. For the foreseeable future, Clara's sofa would be my home. However, she had a caution for me. "As soon as you judge me, you're out." As she said this, her blue eyes flashed as if they had caught fire.

"I've already judged you," I told her. "And the verdict is a positive one."

At this, she softened. When she told Poye about the arrangement, he perked up. Perhaps he thought I would keep him out of trouble. In any case, at my first opportunity, I went down to the college and put in for unpaid leave. I was surprised, and not a little disappointed, by how promptly my request was approved. As if they were happy to be rid of me for a year.

As for Poye, he girded himself and returned to the classroom. Every evening he made a full report of his teaching experiences, and I scribbled away as if taking dictation. He had lectured about the various forms of life and how they were related but steered clear of the shoal waters of how those relationships had come to be. He talked about the structure of DNA but not about how DNA could be used to establish evolutionary relationships among organisms. In other words, he judiciously neglected to mention that human and chicken DNA are 92% similar, pointing to a close evolutionary relationship. And in the rare instance when he experienced a slip of the tongue and referred to such things, he did not dwell upon it but rather hoped the students would chalk it up to either coincidence or inexperience.

This is where I need to point out — for the umpteenth time — that the issue here is Perspective. Poye knew the truth. He knew the facts. He had been well educated, albeit by a discredited professor. But Clara had convinced him to soft-sell these assets — for the moment. She had, in other words, placed things in Perspective, because she had the feel for the bigger picture that Poye lacked. By contrast, Poye had pawned Perspective in the hope of recovering it later. So you see, the whole idea of Perspective can get pretty complicated. I should know. I made a living from it.

NINE
HOPE

As the days unfolded and I grew accustomed to my new living situation, I was sometimes tempted to tell Poye about the Spong. That it had been they who had shone that paralyzing light on us at Debec Pond when we were twelve. But I relented, seeing how he had his hands full with Clara. Besides, I needed to maintain my dispassion as Earth's final biographer.

In the meantime, Clara had grown restless. She had dedicated herself to Poye for two months now, and it was clear she was beginning to feel constrained. Without preamble, she returned to her sporting ways. I saw it down in Briody's, where she surrounded herself with drunken, stumbling men. And I was witness to it in the apartment when Poye was out. Clara freely brought men to her bedroom without giving me a look while I sat at the table scribbling my notes. I observed these characters closely, and they had a common thread. All of the men Clara carried on with behaved as if they were in control of affairs. But they were deluded. Clara was in control because she wouldn't have it any other way. With Poye, though, she behaved more like a pioneer exploring a young and unfinished land. In him she had something to work with because, in my opinion, for the first time in her life she felt responsible for what another human being might become. She seemed fascinated by Poye and didn't want to lose him, so it was he to whom she returned every night.

As for Poye, he was nothing if not diligent and conscientious in studying his textbook and preparing his lectures. *A Miraculous World* had been approved by the President's Council on Right Thinking. Some of the basics were pretty innocuous and familiar to Poye: living things were composed of cells; plants carried out photosynthesis; genes were made of DNA. But when he read the text's sidebars, he began to get an inkling of the book's intent. I watched as he shook his head. He communicated his consternation to me. For example, he pointed out that although the text acknowledged that genes transmitted heredity, sexual reproduction — "intermingling of the genders" was how the text phrased it — was couched in terms of the mystical, or miraculous:

The pinnacle of creation is the wonder of human reproduction, during the course of which the intangible entity known as the soul takes up residence in the biological substrate, the body, of a new human.

Poye bristled. "How can I teach such a thing, Nest? Professor Todelaw said that science was the art of quantification. Counting cells, measuring genetic outcomes, calculating reaction rates. How on earth can I quantify the soul?"

I wished I had an easy answer for my friend, but I didn't. "You've got to be creative," I told him. "Get the truth in edgewise, so that they don't even suspect they're learning. It's the only way to preserve your self-respect."

The thing was, it wasn't just the schools that had changed. The entire country had experienced a tectonic shift. First of all, the two major political parties had been dissolved and replaced with one party, the Star Nation. Then a constitutional convention had been convened and had released a Reinterpretation of the hallowed document. Remember what I said about people needing to feel afraid? Well, the proof of the pudding is that the convention re-wrote all of the amendments in terms of security. Here are a few examples:

Amendment #1: The Theocratic Union of American States is acknowledged to be a Christian nation, the precepts of Christianity informing its moral sense. In this light, free speech, a free press, and free association shall honor, and be informed by, the fundamental teachings of Christianity as expressed in the New Testament of our Lord and Savior Jesus Christ. In this manner, the nation shall create a secure sense of self.

Amendment #2: A secure state being necessary for the free expression of a democratic people, the right to own and bear firearms shall be absolute and their possession by all Christians over the age of twelve obligatory.

Amendment #3: When deemed necessary for the security of the state, soldiers may be freely quartered on private property.

Amendment #4: When deemed necessary for the security of the state, searches may be conducted of private persons, their properties, and effects, without prior notice or impedance by a warrant.

The upshot of all this was that Poye felt very much alone, schooled as he was, by teachers such as Professor Todelaw, in the ways of freethinking and pointed inquiry. Which is why Poye clung all the more tightly to Clara, his still point, his anchor, his chained-to-the-bottom-of-the-ocean buoy with its bell clanging through his eternal fog of self-doubt. Is it any wonder that he was confused when we returned to the apartment one day and he spotted a man's tie — spattered with tomato sauce — draped over a chair? A ruckus was emanating from the bedroom — deep, mammalian, male grunts and a counterpoint of wild, womanly cackles of delight. I was at a loss for words but felt profoundly sorry for my best friend. I lay down on the sofa, covered my face with my hands, and tried to turn my thoughts elsewhere.

For his part, Poye, who had always been remarkably inept at drawing conclusions, simply sat down at the table, pulled out *A Miraculous World* and began to work on his lesson plan for the transportation of substances across the cell membrane, while the bacchanalia in the bedroom continued unabated. Fifteen minutes later the door flew open, and a bald, portly man staggered out. He had a self-satisfied smile on his face, like someone who had just eaten a banana split. He glanced at Poye, reddened, grabbed his tie, and stumbled out of the apartment.

Clara stood in the bedroom doorway in her panties and a brassiere that barely restrained her breasts, posing with one hand on the jamb and another on her hip. She flipped her lighter and ignited a cigarette. She had never learned how to give ground, and she wasn't going to start now, so she met Poye's stare with her own. "Well?" she said. "What are you looking at?"

Poye was nonplussed by her comment. He glanced at the door to the apartment, then at Clara again. Then he shrugged, suggesting that maybe there was nothing to be concerned about. This is what I came to refer to as "Poye's Hope." After all, Clara was still with him. In fact, she marched over to him, grabbed him by the hair, and dragged him off to bed, where she ravished him with abandon.

While all this was going on, I recalled what Poye had told me about Professor Todelaw, about his saying that science is the art of quantification. But maybe not everything could be quantified, in which case there might be a soul after all — something that went beyond our poor ability to measure. Was the soul synonymous with sexuality? Given her inexhaustible supply of this resource, perhaps Clara was a holy woman, or a saint.

TEN
TENURE

I was reasonably happy at Wytopitlock College, but I worried about Poye. I don't think his experience was anything like mine, no doubt because he was an adjunct instructor which the administration played like a pawn. I, on the other hand, was not only a tenured professor in the philosophy department, I *was* the philosophy department. Among students in general, the number of philosophy majors had steadily decreased over the years, in tandem with the rise of web-based pornography. As the number of philosophy majors decreased, so did the once-vigorous phalanx of grizzled philosophy professors whose sepia images hung in oval frames in the hallway of the philosophy building. It's a known fact that of all the faculty, the musicians and philosophers live the longest. The musicians usually drop dead at advanced ages in front of an audience, and the philosophers ossify at their desks because they feel they are misunderstood and unappreciated by the administrators, so they persist out of spite.

Take me, for example. I was the last of my species at Wytopitlock College. When I wrote *Perspective for Idiots,* it was quite a hit. I actually made a lot of money. I think the higher-ups expected me to build a recreation center or endow a faculty chair. But I didn't. Because I felt misunderstood and unappreciated. So I spent the money on myself. Out of spite.

Please don't take me for cold or selfish. As a philosophy professor, I often lay awake at night, wrestling with the question of self vs. other. But I also lay awake because I worried so much about Poye. Not to mention the Spong and what exactly they had in mind. Speaking of whom, when I told them about Poye's tribulations with evolution, they were astounded that it was an issue on Earth, or at least in the Theocratic Union of American States. After all, the Spong had shown themselves to be masters of Perspective. For them, evolution was a given. In their highly advanced minds, the controversy over evolution was as foolish as arguing about gravity, or air. They couldn't imagine anyone saying, "Don't give me that gravity stuff. I've had it with gravity. Gravity is the biggest lie ever told." Their only reservation about the human understanding of evolution — and this was a very big reservation — was that it didn't address the question of origins. More to the point, it didn't attribute a superior intelligence with originally seeding life on Earth.

And so Poye suffered along, hounded by the sense that in not teaching evolutionary theory he was failing himself by not standing by the scientific beliefs inculcated in him by the sainted Professor Todelaw.

•   •   •   •   •

The years passed, and I continued to take assiduous notes, filling legal pad after legal pad. Poye celebrated his fifth anniversary at Wytopitlock College by taking Clara out for a lobster roll, with me taking up the rear. Yes, that's right. For five long years Poye and Clara had persisted as a couple and, more remarkably, I continued to live with them as a sort of crazy uncle, playing James Boswell to my very own Samuel Johnson — Poye Trubb. We were quite a triumvirate. The college was also willing to grant me leave after leave, giving me the sneaking feeling that they were happy to live without me. The Spong, for their part, continued to supply me with enough cold, hard cash to meet my meager needs.

As for Poye, there was a bit more to see now. Both he and I had turned thirty-one. He no longer looked like an adolescent. He had filled out, straightened up, and ceased to shuffle. He had a touch of gray along his temples and had developed a tendency to squint, especially when he was thinking hard about something. Even though he was still, yes still, an adjunct biology instructor, he dressed like the stereotype of an established college professor, natty in his chinos, penny loafers, and cardigans. Contrast this with me. I looked like a bum, in the hallowed tradition of philosophy professors. But I was comfortable in my tattered, low-slung jeans with the torn-out knees, my gray, hooded sweatshirt ripped down the front, and my worn-out sneakers through which my toes protruded. You might think I dressed like this because I was preoccupied with higher thoughts about important things, and therefore didn't dwell on physical appearance or even hygiene. The truth is that I was simply lazy.

The biggest change in Poye was that he had learned to speak his mind with Clara. Where he used to allow Clara to haul him off to bed at her whim, he had now become more selective about love-making. The first time he said to Clara, "Not right now, love. Maybe tonight," she tried to drag him to bed by the hair, but he did something unprecedented — he grabbed her wrist. "Not now, love," he repeated. And she relented. In fact, although she would never admit it, Clara seemed to like this development in Poye, who had, in my eyes, become her match.

Clara was now fifty, but those years had meant little as far as her physical appearance was concerned. Her hair was still a deep, lustrous red with not a strand of gray, her jawline was clear, her neck tight, and her bosom remained high and protruding, like the bow of a frigate. Her energy was still prodigious, her laugh operatic, her temper hair-trigger. She still cooked as if possessed, clattering pots and pans like a smithy hammering out armor, while clamping a smoldering cigarette between her blood-red lips, and the bedroom was still her preferred playground. Poye's becoming pickier about the time and frequency of their couplings only whetted her sexual appetite. She was not used to being denied, and the pent-up energy drove her to the far reaches of passion so that the times when they did make love were wild binges which left Clara licking her lips, like a predator that had tracked, killed, and finally devoured its prey.

With regard to Poye's work, Clara had been prescient. Over the intervening years, Poye had whittled away at an online doctoral program and had finally completed a dissertation on a new species of mite that inhabited the anus of the honeybee, and which he had named *Clara elegans*. Shortly thereafter he was finally invited to apply for a tenure-track position that had opened up. Wytopitlock College was very grudging with tenure, as it had the potential of creating a faculty member who, if he became "difficult" in some way, would be hard to dislodge. But the elderly, tenured Professor of Biology Lester Lomax had finally died, and the college thought it unseemly to have all the bio courses taught by adjuncts, who tended to have little allegiance to the institution. For appearance's sake, they needed to be able to boast of at least one tenured professor of biology with a Ph.D. Poye was the only in-house choice, unless the college wanted to run the risk of hauling in an unknown entity from the outside. Besides, Poye had, as per Clara's counsel, judiciously kept his nose clean. He had dutifully taught his abridged version of biology, carefully avoiding the Scylla and Charybdis of evolution, and had insulted neither administrative nor student sensibilities.

And so Poye made his application. Not long after, I accompanied him before the tenure committee, as his advocate. The committee was chaired by Dean Wilmot, who uttered a cursory "Hosanna" upon seeing him, to which both Poye and I replied, half-heartedly, "Hosanna." To Wilmot's right and left sat two of the men who had presided over Poye's hiring as an adjunct. All wore resplendent cross pendants. Poye's, by contrast, was tarnished, which brought the dean to comment, "Please take more pride in your identifier." Poye's only response was to bite his lip. The distasteful looks on the faces of the committee members communicated a sense of this being dirty business which, nevertheless, had to be conducted.

Eulalie Wilmot turned to me. "So you're advocating for Mr. Trubb?"

"With honor," I said. Poye threw me a grateful look.

Dean Wilmot looked me over. "Your pendant contrasts strongly with your general appearance," she said, noting a fresh salsa stain on my sweatshirt from the fish taco I had just eaten.

I looked at myself and straightened my sweatshirt, which, I had to admit, smelled a bit raw. Then I pulled my cross pendant to my mouth, misted it with my breath, and rubbed it to a bright shine on my sleeve. "I want to make a good impression," I said, all the while reveling in my tenure, my shield, my assurance that almost nothing I said or did would risk my cushy position at Wytopitlock.

The dean ignored my comment. "Do you know of any reason why Mr. Trubb should not be awarded this tenure-track position?"

"None whatsoever, Dean," I said without hesitation. "He's done his five years in purgatory and is now ready for paradise."

Wilmot straightened up and took a deep breath of exasperation. Poye glanced about, first at me and then at the committee. I threw my friend an affirming look, nodding approvingly and noting how picture-perfect he was in his blue cardigan with the cowrie buttons, and the loafers into which he had slipped shiny new pennies, for luck.

The committee conferred while we hovered in silence. I crossed my ankles and threw an arm over the back of Poye's chair, while he sat at attention, on his hands. I couldn't shake the feeling that the committee members just didn't like Poye. Perhaps they would conclude that the easiest thing to do was to give him the miserable tenure-track position and send him on his way.

Which is exactly what they did.

Because, it turned out, they had Perspective. At least, this is how my expert's eye saw it. My take was that they viewed Wytopitlock College as a playground for their personal interests and had found an inconspicuous corner of that playground for Poye, whom they had labeled "harmless." He was, to them, not a part of the big picture, but only a minor functionary. As insignificant as a dust mote, he would continue to occupy himself with his microscopes, test tubes, and struggling students, then submit his grades and repeat the process over and over until, one day, he would follow the late Professor Lomax into the oblivion of either death or retirement. At which point Poye, too, would be replaced with another pliant soul.

After a lecture about Poye's responsibilities as a tenure-track assistant professor of biology, Dean Wilmot made smacking sounds, as if clearing her palate for the next course, and said, "Okay." After a pause, this was followed by, "I hope you will acquit yourself well and make the college proud of you." In other words, she was hoping Poye would continue to mind his business and stay out of her hair.

"And as for you, Professor," she said as she looked me over, "clean yourself up." In response to which I stroked my beard and offered a hearty "Hosanna."

To Poye, the whole thing seemed anticlimactic. He sat there, before the immense desk, still with his hands under his thighs, like a schoolboy. He looked from face to impatient face. Getting up, he uttered a meek "Thank you," turned, and left.

Once outside, he asked me, "Am I supposed to feel something?"

"Well," I said, "what are you thinking about at this very moment? Maybe that will help you understand how you should feel."

His answer was immediate. "Clara," he said. "I want to go home to Clara."

Eleven
Epiphany

Poye and I were living in an academic world which had been transformed by the Reinterpretation and the Education Reform Act. Wytopitlock College, like all schools, from pre-K on up, had been skinned, gutted, and stuffed with new material. It was a microcosm of what the wider country had become — theocratic, ideological, and, of course, armed. As a scientist in an anti-science climate, Poye was more profoundly affected than I.

The Theocratic Union of American States was not the same country we had been born and raised in. Distrust of the government had undone the United States, and was replaced with a slavish, almost sexual attachment to the Theocratic Union and the Star Nation party, touted as representing everybody's interests, when in reality it favored the Christians, who had become the privileged class. Those who were affiliated with other faiths felt branded by their pendants, which was the first thing others noted in any encounter. Many of the non-Christians could not bear up under the pressure of having to ejaculate "Hosanna!" — especially when interacting with government officials, who now seemed to be everywhere. So they either killed themselves, attempted to flee over the border or, less dramatically, swapped their pendants for the cross variety worn by the majority Christians, which required an oath of allegiance to the new set of beliefs, and — *bingo!* — all their troubles disappeared. Suddenly the doors opened and opportunities beckoned, all as a result of a fleeting "Hosanna," which they learned to mumble with the same fortitude as a child swallowing cod liver oil.

As for Clara, she refused to wear the pendant. "But aren't you afraid?" queried Poye one day, expressing a sense of dread.

Clara, who was lying in her bathrobe on the sofa — my sofa — with her legs up at the time, scoffed. "Afraid? Me? Of what?" And then she looked to me for a second opinion. "What do you think, Nestor? Should I be afraid?"

I was sitting in the easy chair, cleaning my fingernails with a penknife, trying to stay out of it. But Clara had cornered me, so I put on my philosopher's hat and struck a philosopher's pose, gazing up as if contemplating a truth which hovered somewhere in the ether. "Oh, I don't know," I hedged. "Fear can be either life-sustaining or debilitating."

Clara frowned. "Thanks," she said. "For nothing."

Poye, watching her from the kitchen table, ventured, "Maybe you should wear the sad face, then. At least you'd be complying with the law, and they'll leave you alone."

Clara sat up and glared at him. "Poye," she said, "there's something you need to learn. They never leave you alone. Yes, I could wear a pendant, but then they'd find something else. They'd come after me for not saying that ridiculous 'Hosanna'."

"Maybe you should say 'Hosanna,'" peeped Poye. "Just to keep them away."

Clara slowly shook her head and registered a look of abject disappointment. She lit up a cigarette and dragged deeply. Then she blew a smoke ring which dissipated before it reached Poye. "You didn't hear a word I said. There's always something. Just remember that."

"She's right, Poye," I noised.

Clara threw me a look of disgust. "Oh, shut up, Nestor."

I did as instructed and returned to my nails.

"I will remember," said Poye. "But Clara, love, and forgive me for mentioning this, there's a little something in me that still wishes you would give the pendant a second thought."

Clara softened. "Poye, babe," she said, cloyingly and almost in a whisper, "I don't have to. Really. Because the Minister of Pendantry is very close to me."

Poye's eyebrows took flight. "Close?" he inquired.

Clara smiled and nodded. "Yes. Very, very close." Then she glanced at the clock. "In fact, I'd better get down to the bar, or he'll wonder where I am."

For the sake of the Spong, I noted all of this with great care. When I was alone, I took out the servo and submitted my reports with cautious abandon, because the Spong could be very touchy, not to mention skeptical. On more than one occasion — such as when I wrote about the clarified and fortified second amendment, which required all Christians to carry guns — they were so disbelieving that they threatened to relieve me of my position as earth's final scribe. "But even the president carries a pistol," I affirmed by showing them a video clip of the head of state waving a nine-millimeter at the editor of *The New York Times*. The Spong relented, shaking their tentacles dolefully. "Poye and I, of course, refuse to carry a weapon," I added, "but so far we've gotten away with it."

It wasn't easy for Poye to maneuver in this world of pendantry, hosannas, and sidearms. As he grew in confidence as a teacher and came to dwell more and more on the example Professor Todelaw had set, he became increasingly restless. He had grudgingly avoided the taboo topic of evolution for two reasons: one, he feared for his job; and two, all of his students were armed Christians, their pendants blazing on silver chains around their necks. He therefore feared the loss of either his career or his life if he got off the path prescribed for him by the dean and The President's Council on Right Thinking. So he kept his cross pendant polished and facing forward, but was careful never to let Clara see him devoting attention to it.

One evening while Clara was working late, Poye and I were sitting in the apartment enjoying cups of Earl Grey tea. He reflected on how much things had changed since we were undergraduates, not all that long ago. "Nest, I remember one day when Professor Todelaw asked the class how many of us had been raised in a religious tradition. There were about seventy students in that lecture, and maybe forty or fifty raised their hands."

"Were they holy rollers?" I asked.

"No, no, nothing like that. They didn't offer anything like resistance to Professor Todelaw's lecture. Everybody was willing to at least consider the evidence for evolution."

"But I thought Todelaw lost his job over the issue."

"Yes," nodded Poye as he cradled the steaming tea in his hands, "but the critical, career-ending objection came from the university's administrators, not the students. What a loss of a great teacher."

All of this had me wondering if Professor Todelaw's fate should be a cautionary tale for Poye. He told me that seething subterranean fundamentalism percolated to the surface whenever he drew near anything resembling evolution. Once, when he had uttered the words, "When amphibians first appeared..." the entire class leaned forward in their desks, which caused Poye, in tandem, to lean back on his heels. The moment passed, and no shots were fired, so Poye lived to teach another day.

Poye was troubled by what he came to regard as his duplicity — believing himself to be a scientist yet afraid to teach a cornerstone concept of science. He divulged this personal conflict to Clara one evening as we were eating a brisket of beef. She listened as long as she could bear to as she sucked a cigarette down to its filter. Then she flicked the butt into the sink and made her pronouncement. "You don't have to toe their line anymore," she said as if giving Poye release. "Your time has come." This made me halt in mid-chew.

Poye stared at Clara. "Those are big words," he said. "It's not so simple."

Clara was unimpeded. "Surely you must have allies, babe."

Poye paused to consider this. "I have Nest," he said, glancing at me.

"That's right, Clara," I said, "although I'm not on the battlefield at the moment and am of little use to Poye, except for moral support."

"Good for you," said Clara dismissively.

"I have only a nodding acquaintance with my colleagues in the sciences and across the disciplines," continued Poye as Clara listened. "I have no idea what their feelings are about academic freedom in general or evolution in particular. I have never felt so alone."

Clara was dumbstruck. "Thanks a lot," she said, clattering her utensils onto her plate and twisting sideways in her chair.

Poye smiled sweetly. "I'm sorry, love," he said. "You are my rock."

That's when Clara got an idea that — little did she know at the time — would alter Poye's trajectory and give him the sense of direction and resolve that had, thus far, eluded him. "We're going on a vacation," she announced.

Poye squinted and then raised his eyebrows. "I've never been on a vacation. Is such a thing possible? What does it entail?"

As in all things, Clara knew her own mind. "Let's just drive," she said. "South. We'll stop whenever something looks interesting. Nestor, you're coming with us, of course."

"Of course," I said, looking from Clara to Poye.

Poye couldn't think of a reason not to go on vacation. Spring Break — a glorious two weeks of respite from teaching — was just around the corner. So he nodded his assent. The next morning, Clara brought the Rambler to a mechanic to make sure it could withstand the journey.

A week later we set out, with Clara riding shotgun, a sackful of fragrant clementines in her lap, which made the car smell like orange blossoms. I was spread out in the back seat, daydreaming and observing the passing landscape. Poye leaned forward in the driver's seat and gripped the steering wheel with the intensity of a man piloting a boat through thick fog. He had never driven south of Portland, so this was a real leap into terra incognita. As we passed over the Piscataqua River Bridge into New Hampshire, Poye looked as if he were moving beyond earth and into outer space. "Relax," was Clara's counsel as she ate one clementine after another and tossed the rinds out the window. "We'll have fun."

We traveled down the congested highways of Massachusetts and New York, past billboards with slogans such as *Thank Jesus that you live in the T.U.A.S.!*, past the flaming towers of the New Jersey flats, through the nowheresville of Delaware and into the broiling south where increasingly hot summers had turned the landscape an uninviting, pancake brown. For Poye, he might just as well have been traveling among the planets. That's how alien everything seemed to him. On several occasions, Clara offered to drive, but Poye noised that he needed to conquer this particular phobia, so he pressed on, gripping the wheel for dear life and squinting dead ahead through rolling, anxiety-inducing headaches. Along the way, Poye and Clara made love on the fly in cheap roadside motels with free adult movies, while I rested in an adjoining room. We ate desiccated meatloaf in diners with buzzing neon signs and walked the forlorn streets of towns like Hurlock, Maryland, and Paw Paw, West Virginia. As the traffic thinned and the countryside became more open and expansive, Poye visibly relaxed. Clara noted this. "There," she said as she peeled a clementine for him. "Feeling better?"

It had been three days since we left Maine, and yes, for the first time since our departure Poye benefited from a blessed sense of distance which gave him some semblance of Perspective. This came to him as the three of us sat on a park bench in Krypton, Kentucky. The day was a warm one, and Poye closed his eyes so he could focus on the calm. "It's true," he finally said. "The idea of physical distance clearing the mind."

Clara clapped him on the shoulder, breaking his reverie. "That's the spirit," she chirped. "Didn't I tell you a vacation was the ticket?"

Poye nodded. "Yes, love." Which prompted me to ask, "Where to, now?"

The answer arrived on the side of a passing bus. It bore a poster for something called the Genesis Museum. Poye pointed to it. "There," he said. "That's where we'll go next."

"Sure," said Clara with a cackle. "Wait until they get a load of me. Are you game, Nestor?"

I always appreciated being consulted, even if a decision had already been made. "Anything you say, Clara."

"Don't give me too much leash, or else I'll dump Poye and throw you in the sack," she said with a wink. At which Poye registered a sick smile.

We drove to Petersboro, arriving at a futuristic-looking building, in front of which was a statue of what appeared to be a brontosaurus. It was being petted by a caveman mannequin in a loincloth. "This looks fascinating," said Poye as he parked the Rambler. "Let's go in."

Clara remarked that she had never been in a museum, but she seemed to sense the need to indulge Poye in this. When we went to pay the admission, however, the elderly man with the gray, pomaded hair and starched white shirt stared at Clara's chest. "Look, but don't touch," she quipped.

The man reddened. "Where is your pendant?" he asked, befuddled, as he clasped the three tickets, vicelike, in a beefy hand speckled with black age spots.

"Oh, my goodness!" said Clara, throwing her hands to her face and feigning alarm. "I'm sure that man who groped me took it. What kind of place is this? Police!"

The ticket master made patting motions as he looked around in embarrassment at the heads that had turned Clara's way. "It's okay, ma'am," he said with a soft Kentucky accent. "Get another one as soon as you can. Here are your tickets. Enjoy the museum. Hosanna."

We turned and entered the exhibit area. "That was a close call," said Poye, but Clara made no response. She had said everything she needed to say.

The place was swarming with large, pasty, rather heavy-set visitors and their progeny. It was also packed with dioramas and animatronic figures of dinosaurs and biblical characters. One display showed people and dinosaurs cavorting together. Poye stood in front of it and hummed disconsolately. "What would Professor Todelaw say?" he voiced to himself. Then we came to a fossil, accompanied by a placard asking, *Can you tell how old this fossil is?* Clara looked on as Poye darkened. "Something wrong, babe?"

Poye shook his head. "Clara," he said, "how old do you think this fossil is?"

Clara threw her head back and cackled, eliciting stares from other visitors. "I don't know, and I don't care," she said. "Let's find a motel and go to bed."

Poye smiled, still examining the specimen. "Look," he said, "there's a clue." He read it out loud: *God was there from the beginning, and He wrote down in the Bible when and how He made everything.*

"Okay," said Clara impatiently. "So how old is that rock?"

"What do you think? Make believe you're one of my students."

No one had ever asked Clara to do much thinking about anything. She was all action. She waved her hands as if erasing something from the air. "Oh, I don't know, Poye."

Poye traced his finger along the answer to the question and read it out: *The earth is just thousands of years old so the fossil cannot be millions of years old.*

Clara nodded in exaggerated fashion. "Okay, so there it is. Your rock is thousands of years old. Happy?" She turned to me. "Are you happy, Nestor?"

I smiled. "I'm always happy."

Poye glanced at Clara with an abiding devotion. "Let's look at something else, love."

The something else we came to was called the Room of Awe, which detailed an idea called Intelligent Design. Poye read the information while Clara hovered, tapping her foot. She and Poye hadn't made love for two nights, and she was having one of her sex retention headaches. "Babe..."

"Shh. I need to read this." It was the first time Poye had ever shushed Clara, and this, too, was new to her. She had had enough. She grabbed Poye's arm and dragged him away. "That's it," she said. "I have needs too."

Poye continued to read as Clara pulled him and I looked on, helplessly. "Wait, love," he said. "Look here. It says that because life is so complex, a higher intelligence must have designed it."

Poye didn't know it at the time, but he had come to a watershed moment. Of course, he could never have guessed about the Spong. Later, when I told the Spong about the Room of Awe and Intelligent Design, they were pleasantly surprised that such a nuisance species as humans could have stumbled upon the truth. It made me wonder whether they still considered us a threat or a mistake and whether the concept of Intelligent Design had brought them to a new appreciation for us. Whatever their feelings in the matter, they did not communicate them to me at the time. The Spong, I had come to learn, played their cards very close to their tentacles.

"So what do you think, Nest?" asked Poye as Clara continued to tow him.

"About what?" I said, hurrying to keep up.

"Intelligent Design. Do you think some higher power had a hand in creating life on earth?"

"Well, I, er..."

Clara emitted a sigh of exasperation. "What the hell does Nestor know? He's got his head in the clouds."

When we exited the Genesis Museum, Poye told us that his brain was swimming with ideas and images. He seemed so distracted by these thoughts that Clara had to physically maneuver his body to get him to walk in a straight line. When she got him back to the motel, she unleashed her passion upon him, her exertions bringing the guests in a neighboring room to bang on the wall. From my own room, I pictured Poye as being only passively cooperative, staring up at the ceiling with his hands behind his head, trying to process all that he had seen that day. Through the paper-thin walls I heard him utter, "I know what I have to do now.".

"So do I," gasped Clara as she worked away at his body. "So do I."

Needless to say, her headache had disappeared.

TWELVE
CONVERSION

The Poye Trubb that returned to Maine was an upgraded model. The Genesis Museum had changed him, gotten his wheels turning, and relieved him of the hand-wringing uncertainty that had characterized his life. All of a sudden he seemed to know his own mind, not only in pedagogy but in everything else as well. Where his usual response to Clara's questions — such as whether she should buy the soft or the extra-soft toilet paper — had invariably been, "I don't care," now he did care. About everything. Life suddenly had focus, intent, import. He was more confident, more energetic, jazzier, and therefore more interesting to be around. At first, Clara was put off, because such changes made Poye more like other, driven men, taking the shine off the things that had attracted her to him in the first place. But when his newfound sense of purpose, his industriousness, and his verve accompanied him into the bedroom, she experienced a Nantucket sleighride of delight. Where previously she had had a pliant lover to mold and manipulate, now she found herself grappling with a sexed-up Ahab riding her great white thighs to ecstatic, crazy perdition.

But a reservation also began to simmer. One day, as I was getting up from the sofa, I caught sight of Clara standing before the mirror in her bedroom, looking wistful as she slowly twisted and dipped and ran her hands over her face and body. Had she become aware of the age difference between herself and Poye? Of the fact that she was fifty to his thirty-one? I had never heard Clara refer to her age, perhaps because she had seemed to defy time's affronts to the body. What Clara had was a body that, rather than plumping, had seemed to grow more resilient, more robust, more energetic with the years. Her hair had darkened to a deeper, bricker red, her eyes had become more brilliantly blue, her edges sharper, her mind more agile. It was as if the years had whetted her God-given assets. But still, as she examined herself in the mirror, her doubts were palpable. Could it be that when she was lying with Poye, she had a younger standard to compare herself to? Did this lead her to believe that any self-assessment of the stability of her endowments might have been a tad generous? There, beside her, was thirty-one-year-old muscle, thirty-one-year-old skin, a thirty-one-year-old mind, and a hair-trigger body that responded to the slightest touch. The gulf between thirty-one and fifty was still manageable, but how would it be when Poye was forty and she almost sixty? She knew sixty-year-old women and was not stinting in her assessment of them.

"They come into Briody's all the time," she once told me as she stared out the window, a Tiparillo smoldering between her index and middle finger. We were sitting across from each other at the kitchen table, and I noted how the western light played up auburn touches in her hair. Clara had turned to me, her eyes soft. "They're females, but they're not women," she said.

I had seen them too. They were plodding, stodgy, giggly things, balancing precariously on high heels, sitting bolt upright on the bar stools, gripping their handbags. They ordered strawberry daiquiris, sipping them with honeyed smiles as their worn, ashen, uninteresting husbands ogled younger women. Sometimes, in a last, futile bid to seize upon a youthful appearance, they dressed in faux buckskin outfits, put purple highlights in their hair, or invested in a small, tentative tattoo of a butterfly or rose, usually on an ankle, where it could be covered with a sock in the event of regret.

"I will not be one of them," she had said, and I acknowledged her desperation. In truth, she would never be one of them. She would never be cautious, halting, circumspect. She would never sip her drinks.

Clara drew away from the mirror and joined me at the table. "Have you noticed how Poye has changed?" she asked. "I feel like I'm living with a different man, like he´s become his own more lively, more interesting brother."

"He still loves you," I offered.

Clara threw me a curious look. "I know that," she said with gentle alarm as if my saying it had raised that very doubt. A mask of worry drew over her face.

What was this? Fear? The fear of losing, of all things, a man? Clara had spent most of her life dealing in men, using and discarding them at will. But now she found herself attached to one. "I'm not letting him go," she said with resolve, intent on having the new Poye on her terms. Perhaps she suspected that he was bound for something notable. If so, she would be sure to garner her share of the credit.

Clara rose from the table, placed a hand on her hip, and threw me a solicitous look. "Nestor," she said, conjuring her smoky voice. "Do you find me attractive?"

My being seated at the table did a nice job hiding the evidence of my arousal. Nonplussed by Clara's query, I was nonetheless quick to respond. "You're the cat's meow."

She forced a smile. She came over to me and ran her fingers through hair that had once been so thick that my mother had to cut it with garden shears, but was now more like eiderdown. "Care to put that in physical terms?"

Oh, Lordy. Of course I did. But I was the victim of a cruel and unrelenting superego which would not let me betray a friend. I was also reluctant to disturb the pleasant stasis of our triumvirate, not to mention risking the loss of Clara's scrumptious cooking. And so, girding myself, I meowed like a tomcat in heat and asked, "Can I take a rain check on that?"

It sufficed, and Clara drew away from me and pulled herself together for her day.

When Poye returned to Wytopitlock College from our inspiring road trip, the place looked very different to him. Instead of a confining box, it was now the open range where anything could happen. He had become a self-possessed man of great confidence in his newfound abilities. He didn't know what awaited him. But he soon found out. Here's how it happened.

Poye invited me to sit in on his class. "I'm always open to constructive criticism," he said as we entered the room. I took a seat in a back corner.

Poye's twenty-five or so students, with their shining cross pendants, were waiting for him. I had seen Poye teach in the past, but only in snippets when I was walking down the hallway and took a moment to pause and listen. I had seen enough to know that his usual manner of instruction was halting and apologetic, eliciting little in the way of student enthusiasm. He had always lacked *oompf.* Well, now he had *oompf* big time. He marched to the front of the classroom and, *sans* the notes on which he had always been dependent, embarked upon a summary riff through all the topics they had covered to date: cell structure and function, animal behavior, ecology, photosynthesis, species diversity, and DNA structure. And then he stepped into it, willfully and with full consideration of the potential consequences.

Poye asked the following question: "Can you think of a word, a concept, that ties all of these things together?"

Poye had told me that his students hated it when he asked them to think. It was one thing to ask questions with discrete answers, such as, "Who invented the microscope?" But it was another thing entirely to ask students to put ideas together, find the critical nexus, and synthesize disparate observations into one overarching theme. But this is just what Poye was doing when he asked them to come up with the magic word he was looking for.

Poye's question was met with bewilderment. But I strongly sensed what he was after. The students looked at one another, or down at their desks. Casting fate to the wind, Poye crossed the Rubicon. He said one word.

"Evolution."

And the shit hit the fan. There was a collective gasp, but Poye charged on before his students could exhale. "It's something I should have mentioned at the beginning of the course. Because evolution is the glue that holds everything together. Without it, biology is just a grab bag of animals and plants and bacteria and slime molds that bear no relation to one another whatsoever."

I couldn't help but smile. Where had this Poye been all my life? Certainly not at Debec Pond all those years ago, when he had forgotten the Hail Mary.

One student finally erupted, sputtering, "What the…?" He was twenty-fiveish, short, and chubby, with a cap of black hair cut into a severe line of bangs across his broad forehead. He struck me as inarticulate, his face contorting as he attempted to excavate the words he was groping for. I would later learn that his name was Jared Hennemyer, a so-called "non-traditional" student who had made several attempts to succeed in college. He was from the Maine woods and was a communicant of the small, clapboard, white-washed Church of the Happy Clappers, presided over by someone named Brother Eevin. Jared's major was dental hygiene and, grade-wise, he was barely hanging on. Poye told me he rarely spoke up in class because he couldn't seem to get his words in a row. Poye's mention of the E word would cure him of this malady, but for now, he was sputtering.

Poye paused momentarily to allow Jared time to pull himself together. Finally, the student came out with, "You are forgetting the biblical account of creation."

I didn't know from what deep well Poye's response erupted, but erupt it did. Confidently, and in a low voice, he looked at Jared and said, "I don't think so." And then, evidently pained at having put one of his students on the spot, he attempted to mollify him. "Look," he said, "I admire you for having faith in a world that constantly lets us down. But this is a science course, and my job is to help you understand what science tells us about the relationships among living things."

Poye said this with such conviction and authority that Jared once again became tongue-tied. He soon found his voice, however. "I - I'm taking this to the dean," he stammered, his eyes blazing with intent.

"Well," said Poye, leveling his own gaze at the young man, "that's your right."

As soon as Poye uttered this, I could tell he wanted to take it back. He wanted to leap into bed with Clara and say, "Love me." I knew, with the perceptiveness of the tenured professor that I was, that Poye was no longer doing the job he was hired to do. He was not the Poye Trubb who had sat on his hands before the selection committee years before, obedient and yielding, or the nodding man who had sat before the hiring committee for the tenure-track position. He wasn't sure what would happen when Jared Hennemyer approached the dean. But he was going to find out.

Thirteen
Dean

I couldn't decide whether the rest of the day following the altercation in class was, for Poye, one of consternation or simple resignation. He seemed folded into himself, but there was nothing indicative of regret. Clara was working late. When we returned home she wasn't in the apartment to hector him. As for me, I kept my peace and allowed Poye the emotional time and space to work things out in his own mind as the night wore on.

The next morning was also quiet, eerily so. I accompanied Poye to his office, where I finally decided to break the silence. "You haven't said a word about that performance in your class."

Poye looked up from the papers he was shuffling and shrugged. "Mine or the student's?"

"The whole show."

"It's intellectually trivial. This whole anti-evolution business. It's such a little thing."

Ah. There it was again. Yes, a little thing. But the problem was people like Jared and the dean who were willing to make it into a big thing. Such are the wages of the loss of Perspective.

The phone rang. Poye seized the receiver, perhaps too quickly, as if wanting to get it over with, whatever "it" would turn out to be. "Yes," he said. "On my way." He turned to me. "I have to see the dean."

Poye's relationship with the dean was delicate. He couldn't say that he liked or even respected her. In truth, he wasn't sure what to think of her, although she seemed to be even more naive about the world than he, if such a thing were possible. Once, at a faculty breakfast, someone mentioned that there had been a mugging outside a popular coffee shop in town. Dean Wilmot had tsked, looked desperately from face to face, and asked, "Who does these mugging things anyway?"

And now she had summoned Poye to her office. I offered to go with him.

Poye's stride was long and determined, so I had to sort of hip-hop to keep up. "Well, I'll stick with you," I told him. "I always have. I don't see a reason to quit now."

Poye turned his head and smiled at me without breaking his stride. "I cherish you, Nest."

I wasn't very good with sentiment, so I kept my peace and continued to hip-hop along.

We entered Rockland Hall and made our way through a dim corridor. Rockland was as stuffy as old college buildings came. A red brick affair — complete with ivy-covered walls — that had been built in 1911, it was full of old wood and cheap industrial floor tiles that had been buffed to thin, brittle wafers. It was claustrophobic, with a small number of long, narrow windows and, hanging from the ceiling, large, Depression-era milk glass globes that did little more than filter the low-wattage light within. In short, the place had the ambiance of an armory.

The dean's administrative assistant was an older German woman named Mrs. Depper. Unvaryingly dour, she wore her gray hair in a spun braid on top of her head. She feigned industry when Poye approached her desk. I was already on her shit list and had nothing to lose. "Hosanna and how ya' doin', Dep?" I said. She pursed her lips and narrowed her eyes at me.

"Hosanna, Mrs. Depper," said Poye in a more respectful tone. "The dean wanted to see me."

The grim sentinel seethed. "Hosanna. I'll see if she's in," she said, giving each syllable equal weight.

I cast her a beguiling look. We all knew that there was only one door to the dean's office, just behind Depper's space, so she had a very tight tab on Wilmot's coming and going.

Poye hovered by the desk as Mrs. Depper orchestrated an inquiry with the dean behind closed doors. After a minute she emerged. "She will see you," she said.

"Thank you," said Poye. "I do have an appointment."

Mrs. Depper eyed me coldly. "I believe she wants to see only Professor Trubb."

I brushed the comment aside. "I have to go in too," I said. "Union rules. But thank you, Mrs. Depper."

We stepped through the door and found Eulalie Wilmot sitting behind her desk with her hands neatly folded before her. She seemed to be straining to sit up straight, as if seeking relief from a bad back. Her broad, pale face would have been brightened by a smile. "Hosanna, Professor Trubb," she clipped without changing her blunt expression. "Have a seat." Then she turned to me. "Hosanna, Professor. I see you're here too."

"I'm his emotional support animal," I said, and she arched her eyebrows.

Poye sat down in front of her desk and reverted to his customary pose of sitting on his hands. Then he murmured, "Hosanna."

"Okay," said the dean by way of preamble, placing her hands flat on the desk and examining them. "We've had a complaint..."

"From Jared Hennemyer," inserted Poye.

Dean Wilmot ticked her head to the side, birdlike. "Yes, I guess you would have anticipated his visit, based upon the incident in your class yesterday."

"I wouldn't call it an incident," I said.

The dean, annoyed, turned to me. "Well, you weren't here when the student registered his complaint."

"But I was there in the classroom, observing. Poye handled himself quite well. Most respectfully. And, I might add, appropriately."

"I don't understand," said Poye, his expression pleading. "What did he tell you? That I was trying to destroy his faith?"

Eulalie Wilmot hummed. "Something like that."

"I still don't understand. Evolution is part and parcel of any course in biology. I've found it difficult to go on without explaining what it means. Surely the students can accept or reject it if they wish. But they shouldn't be ignorant of it."

The dean clamped her mouth shut, as if reluctant to breathe the same air as Poye. Then she launched her volley. "You are not a free agent," she said, leaning forward, her hands still splayed out on the desk. "You can't just say everything that comes to mind. And, may I remind you that you are violating your teaching agreement? Not to mention the Education Reform Act."

Poye stared at her. We both watched as Dean Wilmot produced a file folder and pushed it across the desk. "Please read this."

Poye fetched up the folder, opened it, and glanced at the title page within: *The President's Council on Right Thinking — Curriculum Guidelines for Public Institutions of Higher Education in the Theocratic Union of American States.*

"Please read the part I have highlighted for you," said the dean.

Poye closed the folder and laid it back on the desk. "I don't understand," he said, in what was becoming a routine refrain. "This isn't a public college. I don't think I'm bound by whatever guidelines might be in this document."

"They're not guidelines," said the dean. "They're directives. Standards. We may be private, but a lot of federal money flows our way. If we don't comply, we will lose that money. Besides," she added, darkening, "we are not exempt from the law."

Poye took the file folder and opened it on his lap while I craned to read it too. A paragraph was highlighted in fluorescent green: *The Teaching of Evolutionary Theory:*

It cannot be emphasized strongly enough that the beliefs, ethics, and sensibilities of students of faith must be held in the highest regard. No student should feel alienated because he or she holds a belief not in concert with scientific conjecture about the origins and relationships of living organisms. To this end, the instructor will not threaten the religious convictions of any student by suggesting origins of life that do not concord with the record of the Christian Bible.

Poye's mouth fell open, forming the same shape as the breathing orifice in the foreheads of the Spong. He was not good at either debate or repartee.

Dean Wilmot demanded, "Are we clear?" Poye nodded. Then she eyed me. "I'm glad you were here. As a witness. Perhaps you can reinforce my message to Professor Trubb."

"I think you're making a fuss about nothing," I said.

The dean took a deep breath and slowly released it. "Be careful about which battles you choose to fight," she said. "Hosanna."

Poye and I got up and walked out of the dean's office, past Mrs. Depper's desk. The old woman nodded at us in a *Put that in your pipe and smoke it* manner.

Poye was already wringing his hands as we walked out into the day. "That didn't go well," he fretted. "Not well at all. My mind is a complete muddle."

"For the moment," I told him, "everything is cool. Let's see if this thing blows over of its own accord."

Poye bumped up against me in a brotherly fashion. "You're still my best friend, Nest."

"Don't let Clara hear you say that."

In short, the new, assertive Poye, the product of a visit to the Genesis Museum, was already dissipating, and the old, indecisive Poye was reasserting itself. This was the Poye who needed to go to Clara to ask what he should do.

FOURTEEN
CREATION

Clara welcomed the doubting, dependent Poye back with open arms. She relished again being the woman in charge and manhandled him with alacrity. She sat him down, stood him up, looked him over, and finally fell onto the sofa with him before I had a chance to claim my space. I sought refuge at the kitchen table, in the hope of scoring some leftovers, but I was upended when Poye said one word that put Clara off.

"No."

Clara sat up, straddling his belly. "No?" she echoed. "You come home to me hangdog, looking for comfort, and you say no? How dare you." And then, pointing to me, "I've got a back-up here, and he's a willing one."

Poye's eyes widened. "Nest?"

I threw up my hands. "Please don't drag me into this. I'm just noodling around for a few scraps."

Poye tried to sit up, but Clara put her hand on his face and pushed him back down. "Now you listen to me," she said. "You've got to make up your mind about me. Do you want me or not?"

Poye's response was immediate. "Now more than ever."

"Then get those pants off," she whooped, reaching for his belt. But Poye stayed her hand.

"People!" I called out, averting my eyes. "At least wait until I'm out of the apartment."

Clara turned and glared at me. "You're never out of the apartment," she growled. "That damned eternal leave of yours. Aren't you supposed to be working on a project or something?"

How could I tell her that I *was* working on a project? And that it involved aliens? She'd have me out on my ear, without so much as a take-home Tupperware of her exquisite manicotti.

"Clara," said Poye, almost in a whisper. "I do want you. But right now I need advice."

"Advice?" echoed Clara. "That's what the drunks at Briody's say before they get down to business." But she must have known it was different with Poye. If he said he needed advice, then that's what he needed. Clara rolled off his belly and closed her eyes, like a mystic seeking communion with the spirit world.

"Clara," intoned Poye, looking intently at her, "the dean told me not to teach evolution. I mentioned it in class today, and a student complained."

Clara hummed disconsolately. "Oh, Poye," she moaned, eyes open now, "I thought I had solved this for you years ago. I said that when you got tenure, you would be able to go off on your own."

Poye shook his head. "I'm on tenure-*track*," he corrected her. "It's like probation." And then, "She showed me the federal standards from The President's Council on Right Thinking."

"So?" returned Clara. She propped herself on an elbow and examined Poye's face, noting his pained expression. He once again had the look of a bewildered adolescent, his smooth cheeks still sporting the merest fuzz. "Your visit to the Genesis Museum changed you, babe. At first, I didn't care for the new you, but then I learned to live with it and even like it. I don't believe that you changed only for the moment. I think the Genesis Museum gave you a mission. That's why you mentioned evolution today. You've got to get back your feeling for that mission. You've got seniority now. Use it. If the school wants to make an ass of itself, then let it. You've got to live with yourself." Then she added, as an afterthought, "And me."

That did the trick. I watched the energy and conviction flow back into Poye. He rose from the sofa, Lazarus-like. Looking down at the recumbent, expectant, frustrated Clara, he said, "We weren't planted here like sunflowers."

Now, looking back, it might appear that this was one of those pivotal moments in Poye's education, that he had had another breakthrough. And you would be right, but not for the reason you think. It's not that Poye had struck upon the right answer. He hadn't. In fact, he was dead wrong, and the Genesis Museum was right. We *were* planted here like sunflowers (if only by accident). And this message would be delivered by two gentlemen who found their way to Poye's office the next day. It was a momentous meeting, and it would solidify and highlight Poye's false trajectory.

I had dropped by Poye's office to offer a few words of encouragement before he returned to his class. As I turned to leave there was a tentative knock on the jamb of the open door. Now I had a reason to stay, my curiosity piqued, my responsibility to take thorough notes for the Spong uppermost in my mind. Two smiling men introduced themselves too warmly as Rate and Brother Eevin, who, in unison, greeted me and Poye with a hearty "Hosanna!" Yes, this was the same Brother Eevin who had spawned Jared Hennemyer. Rate was the older man. He wore a cheap gray suit that couldn't be buttoned around his paunch, so it just swung open, revealing a wrinkled, button-down shirt and a red string tie with a blue onyx clasp. Bald and red-faced, he had a startling set of blazing white false teeth that looked like they had a mind of their own and could jump right out at you.

Brother Eevin was straddling forty. He had hair like Stalin but dyed black, black, black. In contrast to the beefy Rate, he was thin and wiry, with large hands. His suit was also gray but tailored, and he wore a purple, button-down shirt and white clerical collar. His teeth, however, were his own and fit his face. Both men had sidearms slung in hip holsters and, needless to say, they wore the cross pendant, only theirs were pimped with a bordering crust of cubic zirconium. "Do you have a minute, Professor?" asked Brother Eevin in a lazy southern accent.

Poye, seated at his desk, stared at the two beaming men as they teetered on the threshold. And then he said what he said to all visitors: "Always." He noticed them glance at me. "This is Nestor," said Poye by way of introduction. "He's okay."

Both Brother Eevin and Rate shrugged and smiled affably. They looked at each other with bright expressions and pulled up two chairs normally reserved for student supplicants. I took a seat opposite them, behind Poye, my pen hovering above my legal pad. I had, in my travels, met churchmen such as these, who were accustomed to having doors slammed in their faces when they attempted to communicate the truth of Scripture to the uninitiated, so they seemed pleased with Poye's response. "Well," said Brother Eevin, "this is a nice welcome."

Poye continued to stare at them with his po'boy face, while I wondered what had brought southerners so far north to the wilds of Maine. Finally, Rate spoke up. "Do you know a student named Jared Hennemyer?"

Poye sat up a little straighter. "I'm sorry," he said. "I'm not allowed to discuss students by name with outsiders."

Rate and Brother Eevin chuckled good-naturedly, adjusting themselves in their chairs. "It's all to the good. We can go about this another way," said Rate, like a surgeon looking for the best place to cut.

When Poye continued to stare at the men their smiles faded, and they started to poke and prod. Rate took hold of the onyx clasp and began to fidget with it, sliding it up and down the tie strings, as if tuning an instrument. "We understand you introduced the topic of, er, evolution in your class," he said, smoothly, and without rancor, his voice dropping when he said "evolution."

Poye nodded. "It's central to understanding biology."

Brother Eevin's shoulder jumped as if he had a tic. "May I ask how you think we got here, Professor?"

Poye didn't grasp the question. "We?"

"Yes," said Brother Eevin. "Us. All of us. I mean, in the first place. In the beginning." As he said this he looked up, and Poye followed his gaze, squinting. Poye leveled his eyes again and, as if reciting from a catechism, said, "We descended from lower orders of living things."

"Ah!" ejaculated Rate, slapping his knee. And then, leaning toward Poye, "Could you provide evidence of this?"

Poye looked around his office, as if the evidence might be somewhere on a shelf, or hanging on the wall. Then he returned his gaze to the two men, who were smiling in a "gotcha" kind of way. "I suppose," he said, "I could provide DNA evidence showing how closely related all living things are."

"Ah!" gushed Rate again, like a chess player who had checked his opponent's king. "Couldn't you also say that because some higher intelligence created all things, it used the same basic materials and that's why all beings seem so closely related?" Rate glanced at Brother Eevin for approval, and the cleric closed his eyes and murmured an almost imperceptible "Amen." For my part, I was scribbling assiduously on my legal pad, anxious for my next communion with the Spong.

Poye's wheels were turning. I could see it in his eyes. It did sound logical. Reasonable. Rate did not seem to be a maniac in any way. He seemed more childlike, eager for approval. But Poye saw no reason to approve. Finally, he came up with, "I don't know what you want me to say."

Rate became playful. "Have I stumped you, Professor?" He turned and grinned at Brother Eevin, who beamed in response.

"Stumped?" echoed Poye. "I don't think so."

The visitors weren't used to such candid passivity. Like most itinerant churchmen, they were no doubt used to either preaching to the choir or eliciting angry responses from people who told them to get their ignorant asses off their porches. Rate produced a prop that put the conversation back on track. "Here," he said as he held out a slim volume to Poye. It had a beige, nondescript cover with the words *Intelligent Design* embossed in gold.

Poye took the volume. His face immediately lit up. "I know this," he said. "I saw this information in the Genesis Museum."

Both men's blood quickened. They moved to the edges of their chairs. "Praise the Lord!" sang Brother Eevin. "You are an enlightened man. An honest man. You sought out the other side of the story, didn't you? We respect that. Don't we, Rate?"

Rate nodded aggressively. "We certainly do, Brother Eevin."

Both men looked at me as if inviting me to join the eager chorus. Instead, I gave them my poker face.

Poye watched the two men as they waxed euphoric. Then he looked at the book they had handed him. "What should I do with it?"

"It's a gift," piped Brother Eevin. "We hope you will read it, digest it, and perhaps incorporate it into your course. Naturally, you are welcome to ask us questions as well."

"I think it will set you straight," said Rate, perhaps a little too precipitously. And then, "That is, after you read it maybe we can continue our discussion."

Poye, deadpan, nodded, "All right."

The two men exchanged glances, smacking of satisfaction, like used car salesmen who had found a potential buyer open to giving their jalopy a spin. After a few concluding pleasantries, they got up, shook Poye's hand, and headed for the door, not even bothering to acknowledge me. "We shall be back," said Rate. "Give our regards to Brother Jared."

Brother Jared?

Poye flipped through the book Rate had given him. "There's stuff here about DNA and change and the variety of living things," he murmured.

"Let's have a look."

Poye handed me the volume, which I briskly leafed through. My beat was Perspective, not molecular biology, so I could have easily been a sucker for what looked like an impressive intermingling of God, genes, and miracles. "What are you going to do with it?" I asked as I handed it back to him.

Poye responded by slipping the book into a pocket of his jacket. "We shall see," he said in his typical, non-committal way.

I left the office with my notes and locked myself in the men's room, where I took out the servo and reported this incident to the Spong. I have to say that they were completely riveted. They asked me, "What was in the book?"

I explained what I knew about Intelligent Design. That humans had been manufactured by what the creation scientists referred to as "a superior intelligence." "That would be Spong," said Spong 1. "So what is the issue here?"

I explained that Intelligent Design was a way of saying "God" without saying "God," to which Spong 2 replied, "What is God?"

"Whew. That's a biggie. How much time do you have?" I asked them.

In unison, they shrugged with the parts of their rubbery bodies that passed for shoulders. They asked, "How much time do *you* have?"

Well, I was on extended leave, so time was my oyster, right? I commenced my odyssey through the history of God. I explained how he had planted a naked man and lady in a beautiful garden in Iraq, then how they deceived God, and how God punished them. I talked about how Abel's brother murdered him, how God had drowned almost everybody in The Flood, and also turned a woman into salt. I described daughters having sex with their holy fathers, and how God told us to kill people who worked on the Sabbath. Then God killed Er because he was wicked, and said that witches should be killed. And if a man has sex with another man...well, you get the picture.

When I was done, the Spongs' orifices were hanging wide open. They scratched their apices with their tentacles and looked at each other with the eyes that were at the ends of those tentacles. "So let's get this straight," said Spong 1. "You say God put the humans on earth, and then he killed them."

"Not all the time."

Spong 2 asked, "When?"

"Only," I said, "when they displeased God."

The Spong hummed in unison. It was quite beautiful, like singing. "When did they displease God?" they asked.

"That's easy," I said. "When they weren't perfect." (It's easy to feel you know a lot about the Bible when you're talking to those who have never heard of it.)

The Spong fell into a sort of commotion. They were all talking at once, waving their tentacles and breathing heavily through their orifices. Then Spong 3 turned to me. "Why," he asked, "do they call the creator God and not Spong?"

Now, there was a stumper. "I don't know. Maybe it's your fault. I mean, did you ever give humans a book of answers the way God did?"

Spong 1 was quick to respond. "Spong didn't even know you were here until we returned. Four billion years is a long time to be away."

I picked up the servo, raised it to my eyes, turned it about, and considered what a wonder it was. "Well," I said, "you weren't minding the shop so what did you expect? Someone had to take your place, right?"

The Spong congratulated me on a competent, if disturbing, report. They told me to continue my observations, as they were now concerned for Poye. "It seems," they said, "that Poye and those two men have a lot in common. We think that the book they gave him says 'superior intelligence' because the person who wrote it is a genius. Do you think those two men, who seem closer to the truth, are a threat to Poye?"

"I don't know," I said. "I haven't thought about this possibility. I will watch Poye closely and get back to you."

The Spong waved their tentacles and signed off, leaving me with a pile of fresh cash. I considered that the Spong held me in very high esteem. Maybe they thought I was the most intelligent man who ever lived. Maybe they thought I was something like God.

FIFTEEN
WATCHMAKER

I went back to the apartment, leaving Poye to spend some time reading and brooding over the book that Rate and Brother Eevin had given him. When he arrived home, he was still reading it and tripped over the threshold in his distraction. "It sounds so logical, Nest," he announced as he snapped the volume shut. "The whole thing seems to revolve around the example of a pocket watch. Basically, the book is asking, if you found a pocket watch lying on the ground, picked it up, examined it, and noted the intricacies of its mechanism, you would conclude that it had been made by some intelligent entity, right? That's the way this book says it was with humans. We're like watches, with so many parts working flawlessly together. How could anyone conclude that the pocket watch was an accident, or that, by extension, human parts had coincidentally associated with each other in such a way that they were able to produce something like a man? There must have been a designer."

I stretched out on the sofa, scratched my beard, gave a generous yawn, and folded my hands on my chest as I gazed up at the ceiling. "I'm no biologist, Poye, but it doesn't sound right to me. With humans, doesn't the environment have an influence on how we evolved?"

"Sure," said Poye. "That's the whole ball of wax."

"Well," I said, still staring up, as if taking dictation from a higher intelligence, "I don't think a pocket watch gives a damn about the environment."

Poye emitted a pronounced "hmm." Then he abandoned the subject to inquire after Clara's whereabouts.

"She's in the bedroom," I said and left it at that. I saw no need to tell him that she had just finished entertaining a one-legged man. Poye, for his part, drifted over to the kitchen table, where he delved into his book again.

As for Poye's musings on the subject of Intelligent Design, this is precisely where he lost his Perspective. And as I've explained over and over, the loss of Perspective has been the cause of every misguided adventure in human history. Think of World War I. It happened because some kid shot an emperor's nephew. Or Nazi Germany. Who could have imagined that the country that produced Beethoven and Einstein would decide to follow an army corporal named Schicklgruber? (*Heil, Schicklgruber!*) Think of pet rocks. (My cousin Dooey, who was as loose as ashes, bought one of those.) And then there was the fashion tragedy of leg warmers. All of these things may have seemed reasonable at the time, but now we look back and shake our heads.

So it was with Poye. He allowed something that sounded reasonable — Intelligent Design — to preoccupy him and harden him against a broadening of his understanding of evolution to consider the issue of origins. Clara, of course, picked up on his consternation. She emerged from the bedroom as she was putting up her hair. "Whatcha got there, babe?" she asked as she moved seamlessly to the stove and started to chop a zucchini, a cigarette pasted to her lower lip.

"It's a book," said Poye.

Clara clucked. "Why the puss?"

Poye attempted a pathetic smile. "I had a visit today."

"Lay it on me, babe."

Poye went over to the stove and watched as Clara chopped, chopped, chopped the zucchini in uniformly thin slices. "Two men," he said. "They said they wanted to set me straight."

"Oh, babe," lamented Clara as she wiped her hands with a dish towel and threw a pot of water on the burner. She grabbed a fistful of linguini and snapped it in half. Poye winced. "They say you shouldn't break pasta before boiling it."

Clara cackled. "You think I give a rat's ass what 'they' say? Don't distract me. Why did those two guys think they had to set you straight?"

Poye shrugged. "I don't know. They gave me this book," he said as he produced the volume. "It's about something called Intelligent Design. The same thing we read about in the Genesis Museum."

"Oh, that," said Clara with a wave. "Didn't make an impression on me." She sucked on the butt with deep concentration, squinting as she blew a fog of smoke in Poye's direction. "You know, I think I'd like to be a professional chef in a snooty restaurant."

"I was with Poye when those two guys showed up," I chimed in.

"Oh, yeah?" said Clara. "So why didn't you defend him?"

"He held his own," I said. "You would have been proud of him."

"Clara, let me ask you a question," said Poye. "If you were wandering in the desert and found a watch, what would you think?"

"That's easy," she said. "That somebody lost it."

"That's not the answer I was looking for."

Clara drew back. "Sorry, babe," she said, indignant. "Tell me what answer you want."

"It's not like that," continued Poye as he stroked the book's cover. "I mean, how did that watch become a watch in the first place?"

Clara looked as if she were at some disadvantage. She didn't like being probed. She was used to being the one in charge, in or out of bed. But, perhaps because she sensed Poye's distress, she decided to go along. For a little while, at least. "Somebody made it?" she suggested, tentatively.

"Yes."

Clara huffed. "Is this supposed to be a hard question? Didn't I give you the right answer? Just because I dropped out of high school doesn't mean I'm stupid."

Poye reached out and laid a hand on her arm. "No, no, of course not," he said. "You've got a wisdom I've never found in anybody else. It's a gift."

Clara softened. She dumped the linguini into the boiling water and threw the zucchini into an oiled pan. "Thanks, babe. But what's this all about?"

"Those two men. This book. It says that humans are like watches. Someone or something must have made us."

"I just don't understand why they came to you."

"They want me to teach this in my biology course."

"So? Are you going to?"

Poye looked at the zucchini as it sizzled and snapped in the hot oil. "No," he said. "There's no higher intelligence that accounts for how we got here."

And that's where Poye lost his Perspective in a big way. I was bursting, just bursting, to tell him the truth as revealed by the Spong, but I held my peace. He didn't know it at the time, but he was about to set off in precisely the wrong direction, and all because the idea of evolution he was so invested in was all but mum on the subject of origins. Rate and Brother Eevin were closer to the truth, even though they said "higher intelligence" instead of "Spong." I left the apartment to make my report to the Spong, who said that those two men had insight and were probably geniuses, like the man who wrote the book. They directed me to keep track not only of Poye Trubb but of Rate and Brother Eevin as well. They told me, "Maybe those two will be worth saving. It seems that they would be open to the idea of Spong."

When I returned to the apartment, Clara came over to me and lifted a wooden spoon to my lips. "Here," she said. "Taste this." I sat up and did so, and the sauce was so delicious that I concluded that a higher culinary intelligence had created it.

Sixteen
Inspector

Although I couldn't tell Poye about the Spong, for fear of altering the course of events, I had to tell him something, because he was starting to wonder why I tagged along with him so much. "You're on leave, Nest," he said as we alighted from the Rambler and headed for his classroom. "You should be off somewhere, indulging yourself."

"What? And miss out on Clara's cooking?" I feinted.

Poye regarded me with a questioning eye. "I am grateful for your friendship," he said.

"Aw, you don't need to tell me that, Poye. You've been saying it since we were kids."

"What I'm saying is that our friendship could weather a bit of distance. I think it's that strong."

Hmm. What did he mean? That he no longer wanted me around? That his relationship with Clara meant three was a crowd? Cognizant of my obligation to the Spong, and not wanting to risk the loss of their gracious bankrolls, I had to tell him something to justify my constant propinquity. I took hold of Poye's arm and stopped him for a moment. "Listen," I said, "remember when Clara asked if I had a project to pursue? Well, I do. I'm writing a biography."

"A biography," echoed Poye, his face brightening. "That's great, Nest. Who's the subject?"

"Brace yourself. It's you."

Poye pointed to himself and raised his eyebrows. "Me?"

"Yes. Oh, now you've gone and spoiled it somewhat because you know what I'm up to and I'm afraid it will change your behavior."

"The Heisenberg Uncertainty Principle," recited Poye. "You can't know everything about the electron because your attempts to do so affect its behavior."

"Yes! Yes!" I rejoiced, having reeled him in but good. "I'm writing about the challenges of teaching science in the current social and political climate. And since we're already good friends, I felt that you were handed to me on a silver platter. So all I ask is that you go about your business as if I weren't around. Just do what you normally do and leave the note-taking to me. Please tell me you'll cooperate and not ask any more questions, okay?" As I said this, I had on my little-lost-boy face.

Poye assented with a couple of nods. "Okay, Nest," he said. "I'll try to be myself."

The recent classroom altercation couldn't have been far from Poye's mind, nor from Jared Hennemyer's. As soon as we entered, Jared narrowed his eyes. Poye cast him a fleeting look, sighed, and turned to his other students. "Now, where were we?" he asked as I snuck off to my corner.

At that moment a vaguely familiar woman appeared at the door. She was fortyish, stout, with brown, shoulder-length hair and muscular arms. She signaled to Poye. He excused himself to his class and went over to her. "I'm teaching," he said, stating the obvious.

The woman was apologetic. She identified herself as Trish Tash from Student Affairs. "May I sit in?" she asked.

Poye looked bewildered. "But why?"

"We have a situation," she said.

"Situation?" echoed Poye as his students, and I, listened in.

"Yes."

Poye brought a hand to his chin and dropped his eyes as if doing a quick calculation. Either he could continue to bandy the issue about while standing on the threshold, losing precious instructional time, or he could acquiesce and sort things out later. So he stepped aside and watched as Trish Tash made her way to the back of the room and took a desk three aisles removed from me. Jared Hennemyer was sitting two aisles over from her other side. I threw her a welcoming smile, but she merely winced before turning her attention to Poye, who had resumed his station at the front of the room. "Now, I'd like to continue with our discussion of evolution," he intoned, in contravention of the dean's warning.

Jared Hennemyer jerked his head to the side and stared daggers at Trish Tash.

This didn't escape Poye, who nevertheless stayed on task. "Evolution," he repeated.

Jared shouted through cupped hands, "What if you don't believe in it?"

This unsettled the class and the students started to move uneasily in their desks, their pendants shifting about their necks. Poye looked at Jared. For a moment I thought he was going to retreat, but something deeper welled up in him and cemented his conviction. "I'm not asking you to believe it," he said. "I just want you to understand it."

This appeal to some higher intellectual function seemed to throw Jared Hennemyer off balance. He licked his lips and then launched his next volley. "I haven't heard any mention of God," he said. There were several approving nods.

"Nor will you," said Poye, feeling stronger now, perhaps recalling how energized he was after his visit to the Genesis Museum. He glanced at Trish Tash, who was regarding the exchange coolly. She ran her hand along the chain holding her cross pendant. Was this supposed to be some sort of signal? Perhaps it was a warning.

Jared sprang to his feet. "Then it is my duty to leave." Poye watched the student's hand and its spatial relationship to the pistol that dangled in its holster. Then he shrugged. "Duty is important," was all he said. He watched as Jared marched out. "You haven't heard the last of this," he said, shaking a fist at Poye.

That was an understatement. Poye had lit a fuse. Now the dean would go to war with him for sure. And what about this Trish Tash person? It was an impossible situation. If Poye retreated, he would be betraying his own obligation to convey the truth of the scientific evidence. Not only that, but he would be betraying the wisdom of Professor Todelaw, whom he so esteemed. So he continued on, talking about Darwin, about the variations that exist in any species population, and about how natural selection favors the characteristics that best suit individuals to their environments. In this way, the strongest, fastest, and most beautiful survive to reproduce, while the slowest, weakest, and least attractive have far poorer chances of success. Such laws applied to both man and beast. It was all so simple. And yet some of his students were obviously discomfited, shaking their heads and crossing their arms. When he finished what he thought was a clear and interesting and well-presented lecture, the students shuffled out without a word. Trish Tash, however, remained behind, as did I, my paws clamped over the edge of my desk.

Poye put his notes away and waited for the woman to say something, but she just sat there, contemplating him. Finally, Poye spoke up. "Why are you here?"

Trish Tash remained seated and spoke across the room, blankly ignoring my presence. "Jared Hennemyer filed a formal complaint."

Poye's expression was pleading. "I still don't understand why you're here."

"He cited the President's Council on Right Thinking."

Poye meditated for a moment, looking down at the floor tiles. Then he raised his head. "Am I wrong?" he asked.

"We must all comply."

Poye, childlike, "But I don't want to comply."

Trish Tash was unmoved. "This will make things difficult," she said. "I have my duty."

Everyone has their duty, I thought as I scribbled my notes, concluding that duty might not be such a good thing if it overrode judgment, or required that one carry out harmful policies, or relieved one of the responsibility to think deeply about things.

"Can I keep you out of my classroom?" Poye asked, with no hint of irony.

"I have broad authority to monitor classroom activities."

"Like a political officer," said Poye. I was amazed at his cheek. Perhaps he had a capacity for humor after all.

Trish Tash got to her feet and moved toward the door. "Let me speak with the dean and see what she says."

"She will not like it," said Poye.

"No, I don't think she will," Trish Tash said as she lingered on the threshold. "This would be the second offense."

"But I'm on tenure-track," offered Poye, pathetically.

Trish Tash had no response to that. Poye watched as she disappeared down the hallway.

I got up with my legal pad and approached my friend. "Well, the plot thickens."

Poye sighed. "Which makes your work more like a novel than a biography." And then, "Nest, I fear this thing has a life of its own now. Too much momentum. Do you really expect this biography you're writing will make any kind of difference?"

"Who knows?" I said. "But I've come this far and have no intention of bailing out now."

Poye became dreamy. "I wish we were twelve again, Nest. I wish we were warm in our childhood beds. I wish we were skinny dipping in Debec Pond under a full moon on a hot summer night. I wish..."

"I wish a lot of things too, Poye."

SEVENTEEN
AXIS

When I communicated this incident to the Spong they shook their tentacles in a gesture I interpreted as despondence. Why, they wanted to know, didn't Poye just see that Rate and Brother Eevin were right? Life on Earth *was* the result of a higher intelligence. I tried to explain that Poye's view of things wasn't broad enough to entertain the existence of the Spong, but it was narrow enough to eliminate the prospect of a God. This utterly confused the Elders. "Maybe God is the problem," said Spong 1.

"Many people say that God is the answer," I replied, a bit too neatly. This caused the Spong to throw their tentacles around one another and huddle in a sort of rugby scrum. I realized that it was they who were responsible for this whole mess because they had somehow mis-seeded the planet, inadvertently creating a species that wanted to do more than just snuffle around for food and sex. Although they were billions of years more advanced than we, they were surprisingly naive. I didn't tell them this, however. I wanted to keep my job, and my supply line of cold, hard cash.

When Poye and I returned to the apartment that day we found Clara lying on the sofa in her bathrobe with one exposed leg thrown up on the backrest. She was reading an *American Cowgirl* magazine. "You know," she said without preamble, "I think I'd like to be a cowgirl. I like the style."

"That's nice," offered Poye as I plopped down at the kitchen table in hope of stimulating the appearance of food.

Clara dropped the magazine on the floor and extended her arms to him. "Wanna roll?" she offered. "I'm up for a few tricks."

"Not now, love."

She craned her neck toward me. "How about you, Nestor? Let's see what kind of man you are."

I looked down at myself, at my worn, low-slung jeans, my stained hoodie, and my dilapidated sneakers. "Not much of a man right now," I said.

Poye's increasingly frequent denials only magnified Clara's desire. I knew she could muscle Poye into the sack, but she didn't seem to want to have to do that. In any case, when Poye wasn't around she had no trouble finding release in the bar patrons she dragged home. "Another bad day?" she queried.

Poye sat down in the easy chair opposite Clara. "Yes," he said. "I took your advice and continued to lecture about evolution, but I think it's only making matters worse. An administrator sat in my class today to see what was going on."

Clara shrugged. "And...?"

"I don't think she liked it."

"Did you tell her you're on tenure-track?"

"Yes. But I don't think it impressed her. I don't think it makes a difference. Even actual tenure would be like a paper shield."

Clara sat up and pulled her hair back behind her head. "You want me to go in and make things clear to her?"

Poye fixed his gaze on Clara and smiled. He clearly loved her. She could have any man she wanted — and, I suspected, she had — and yet she stayed with Poye. Five years. That's a good chunk of time. "No, no," he cooed. "I appreciate the offer. I think this is a battle I have to fight on my own."

Clara didn't like to waste time arguing. She was used to having her way. Her combination of wiles and brawn proved irresistible in most situations. "I'm here if you need me," she concluded before fetching up her magazine again.

"I know, love."

Poye, in his biology course, was dealing with evolutionary change across millions of years, but he didn't seem able to consider the change that can occur overnight. When we returned to his class a couple of days later, Jared Hennemyer was sitting rigidly in his desk. He and several other students were wearing purple armbands, each bearing an illuminated yellow cross. Jumping out from the cross were yellow squiggles, like lightning bolts. Poye didn't voice any questions.

Courageously, he continued with his lecture on evolution, describing how modern species — such as the many species of sharks — could have arisen from a common ancestor. But a peculiar thing happened. Every time he said "evolution" the armbanded students hummed. And each time they hummed they hummed louder. Poye finally turned from the board with a sick, questioning smile. When he opened his mouth to speak, the armbanded students hummed. He tried again. They hummed. I felt desperately bad for my dear friend. Maybe he should have brought Clara along after all. But no, that wouldn't have turned out well. He still had an obligation to teach his class, so he did a remarkable thing: he wrote the rest of the lecture out long-hand, word-for-word, on the blackboard. Jared's face registered alarm. His toadies looked to him for direction. He had none. What was the point of humming if there was nothing to drown out? Poye finished the lecture, filling four blackboards with his cramped, but legible, script. He rubbed his arm, which must have been terribly sore, but he had finished.

Trish Tash had been standing in the hallway outside his classroom. "What was all that humming?" she asked as the students filed out past her.

Poye shook his head. "I was hoping you might be able to tell me."

Is it any surprise that Dean Wilmot wanted to speak with Poye again? Trish Tash conveyed this message and left. Poye drew his things together, and we headed for Rockland Hall. Mrs. Depper was crocheting a sock at her desk but hurriedly stowed it when she saw us approach, as if she were doing something illicit.

I threw a "Hiya, Dep," at the old girl, who squinted savagely at me.

"The dean wanted to see me," said Poye.

"Do you have an appointment?" she asked, bitterly.

I regarded Mrs. Depper with curiosity. Was she like this with everybody? Or just Poye? Finally, Poye blurted, "I think so. Maybe you should check."

Mrs. Depper firmed her lips, got up, and clopped through the door to Wilmot's office in black nun's shoes with square heels. An all-too-brief moment later she returned and seemed to take delight in telling Poye, "They're waiting for you."

They? Poye inclined his head and peered through the open door. There, aligned along the far side of the dean's desk, from left to right, were Jared Hennemyer, the dean, Trish Tash, and a small, elderly, block-shaped, dusty man in a Carhartt work jacket and striped train driver's cap. All four wore a gold cross pendant. Poye was at a deep disadvantage, and I could sense him welling with an uncharacteristic emotion: anger. No doubt because Jared Hennemyer was present. And seated next to the dean.

Poye and I walked in. "Hosanna," said Eulalie Wilmot. "Please sit down, Professor Trubb." Then she looked at me and tsked. "I see you're here as well, Professor. Aren't you supposed to be on leave?"

"Indeed," I said. "Poye is my project."

The four members glanced at each other but had evidently resolved not to be distracted from whatever their goal was, so they abided me.

Poye took a seat in the solitary folding chair that had been placed before the dean's desk, but at an intriguing distance, creating an empty gulf between the two parties. I pulled up a chair next to Poye and crossed my legs, my hands slung in the pockets of my hoodie.

Poye made a conscious effort not to sit on his hands this time, layering them awkwardly on his lap. Jared Hennemyer was already smirking. Despite the student's youth, he had preternatural lines in his face which clashed with his pixieish haircut. But who was that block-like man sitting to the far right, with his arms hanging down behind his seat back and his Carhartt jacket open to reveal dusty blue coveralls? He was squinting at Poye with something resembling contempt. Poye had been disliked by people in his life but never despised. Was he in for another new experience?

"Professor Trubb," intoned Dean Wilmot as she looked down at some papers splayed out before her. Then she turned to her right and extended her hand. "I think you know Jared Hennemyer."

"Yes," said Poye. "I also noticed his armband."

Jared Hennemyer looked down at the armband as if he had forgotten it was there.

"Yes," confirmed the dean. "Mr. Hennemyer is the leader of the Star Nation Campus Compact."

"Compact...?" blurted Poye.

This is where I need to jump in. The Theocratic Union of American States got busy soon after the constitutional convention established Christianity as the official national religion. This meant an aggressive educational program, commencing in the lowest grades. At the college level, this resulted in the fostering of a government-sponsored student activist organization reflecting the positions of the sole national political party. When Dean Wilmot summarized this for Poye, he took a moment to digest it. Then he said, "A small world."

The dusty, block-like man opened his small mouth a crack and growled, "What the hell is that supposed to mean?"

Poye shrugged. "It occurred to me that Mr. Hennemyer used to be a nobody. Now he has apparently found a world small enough to feel big in."

My heart leapt in my chest for my friend, and for his courage in conjuring such assertive language. I couldn't believe his daring. And neither could the committee. Their mouths fell open, except for the block-like man, whose jaw was clamped shut. I could feel Poye's energy surge as if he recognized his moment's advantage. He pressed on. Looking at the dusty man, he said, "I don't believe I know you, sir."

Dean Wilmot thawed and gestured to her left. "This is my father."

It dawned on me who this glaring octogenarian was: Dud Wilmot, owner of a cement plant called Hosanna Castings and an elder of the Church of the Happy Clappers. I also recalled his name from the cover of the Intelligent Design book that Rate and Brother Eevin had given Poye. Dud sat there, motionless, only his rheumy eyes giving any indication that there was a pilot light of life within that massive, rock-like head. His nose was square at the tip as if it had been hacked off with a machete. He was covered in rock dust, which made him look like something sculpted from granite. He opened his mouth and said, "Are you trying to be funny?"

Poye, who had never managed the knack of being funny, looked like a man who nevertheless wanted to take credit for it. He glanced at Dud and shook his head.

Dud didn't budge. Only his mouth moved. "I think you are," he said. "And I am an excellent judge of character."

"Then I will not argue with you," said Poye.

Dud sucked his teeth. "There you go again. Being funny."

Poye seemed to be wondering why, if Dud thought he was funny, he wasn't laughing. He shifted his gaze to Eulalie Wilmot and asked the obvious question. "Why am I here?"

The dean leaned forward. "Because Ms. Tash has reported that you continue to press on with a line of pedagogy that is isolating and disrespecting our students." And, for good measure, she added, "In contravention of the Education Reform Act. Does this sound familiar?"

Poye swallowed audibly. "But I am on tenure-track," he said, and Dud erupted, "Ha!" as a smile finally blossomed on his face. "Now I know you're being funny."

Jared laughed too, and Poye reddened. He had never been laughed at by a student, at least not to his face. And now here he was being mocked by the least capable student he had ever had. In hindsight, though, I think Poye knew he had said a foolish thing. He was like a drowning man shouting to the consuming ocean, "But I can't drown. I have plans!"

A silence set in. No one was saying anything. The tension became unbearable, so Poye blurted, "With all due respect, I don't see what Mr. Wilmot has to do with any of this."

A slow, glacial smile blossomed on Dud's face. He reached up and patted his breast pocket, from which his checkbook protruded. Of course, Poye didn't catch this at all. "Your coat?" he queried, innocently.

Dud's smile vanished. "There you go again. Being funny."

Poye still didn't seem to understand. He threw me a helpless look. If he was being funny why wasn't anybody on the committee laughing?

The truth that Poye was not privy to was something I had learned along the way: Dud Wilmot was a generous benefactor. He was a high school dropout who recognized the lackluster potential of his unmarried, uninteresting daughter, so he decided to shore up her prospects with large private contributions to Wytopitlock College. And now here he was, sitting on some sort of board of inquiry, judging Poye. "You think you're so smart," the cement king said.

Poye raised his eyebrows. "It never occurred to me," he admitted, which brought a rush of air from Dud's lungs. "Ha-ha. Very funny." He jabbed a finger in Poye's direction. "Well, I want you to know that I wrote a book. Perhaps you've heard of it — *Intelligent Design*."

Poye brightened. "Yes," he said, eagerly, moving to the edge of his chair. "I read it with great interest. As a matter of fact, I found it intriguing."

Poye's candor caught Dud Wilmot off guard. He shifted his eyes a few times before settling on Poye again. "Well, well," he said, raising his arms. "So there is light in the *Dummkopf* after all. So you admit that a higher intelligence could have gotten the ball of creation rolling."

"Oh, no," said Poye, leaning back. "I don't admit that at all. I'm just saying that your book attempts a very logical approach to the question of origins. I admire that."

Dud Wilmot looked like a man who had had the air knocked out of him. And yet there was some little something that suggested to him that maybe, just maybe, he had gotten the leading edge of his wedge under Poye's skin.

"This is your final warning," concluded the dean. "Abide by the directives of the President's Council on Right Thinking. To ensure that you do, I am empowering the Star Nation Campus Compact to track your teaching activity and make their reports directly to me." As she said this, Jared

Hennemyer seemed to grow larger as he sat there with his arms thrown around himself, smirking in a self-satisfied manner. "Do you understand me?"

"Oh, yes," said Poye, because it was true. He understood everything the dean had said.

"And Ms. Tash will also be monitoring the tone and content of your classroom."

Both Poye and I looked at Trish Tash, who had not said a word during the proceeding.

We left campus and headed home in the Rambler. "That was brutal," I finally said.

Poye gripped the steering wheel with both hands and leaned into the windshield as if straining to see the way ahead. "How do you think it will end?"

"I'm just a note-taker," I hedged. "But it feels more like I'm writing that novel you referred to."

"Do writers know how their novels will end before they get there?"

"I don't know."

When we arrived home, the apartment was booming. Poye felt the pressure waves of the music as soon as he opened the door. When Clara saw him, she turned the stereo down a bit. "Rammstein," she shouted over the din. "Isn't it great? You know, I think I'd like to get a rock band together."

"That's nice."

She lowered the music a bit more. "Nah?" she prompted. "Was today a better day?"

Poye managed a weak smile. "I think I'm becoming funny," he said.

"See?" said Clara. "All's well that ends well."

Poye sighed. "I'm afraid it's just beginning."

Eighteen
Clappers

Dud Wilmot's evil intent had been clear to both Poye and me. He seemed like he wanted to kill Poye, for making life difficult for his daughter if nothing else and, like most citizens of the Theocratic Union, he carried a sidearm that could do the trick — a 10-millimeter Glock G40 auto with gold filigreed grip inlays. But while Poye recognized Dud Wilmot as a threat, he didn't know what he could do about it.

This is what Poye and I were talking about while leaving his building after he worked late one evening. Out of nowhere, a crummy old Ford woody pulled up. A heavyset man stumbled out and laid hands on Poye. I reflexively grabbed my friend's arm and commenced a tug of war with the assailant. I was on the losing end, my thin, wiry frame no match for the Gargantua who was hauling Poye off like a sack of wheat. He threw him into the car and, as I was attached to Poye, I flew in as well. The woody rumbled off, its broken muffler clattering on the pavement.

The abductor wedged himself in between me and Poye. Physical resistance was futile. Besides, Poye had never in his life physically resisted anything or anybody. We looked at each other around the big man who was staring straight ahead with a grim expression, smelling of perspiration. And then I took note of the driver. My God, it was Dud Wilmot, looking diminutive behind the wheel of the big wagon. He was wearing the same work clothes, covered with cement dust, and his striped train driver's hat, tilted at a jaunty angle. No one said a word for five minutes or so until Dud spoke up. "Don't you want to know where the hell we're going?"

Poye lifted his head. "Would it make any difference?"

Dud growled. "There you go again, being funny." Then, after a moment, "No, I guess it wouldn't." The woody pressed into the night, maneuvering and bouncing on its worn shocks along a winding road studded with signs warning of moose. "I see you got your sidekick with you."

"His name is Nestor."

"He's your sidekick," reiterated Dud, determined to have everything his way.

I glanced out the window but didn't see anything familiar in the landscape, which was heavily forested and repetitious, with roving clouds periodically obscuring a half moon. "Don't be afraid," rasped Dud.

"I'm not," said Poye.

"We're not going to hurt you."

"I know."

"How do you know?"

"Why would you hurt me?"

"We have reasons."

"We?"

Dud Wilmot chuckled like a stock villain. "Just wait."

And so we waited. I noticed Poye staring at the hefty man sitting next to him. Then he registered a flush of recognition. Our abductor's large, pudgy face was pockmarked and stubbled. He must have sensed Poye looking him over because he turned and regarded him with extreme distaste. "Well?"

"My goodness," said Poye. He swallowed audibly and managed, "Hello, Joe."

The man smiled. "We meet again."

I had read stories about playground bullies who matured into decent, charitable adults. But they must have been the exception, because here, right between us, sat Poye's childhood nemesis, Joe Christiani. Apparently, the years in grade school had been a proving ground for his career as a leg-breaker. "It's been a long time, Joe," Poye said without sarcasm.

Joe Christiani turned his eyes front and forward again. "Too long," he said. And then he chuckled. "I've missed you."

Dud cut in. "Shut up, Joe," he said. "You talk too much."

"Yessir."

Poye didn't say another word. He just bided his time until the woody pulled up somewhere in the sticks beside a ramshackle, peel-paint church with a tilted steeple. The home base, no doubt, of the Happy Clappers. Joe Christiani muscled Poye out of the car, and I dutifully followed. We stood watching while Dud struggled out the driver's door, grumbling goddamns as he maneuvered his stiff body to a standing position. As he marched, limping, toward the church, he signaled over his shoulder for Joe and us to follow him.

We descended into an ill-lit basement that smelled of spice cake and moldy carpet. There were two more men seated at a round table under a flickering fluorescent light. Poye brightened when he recognized Rate and Brother Eevin. They smiled in return. "Hosanna," said Rate by way of greeting. "Thank you so much for coming," he added in his easy drawl. As if Poye had had a choice in the matter.

"Amen," pronounced Brother Eevin.

Dud clattered into one of the metal folding chairs at the table, next to the two churchmen. He signaled to Joe Christiani, who pushed Poye into a chair opposite Rate and Brother Eevin. Then he threw me a dismissive glance. "This doesn't concern you, sidekick."

"I go where Poye goes," I said.

"Well," concluded Dud with mock amiability, "then I guess you're going to hell too."

Joe chuckled at that one. I took a seat in another folding chair off to the side, but close enough to leap into any fray that might erupt. Joe sat down just behind Poye. The quiet was pervasive, except for Dud Wilmot's labored breathing. Outside the church, a dog howled in the empty night.

Poye glanced back at Joe, who was seated behind him. Then he looked at the two churchmen. Rate spoke up. "I hope this hasn't upset you," he said with palpable concern. "With all due respect for Brother Dud, I don't think it's a done deal that you're going to hell." And then he glanced at me. "Or your friend."

Poye rested his eyes on Rate. "I'm not upset," he said. "But Clara will be worried about me."

Brother Eevin piped up. "Clara?"

"My companion."

Dud Wilmot said, "We'll take care of Clara."

I thought that Poye was going to smile at that comment. He didn't. But he did say, "Be careful. Clara can be very touchy."

Dud's expression widened. "You're telling *us* to be careful?"

"Clara likes to have things her way," said Poye.

Dud narrowed his eyes. "Well, so do we."

Rate moved to turn the thermostat down. "Now, now," he said, patting the air with his beefy hands. "We're all friends here, so let's have a civil conversation." Then he looked at Poye. "Isn't that what we want, Professor?"

"I don't know," said Poye, blankly honest as always. "I don't know why

I'm here."

"Brother Rate just told you," rasped Dud. "We want to have a civil conversation." He said this with a note of disgust, like a man disdainful of civil conversations.

Poye nodded. "That's nice."

Dud inhaled. "There you go again, trying to be funny."

Poye's look was quizzical, as if he still didn't understand why Dud Wilmot found him so funny yet never succeeded in laughing.

The dog howled again, and continued to howl, as if in pain.

"Goddamn bitch," barked Dud.

"Brother Dud!" exclaimed Rate, throwing the cement king a disapproving look.

Dud turned contrite. "I'm sorry, Brother Rate. I'll give the church five hundred for that one."

Rate beamed.

Dud resumed the thread. "Someone start talking to this man."

Brother Eevin scrunched his shoulders and flashed his full smile. "Professor, do you recall the visit Rate and I made to your office?"

"Of course," said Poye. "You gave me a book."

Brother Eevin turned to Dud. "He's talking about the one you wrote." Dud grunted. "Well," said Brother Eevin, turning back to Poye, "we were wondering what your impressions were."

Poye pulled back a little. The dog howled a good one. It seemed to be coming closer to the church, perhaps drawn by the heavy spice cake odor. Dud Wilmot dropped his hand and caressed the butt of his pistol.

"I found it very interesting. It was so reasonable."

"Well, that's good to hear," said Brother Eevin, warming. "You're making it easy for us. And yourself."

"I still don't understand," said Poye. "Is this meeting about the book?"

"No, goddamnit!" barked Dud Wilmot. "It's about your teaching evolution and denying the existence of a higher intelligence. Who do you think got things started in the beginning? Hmm? Tell me." His hand fastened around the handle of the Glock.

Rate and Brother Eevin registered alarm. Joe Christiani smirked. I leaned forward in my chair, ready to pounce in defense of my friend.

Poye gave Dud's question due consideration before peeping, "I just don't know. I don't think it was anybody in particular."

At this point, I realized that Poye was as set in his ways as the others were in theirs. He saw no reason to insert a higher intelligence into his lesson plan on evolution, and they saw no reason to go on living without one. When Poye made his statement, the dog gave a particularly mournful howl. It sounded like it was in the same room with us. Dud blurted, "Joe, go out there and take care of that mutt. I'm sick of it."

Joe grunted as he raised his heavy body from the folding chair and did as he was told. Poye looked pained. "He's not going to shoot it, is he?"

Dud smiled. "What if he is? Would that bother you?"

Poye nodded. "Why, yes. Yes, it would."

"Why?" pressed Dud. "If we're all just a collection of goo and blood and hair and skin, what's the use of anything? Why don't we all just drop dead?"

To Poye, the answer seemed self-evident. "Because life can be quite pleasant."

Rate spoke up. "We're getting a little off track here," he said. But now that Dud had laid all the cards on the table he found it easier to play their hand. "Professor, you have broken the law by teaching evolution and denying that a higher intelligence is responsible for humankind. To be candid, we acknowledge there are a lot of people who agree with you, but that doesn't make your thinking right. We are trying to spare the law having to deal with you, and the college the trouble of discharging you, which would provide the type of publicity nobody wants."

"Stop it, Rate," said Dud. "You're talking too much. You sound like you're on his side."

"Brother Dud!" said Rate, hurt. He grabbed his onyx tie clasp and ran it up and down the strings. "How could you...?"

Dud put up a hand to silence him, his cross pendant swinging across his chest like a pendulum. "I'll pay for it later," he said. Then he pulled out his checkbook. "Look," he said to Poye, "look here." Poye watched as Dud wrote out a check, tore it off, and pushed it across the table. Poye glanced at it and hummed. "Ten thousand dollars," he said. "That's a lot of money."

Dud huffed. "You better believe it," he said, although the sum was trifling compared to the rock and mineral wealth he had blasted out of the surrounding hills over five decades.

Poye looked up at Dud. "What is it for?"

Dud shrugged. "I don't know. Maybe it's for you. Maybe it's to help you obey the law and teach what you were hired to teach. Maybe it's to make it easier on my daughter, so she doesn't have to see her name in the paper, in the same paragraph with the word" — and here he winced — "evolution."

There was a pained yelp outside the church, but it wasn't animal. It was human. A moment later Joe Christiani stumbled into the room, cradling his hand. "She bit me!" he bleated. "That bitch bit me! I'm sure she had rabies, the way she was behaving."

"Sit down and shut up," said Dud, unsympathetic. Joe complied and sat there whimpering as he cradled his wound. Then Dud returned to Poye. "So?" he said. "Can we go home now?"

"Yes," said Poye, who moved to get up. Joe used his good hand to push him back down.

"Ain't you forgetting the check?" said Dud.

"Oh, I can't take that," said Poye. "It would be wrong. Especially in a church."

Dud's red face pulsed through the gray of the cement dust. "Why, you dirty..."

That's when another player burst through the door — Clara. She was in wraps, her hair wild and her expression lit. "Poye!" she cried out. "Get up!"

Dud recoiled at the sight of her. "Who the hell are you?"

Clara seemed to grow bigger as her anger waxed. "Watch your language," she commanded. Joe Christiani moved to intercept her, but she knocked him down. Then she fetched Poye up by the collar and looked the gathering over. "What is this?" she demanded. "Nestor, get up!" I did as I was told and hurried over to her and Poye.

Things began to move quickly now. Frightened at the sight of this woman in full, Rate and Brother Eevin sprang to their feet, knocking their chairs over in their haste to retreat to a far corner. Joe Christiani tried to get up again, but Clara knocked him back down. He fell to the floor with a dull thud, landing on his bitten hand and screaming out. Dud, in a bid to intimidate Clara, pulled an eight-inch, drop-forged hunting knife from a belt sheath and laid it on the table. This was a grave miscalculation, because at that moment Clara was possessed. She cackled like a madwoman and, in a flash, seized the knife. Before Dud's startled eyes she pulled out one of her breasts and whetted the blade on it. "Come on!" she said, parrying with the knife and spinning about on her heels. "One at a time or all together. It makes no difference to me. I've done four men before. What? No takers? Then you're cowards. Come on, Poye, Nestor. We're going home." She flung the knife into a far wall, where it wagged. Joe tried once more to get up, but Clara pushed him back down with her foot. Then she swept Poye and me up and out the door and into the idling Rambler. We roared off into the night.

Poye, who had been rendered mute by the whole fantastic scene, finally got his voice back. "Clara," he said from the shotgun seat, "how did you find me?"

She laughed wildly, throwing her head back. "Oh, Poye," she said. "I've never had trouble finding a man. You should know that by now."

After the dust had settled, I snuck off and reported this episode to the Spong. I thought the little servo would explode. It danced like a hobgoblin as I detailed the strange adventure. The Spong were all talking at once so that I had to appeal for calm. "Gentlemen!" I said, although I had no idea what gender meant to them. "Please. One at a time."

They couldn't understand why Darwin's evolution didn't concede the essential piece that would allow Poye to accept the idea of a higher intelligence designing life on earth. Which meant he was not open to the idea of Spong. "Rate and Brother Eevin we like," they concluded. "We think we can get them to say 'Spong.' But Dud strikes us as cruel. Still, he wrote the insightful book."

They devoted some praise to Clara as well. Spong 4 was the most enthusiastic. "She is a wild thing," it said. "Her instincts are base."

When the other Elders tried to ask about the ten-thousand-dollar check, or Joe Christiani, or the dog, Spong 4 kept returning to Clara. It wanted to know everything about her. Why her hair was so red. Where her great strength came from. Why she had chosen Poye and not somebody else. Why other human women kept their breasts covered. The other Spong became impatient with it and tried to put their tentacles over Spong 4's orifice, but it pushed them away. "Tell Spong more," it begged me. "Please."

That's when it dawned on me: Spong 4 had a crush on Clara.

Nineteen
Journey

The next day, while Poye was at school and Clara on duty at Briody's, I was surprised when the servo shuddered in my pocket. I had, after all, communicated with the Spong only the day before. Damn, I hated to be interrupted while lying on the sofa and counting cracks in the ceiling, but when duty calls, it calls. I connected, and it was Spong 4. This was unusual because the Elders always acted as a group. Be that as it may, I pulled myself together and asked, "What's up?"

Spong 4 kept looking about with its eight eyes as if worried that someone might be listening. "How is Clara?" it asked in a whisper.

Ah, so that was it. "She's fine, last I checked," I said. "Why do you ask?" Of course, I knew exactly why it was asking, but I thought it best to play it coy. I didn't mind yanking the occasional tentacle.

Spong 4 seemed conflicted. "Spong 4 just wants to know, that's all," it said. "She seems very different from other humans. As if she does not conform to the normal laws of nature."

"Whoa," I said, reminding it that it had remarked about Clara's being a wild thing and having base instincts. "I should think that would make her pretty natural."

"Yes, yes," said Spong 4 anxiously, raising a tentacle for emphasis. "But in the world of nature, she seems like an exception."

Whatever that meant. In any case, I let it slide. "Where are the others?" I asked.

"Elsewhere," said Spong 4.

"So why are you making this call?" (As if I didn't know.)

Spong 4 began to sparkle, which I took for their version of blushing. "Just to say hello," it said.

"That's nice," I replied. "By the way, you got any more of this green stuff? I'm running low."

Poof! A neat pile of twenties materialized. "Gee, thanks."

"You are welcome. Now, please tell Spong more about Clara."

Well, Spong 4 had given me a generous gift, so I paid out. I told it about Clara's sporting ways, her capacity for drink, her military approach to cooking, her chain-smoking, her relationship with Poye — and other men. For good measure, I also theorized about her upbringing — of which I knew nothing — and suggested that she must have had an absent or distant father for whom she compensated by assuming the attributes of masculinity. Of course, I couldn't believe that such pap was dribbling out of my mouth, but I was a philosopher, damn it, and I was intent on philosophizing.

Spong 4 listened in absolute silence as I spoke. When I was done, it wrapped its tentacles around itself, as if administering the embrace it longed for from Clara. "Thank you," it said, and I sensed a deep note of longing in its voice. I could have continued talking about Clara, but Spong 4 shushed me. The other Elders were precipitating. When they arrived and arranged themselves in the proper order, they raised all those eyeballs and ran them over Spong 4. Then Spong 1 turned an eyeball to me and asked, "Why are you communicating with Spong 4?"

I threw up my hands. "Hey," I protested. "Spong 4 was the one who called me."

Spong 4 raised one tentacled eyeball, which stared at me with incredulity as if to say, "Thanks a lot."

Well, what else was I supposed to say? That I had requested a private chat with Spong 4? Then the others would have asked, "About what?" Then I would have had to make up a lie. It would have been a mess. I didn't know what Spong anger was like, but I had no wish to find out.

The other Spong withdrew their eyeballs from Spong 4 and turned them toward me, but I could tell they were unhappy about one of their own going rogue. When they saw the pile of cash in front of me, Spong 1 asked, "Where did you get that?"

What could I say? "It was a gift from Spong 4. It gave it to me in the name of all the Elders of Spong, as a token of gratitude for all the help I've given you."

Spong 1 turned four of its eyeballs toward Spong 4, who was sparkling from the unsolicited compliment. "That was very thoughtful of Spong 4," Spong 1 remarked doubtfully.

I felt that I needed to rescue Spong 4, so I spoke up. "Gentlemen! What can I do for you?"

Spong 1 returned to me, but it kept one eyeball on Spong 4. "We think it is time that you paid a visit to Spong."

"Who? Me?"

"Yes, you," said Spong 3. "Spong has been conferring and has concluded that you might still be wary because you don't understand us. Spong thinks it important that you come to Spong so you can learn more about us."

I reached out and gathered the cash to myself. "Can I take this with me?"

"Of course," said Spong 2. "But it will be worthless on Spong."

Before I knew it — *Bang!* — my heels left the good old Earth, and I was heaven bound with my eyes wide open. I learned that in space I could hold my breath a good long time, and it was hot and cold by turns, and there was a lot of shiny dust and stars and planets and comets and— well, let's put it this way — Lucy in the sky with diamonds.

Before I knew it, I was in a place difficult to describe. It smelled like new-mown hay, and there were two purple suns in a cloudless sky and streamlets of what looked like water everywhere, only it wasn't water. I say this because when I bent down and ran my hands through it, it wasn't wet. It just sort of separated around my fingers, like mercury. There were no buildings or anything, just balls of light — like the one at Debec Pond all those long years ago — and the Spong seemed to live inside these lights because I kept seeing them step in and out of the lights as they came and went. And yes, there were Spong all over the place, and when you consider that every Spong has eight eyeballs, that was a lot of eyes on me. In fact, I soon found myself surrounded by Spong. They ran their tentacles up and down my body like they couldn't believe I really existed. Now, I'm very ticklish, so when I cradled myself and laughed, the Spong began to chatter. I felt like a celebrity.

I wish I could tell the Spong apart, but that was impossible. They all looked alike. One of them laid a couple of tentacles on me and nudged me along, escorting me to an unusually big light, which I entered. I found myself in a blindingly white space, and there, before me, were my four Elders. I pointed to the far left of the group. "Spong 1?" I inquired.

"Yes," it said. "That's right."

I glanced at Spong 4, which turned its eyeballs away as if embarrassed about our earlier one-on-one encounter.

"Are you comfortable?" asked Spong 1.

"Yes," I said. "Just fine. But I have a lot of questions."

"There is not a lot of time," said Spong 2. "We cannot maintain you in our environment for long. Our suns emit rays hostile to Earth life. So you have time for one question."

"Yeah," I said, looking sheepishly about. "You guys all look alike. How do you, you know, reproduce? Make little Spong."

The four Elders turned their eyeballs to one other, then swung them back at me. "It's a simple thing," said Spong 1. "Spong titillates a fibrous bark. Then the new Spong emanate from the bark, separate, and grow."

"Very romantic," I said, rolling my eyes.

"Explain 'romantic,'" said Spong 4.

"You know," I said. "Or maybe you don't. Haven't you noticed that there are two varieties of humans? Males and females. Boys and girls. Him and her. It takes two to tango, if you know what I mean."

The Spong shook their tentacles as if experiencing a collective chill. "Your talk does not make sense," said Spong 3, but I could see that Spong 4 was captivated, because all eight of its pupils were dilated and focused on me.

"Don't you know anything about love?" I asked.

"Love?" echoed all four Elders. "Tell us about it."

I let out a deep breath. "Gee. It's a big topic, like God. But let me cut to the chase. Love is a feeling that brings males and females together. Some say love is the greatest thing of all. Others say it is the reason for all unhappiness. It is also the most misunderstood feeling. Sometimes people think they're in love, but they're not. But when things work out, well, the males and females touch in an intimate way. Sometimes a baby is the result."

"A baby?" asked Spong 2.

"Yeah," I said. "A little one. A little human. Then it begins to grow."

"Ah," it said. "Like Spong."

"Well, not exactly," I said. "There's no fibrous bark involved."

At that moment I noticed that Spong 4 was sparkling like mad. It spoke up. "So this is how it is between Poye and Clara. They have love."

"Yes," I said. "Now you're getting it. They love each other. It's kind of a strange love, but yeah, they love each other."

Spong 4's tentacles drooped. "Does that mean Clara can love nobody else?"

"Ha!" I laughed. "Not at all. Clara is remarkable because she seems to be able to love any man."

Spong 4's tentacles rose again. "Then there is hope," it said, and just as quickly fell silent and turned its eyes away from me and from the other Spong. "But Spong is not a man," it said in a tone I interpreted as sadness, and again its tentacles wilted.

In unison the others turned their eyeballs to Spong 4. "What hope are you talking about?" demanded Spong 1. "Tell Spong. Tell Spong now."

Spong 4 swooped its eyeballs around and went on the attack. "Please stop. It was just out-loud thinking. Stop persecuting Spong."

The other three Spong continued to berate Spong 4, but Spong 4 brandished its tentacles with unusual ferocity until, finally, Spong 1 silenced the group. Then it turned to me. "Spong apologizes," it said.

"No, no," I said with a wave. "There's nothing wrong with honest emotion. I like seeing this side of you. It makes you more, er, human."

The Spong looked bewildered by my comment. Spong 1 asked, "What is emotion?"

I slapped my forehead and ran my hand down my face. "Let's just say it's in the same class of conversation as God and love. Can we save it for another day?"

The Spong found this acceptable. "We must get down to business," said Spong 1. "It's time you knew something about Spong's plans."

"Plans?" I echoed. There was something ominous about the way Spong 1 said it.

"Earth was not the only mistake Spong made," it began. "Mars was also a failure. We have reviewed the record of your Mars explorations. Remarkably, not only are your findings accurate but your conjectures as well."

"We can be very clever," I asserted on behalf of my species.

"You are correct that Mars used to be more hospitable. It was warmer and had a freshwater ocean. There were also streams and rivers. It was quite a pleasant place, if a little too red for Spong taste. Be that as it may, Spong seeded it and waited until life began to flourish to meet Spong's future nutritive needs. The problem was that once Spong seeded Mars, Spong neglected it, just as Spong would later neglect Earth. We had the intention of coming back later for the harvest, to secure resources for Spong. But we procrastinated..."

"I'm surprised at you," I chided. "Procrastination is a human failing."

"Spong is not perfect," conceded Spong 3, and then deferred to Spong 1 so it could finish its narrative.

"When Spong returned, eons later, Spong found that the planet had an underproduction of plant life, falling far short of what was needed to sustain Spong in this corner of the galaxy. We soon discovered that this was due to an unanticipated nuisance species, a pest, that was working to degrade the very resources needed by Spong. It, like you, was a very clever species, and big, about twice human size. Like humans, it was a biped, but its knee joints were the opposite of yours, and it was far more agile because in addition to its primary brain it had a brain in each foot, which gave it uncommon equilibrium to leap about the beautiful garden we had established. But it was harvesting more than Mars was producing, working against the interests of Spong and disrespecting our hard work."

"I'm getting a bad feeling," I said as I fumbled in my pockets to make sure my money was still there.

Spong 1 continued. "Aren't you curious about the fate of that species?"

I began to whistle *Brown Sugar* by the Stones. "No," I said, "not really. I'm the least curious human on Earth. Just ask anybody."

"Nevertheless," said Spong 1, "it's important that you listen. And please stop that whistling. Spong finds it irritating."

"Sorry."

"That species was working against Spong plans. Instead of cultivating that garden it was devouring and uprooting it. Spong was shocked by what it found. There was no other solution than to erase the species. In the process, we inadvertently erased all the biota. Spong planned to come back later to try again, but never got around to it."

I swallowed audibly. "My gosh. Why didn't you just show yourself and threaten them with punishment if they didn't shape up?"

"It's not so simple," said Spong 1. "We tried that on another planet, in the Vega sector. It split that single species — a wonderful, leather-winged, flying quadruped with a brain the size of a Rigelian mudmelon — into camps, all claiming Spong as their ally. They went to war over it, shouting things like 'Spong is on our side!' In that case, Spong didn't have to apply any Treatment at all. They did it to themselves. Now that planet is barren of life, so there is nothing to interfere with our harvesting its great mineral wealth." And then, "Would you like to see the laboratory where we keep DNA? It comes as a spray."

"No, no," I said, waving a hand. "I'll take your word for it."

"Well," resumed Spong 1. "It's almost time for you to go. Your skin is beginning to suffer from our suns' radiation. As for Poye, Spong has been very concerned that he thinks he is teaching the whole truth and is willing to sacrifice everything for it when it's clear that Brother Eevin and Rate and Dud are the ones with the insight to know that Earth was indeed seeded by a superior intelligence. It's all for the best that they don't yet identify that intelligence as Spong — remember what happened on the planet with the flying quadrupeds. But we are anxious to see who prevails in this contest and whether people will choose to dwell on evolution and its ignorance on the issue of origins, or see the light of creation by what you call Intelligent Design but what is really Spong."

"I have one more question," I said.

"Yes, go on. But quickly."

"How will all this end?"

The Spong quivered as a group until Spong 1 spoke. "Let's return you to earth. You worry too much."

I fingered the servo in my pocket and the next thing I knew, I was back with Poye and Clara.

TWENTY
TODELAW

I was filled with anxiety now. I didn't like that story about what the Spong did to Mars. If they didn't like the Martians for picking too many flowers, what would they do to us for clear-cutting the Amazon rain forest?

Okay, enough about my anxieties. Back to Poye. When I returned from my journey and entered the apartment, I found Clara sitting at the kitchen table, smoking a Tiparillo and swigging beer from a bottle as she watched Poye eat a bowl of her New England-style clam chowder. When she saw me, she gave a hard swallow. "Where the hell have you been?"

"You wouldn't believe it," I said as I went over to the stove and helped myself to some of the steaming chowder. Then I shuffled to the sofa and began to chow.

"You look terrible," said Clara. "You're all crinkly. Have you been smoking pot?"

"Yes," I said between gulps. "That's it. That's exactly it."

Clara shook her head and went off on another tack. "Okay," she said. "Now that you guys are filling your bellies tell me again what all that stuff at the church was about."

"I can't believe Joe Christiani was there," said Poye as he raised the spoon to his mouth.

"Who?"

"The kid who bullied me in elementary school."

"Did you fight back? Get in at least one good punch?"

Poye picked up the bowl and slurped the remaining puddle of chowder, which brought a rebuke from Clara. "That's bad manners," she said as she rapped him on the knuckles with the beer bottle. "Use a piece of bread so mop it up. Here." She handed him the heel from the baguette she had baked.

Poye took the bread and swabbed the bowl with it before tamping the moist wad into his mouth.

"Could I get some bread, too?" I asked.

Clara slammed the bottle down on the table. "What do you think I am? Get the hell off your feet and get your own bread."

I followed orders, snatching a chunk of baguette from the table, then scurried back to the sofa like a frightened pup.

"Clara, love," Poye began after swallowing the tasty mass, "I just wasn't a fighter. I'm still not a fighter."

Clara blew a smoke ring and looked into the distance. "I think I'd like to be a boxer," she said. "Women box too, you know."

"Yes, love."

We soon heard a rising commotion outside. "What now?" demanded Clara as both she and Poye peered out the window onto the street of the careworn, neglected neighborhood. I roused myself and joined them. A small but raucous parade was marching by. The participants wore the purple armbands with gold crosses of the Star Nation and were banging drums and clashing cymbals. The middle rank held up a banner that read, VOTE FOR HENKER! We watched as the parade disappeared down the street and turned a corner. "Who the hell is Henker?" remarked Clara.

"The election," I said over her shoulder. "He's running for president. They call him Bass Drum Henker because of his deep voice."

Clara looked surprised. "I didn't know you kept up with politics," she said.

"I can't avoid it. Henker says he will be the education president. He's vowing to get evolution out of the schools once and for all. I think the times are about to become more dangerous." As I said this Poye focused on me with a look of intense concern.

Clara shook her head ruefully. "I can't believe Poye doesn't have any allies."

Poye raised his head. "I think I may," he said. "You've inspired me."

Clara flicked her butt out the window and watched it spark on the sidewalk. "That's what I'm here for," she said. "Hey, it's still early. Let's go to bed."

•   •   •   •   •

Poye and I went to the college the next day and, incredibly, he picked up where he had left off, lecturing on evolution, while I sat in the corner, taking assiduous notes on my legal pad. The students' humming was now joined by stamping. They thundered the deck with their boots every time Poye opened his mouth. And so he once again attempted the success he had had the previous class — by writing everything out longhand on the board. But this time the protesting students were ready. When Poye tried to write, they threw overripe strawberries, which splatted against the board. He turned and faced the class. "Now isn't that just a tad immature?" he asked, his face flush with sadness.

Jared Hennemyer spoke up. "Maybe immature," he said, "but not sacrilegious."

Poye gave this some thought. Then he took a chance. "Mr. Hennemyer," he said, "if you can spell *sacrilegious* I will stop teaching evolution."

Brilliant. Straight out of the playbook of Professor Todelaw, who, Poye had told me, was known for clever repartee. Poye waited as the moments passed. Jared Hennemyer's Star Nation Campus Compact allies were looking at him, their expressions pleading for direction. He finally sneered at them. "I won't take orders from a man about to lose his job. Wait until Henker is president!" And with this, he got up and stormed out of the classroom. Curiously, his hangers-on stayed put, looking lost.

Poye ventured to resume speaking his lecture, and this time it went off without interruption from clapping or stamping. It seemed that the snake, without its head, couldn't even writhe. But once again he made his capital error —an error that would solidify the Spong's support of Rate and Brother Eevin. When a student challenged him to explain how and why life got started in the first place, Poye did not cite a superior intelligence. Instead, he struggled with some gobbledygook about chemicals and cell membranes and ocean bubbles. He went on to describe something called the Miller Experiment of 1953, where a grad student at the University of Chicago named Stanley Miller had recreated the conditions of primal earth in a flask and produced amino acids, the building blocks of proteins. "And from there," concluded Poye, "the first primitive cells somehow evolved."

Even Poye sensed that his answer was inadequate, that evolutionary theory just wasn't up to snuff on the issue of origins. But he was not about to suggest that some intelligent hand had reached out and — *poof!* — made Miller's chemicals spring to life. In fact, though, that's exactly what had happened. The Spong had indeed reached out and — *poof!* — gotten the show on the road, thanks to their timely infusion of DNA and other proprietary ingredients, in convenient spray form. If only Poye could have seen and acknowledged this, the whole course of world history might have been altered. At the very least, Poye should have stuck to a simple description of natural selection — organisms change to adapt to changing environments. But instead, he guaranteed himself more heartache by proposing a wrong-headed idea about life's origins when it was Bud Wilmot and the Happy Clappers who had it right — a superior intelligence *had* initiated life on earth. This made them natural allies of the Spong, and it would pay off royally for them when it came time for the Treatment.

In the meantime, Poye followed up on his comment to Clara that he might have allies after all. "Nest," he said as he was packing his things up after class, "I've decided to track down Professor Todelaw, the man who inspired me to teach biology."

Out of curiosity, I had already taken it upon myself to research the background of Professor Henry Todelaw, who had become a sort of folk hero to pedagogues in the resistance movement against the President's Council on Right Thinking. He had been no-nonsense and deadly serious about his discipline, at a time when a shadow had fallen over pedagogy throughout the country, in particular as it related to the teaching of evolutionary theory. He had defied this wave of anti-evolutionism and paid for it with the loss of his job. In the blink of an eye, a tenured, senior full professor of biology was rendered a memory.

"Do you know where to find him?" I asked as we hurried along.

"It was surprisingly easy," said Poye. "I found a newspaper article online about a Good Humor man who used to be a professor. He has a route in Portland."

"A bit of a drive," I said.

"A good investment of time, I hope."

When we left the apartment, Clara shed one of her infrequent tears. She embraced Poye and pushed him away by turns as I looked on. "Love," said Poye as she yo-yoed him back and forth, "I'll be back this evening."

After Poye broke free we got in the Rambler and made our ponderous way south as other drivers beeped at and generally hectored Poye for driving so slowly. Poye completed the white-knuckle trip to Portland feeling tense and exhausted. He used the newspaper article to identify Professor Todelaw's route, and we soon spotted the truck, its bells jingling, plying a quiet, tree-lined, residential street, trying to roust out children in an age when few kids played outside. It was a tough sell. When the bells didn't do the trick, Professor Todelaw played a tinny version of *Turkey in the Straw*, on a continuous loop, blared from a loudspeaker mounted on the hood.

We parked and walked down the street to the truck. When we arrived at the service window, Poye beamed when he saw Professor Todelaw in his white uniform and cap, a shiny steel money changer on his black belt. He turned around and looked at Poye through thick glasses. "What'll it be?" he sang, pleasantly enough. "You look like a candidate for a Creamsicle."

"Yes," said Poye without knowing what a Creamsicle was, still looking on in wonder at the man who had meant so much to him as a student. "That's what I'll have. A Creamsicle."

"Coming right up."

Poye watched as Professor Todelaw opened the lid of his freezer and rummaged before extracting the treat. "Here you go."

Poye took the pop and gave Professor Todelaw a five-dollar bill. When the man went to make change, Poye said, "No. Please keep it."

Professor Todelaw tsked. "I cannot do that," he said. "It is highly unethical for a Good Humor man to accept gratuities." He gave Poye the appropriate change. "There."

Poye firmed his lips. The idea of a Good Humor code of ethics seemed to totally unman him. He stood there, pop in hand, looking at Professor Todelaw, who returned Poye's curious gaze. "Son," he said, "eat your pop before it melts." Then he turned to me. "Let me guess," he said. "An ice cream sandwich."

"I don't eat ice cream," I said.

Professor Todelaw frowned. He pulled back as if getting a good look at me for the first time. "You look like one of those hippies from years ago," he said. "Is that what you are, a hippie?"

"I'm a philosophy professor," I said, running my hand down my unkempt beard.

"Ah."

I noticed that Professor Todelaw was wearing the sad face pendant, the symbol of godlessness. "Doesn't that discourage business?" I said, pointing at the pendant.

"Sure does," said Professor Todelaw. "I'm barely scraping by." He looked at Poye. "Maybe you want to try a Chocolate Eclair as well?"

"Sure," said Poye. Professor Todelaw rummaged again, gave Poye his treat, and waved him off when Poye extended the money to him. "One

Chocolate Eclair on the house is not going to make me any poorer than I am."

Poye stood there like a statue, holding up a pop in each hand. He couldn't stop smiling at his former teacher. "You want something else, son?" the older man asked. "Or are you just going to pose with those things? They're melting all over your hands."

"Professor Todelaw," said Poye, "don't you remember me?"

His response surprised Poye. "Of course I do. You had the laughing fit, and I tossed you out of my class. I see you've gotten over it. So, have you made something of yourself?"

"I think so," said Poye. "I followed in your footsteps and became a biology professor. You were my inspiration. Now I need your advice."

Professor Todelaw leaned out the service window and glanced up and down the street. "Look," he said, volume low, "you're wearing the cross around your neck and I've got the sad face pendant. The twain is not supposed to meet. Someone will see us chatting amiably and will wonder what we might have in common. One or maybe both of us will get in trouble. This is a Star Nation Watch neighborhood, and a lot of eyes are on us at this very moment. There are *gauleiters* everywhere. I'm surprised they let me come down this street at all. At first, I thought you might be a *gauleiter* yourself."

A woman in tight jeans and a baggy pink sweater hurried down the steps of her house with a little boy by the hand. She marched up to the truck. "Hosanna," she greeted. "One Good Humor Bar, please." Professor Todelaw rummaged again. "Here you go, ma'am. Hosanna," he said as he accepted her money. The woman took the ice cream, handed it to the boy, and threw me a disapproving look before moving off.

"She'll make her report," said Professor Todelaw as he watched the woman hurry back into her house. "As I was saying," he continued, "we are being watched. Meet me in the park. It's at the end of this street and to the right. We can talk there."

Poye's ice cream was dripping down his hands and wrists. He did his best to lick the mess up. Then we did as Professor Todelaw directed. We walked down to the park and found him sitting on a bench under a broad maple. "Sit," he said, and the three of us enjoyed a quiet place in the shade. "Now, what can I do for you? But first, here." He handed Poye a couple of Wet-Naps and watched as he cleaned his hands.

"I am under attack," said Poye without preamble. "For teaching evolution. I can't bring myself to comply with the school's demands that I stop."

"Hmm," hummed Professor Todelaw disconsolately, rubbing his chin. He pushed his Good Humor cap back on his head and examined Poye. "Nor should you, if you want to retain your self-respect and professional integrity. But brace yourself. It's going to get worse. This Henker fellow will be elected, mark my words, and then all types of ugly things will happen. I'm afraid it will make life very problematic for you." Then he regarded me. "And what about you, son? What's your role in all this?"

I raised my legal pad. "I'm just a note-taker," I said. "I'm documenting Poye's story."

"Good, good," mused the professor. "Contemporaneous notes have great power. They're admissible in a court of law. That is, presuming we continue to have courts of law."

"I hope it doesn't come to that," said Poye.

"One step at a time," said Professor Todelaw. "That's the best any of us can do."

Poye threw his old professor an earnest look. "It must have been very difficult for you," he said.

"Difficult? You mean getting fired? In a way, it was a relief. Colleges can be the stuffiest and most intolerant places on earth. But now I am my own boss. I drive my route, hand out ice cream, then go home to my books. What could be more pleasant than that?"

"But I don't think I would prefer to be a Good Humor man," said Poye, and then he reconsidered his words. "I mean..."

Professor Todelaw held up a hand. "Don't you dare apologize. All honest work is good. I can't say any more than that."

'I'm sorry."

"I told you not to apologize."

Poye rolled in his lips to keep from excusing himself any further. We sat in silence for a minute before Poye resumed, "So what should I do?"

"Do you have any allies?"

"Just Clara."

"Clara?"

"My companion. She's very formidable. A match for any man."

"Yes, yes," said Professor Todelaw, "but muscle won't deliver you from your dilemma. The question is, are you willing to give up teaching evolution for the sake of your job, or are you determined to tell the truth as you know it for the sake of your self-respect? Have you considered escaping to Canada? Once Henker is in office, there will be a new surge to the north, and the lobos will raise their prices. Mexico is another option. Can you speak Spanish? I sometimes think of Mexico myself. Ice cream sells briskly down there."

Poye digested this information. "I don't think Clara would consider Canada. Or Mexico. And as for my teaching job, if I lose it, I risk losing my peace of mind as well, no?"

"All honest work is good," reiterated the professor. "There must be something else you can do."

"All I know is teaching," said Poye. "What other abilities do I have?"

"You might be surprised," said Professor Todelaw as he touched a finger to the black visor of his snow-white cap.

Poye smiled with great affection for his teacher, and I, too, felt a burgeoning warmth for the old man.

"Professor Todelaw, I want to tell you something I haven't even told Clara. I've had this subtle feeling that I'm being watched. Not in a bad way. In a sort of assessing way by people who could be allies. It makes me feel that I need to keep teaching evolution for these watchers, lest I let them down."

Professor Todelaw regarded Poye approvingly. "Good," he said. "Then continue to teach evidence-based science, even if it jeopardizes your job. Make them threaten to fire you. Put them at risk of bad publicity. You have a lot of support out there, whether you know it or not. Maybe you've been selected by some higher power to be an advocate for truth in science. Like John Scopes. He was a twenty-four-year-old kid, teaching evolution in a backwater, and suddenly found himself the center of attention. He lost his initial court case, but today we remember his name. Who remembers the names of the holier-than-thou's who wanted his head?"

Teacher and student sat in silence for a few minutes, enjoying the fresh breeze, while I went over my notes. I wondered if Poye had obtained the advice he was looking for. All I knew was that he seemed immensely pleased just to be sitting in the presence of Professor Todelaw. Poye didn't realize it, but his old professor had positioned him beautifully to be a reluctant warrior dwelling on higher, righteous, ethical ground. The question was, would Poye rise to the occasion? He nodded appreciatively and said, "Thank you,

Professor Todelaw. I think you've affirmed something I already knew."

"Here's my number," the professor said as he scribbled it down on a piece of paper. "Call me when you need me." Then he checked his watch. "Oh, my. I've got to get back to my route. We have a sale on Strawberry Shortcake bars today. The kiddies go crazy for it."

We watched as Professor Todelaw hurried off, rocking in the manner of a man with a bad hip, the money on his belt ka-chinging as he went.

"I think I am returning home to a buzz saw," said Poye as we walked back to the Rambler.

"I'd love to give you advice," I said, "but I'm supposed to limit myself to taking notes. I don't want to affect the outcome."

Poye turned to me and smiled. "I don't want advice, Nest," he said. "Especially advice about avoiding the buzz saw. I've already resigned to meet it head-on."

As we drove north, again at a snail's pace, with cars honking at us and drivers giving us the finger, I considered the arc of my friendship with Poye. He used to put so much stock in me, in what I said, in what I did. There was a time when he wouldn't blow his nose without asking my permission. But all that had been turned on its head. Now it was I who was caught up in Poye's wake. My sheepish boyhood friend had become a driven man and, rather than resenting the reversal of our roles, I was, in a powerful way, honored to be his biographer.

Twenty-One
Henker

A period of anxious calm set in. Although Poye had once again defied the dean, not to mention the Education Reform Act, and although Jared Hennemyer had once again stormed out of his classroom and, presumably, hightailed it back to Eulalie Wilmot, there was no blowback. Not immediately, at least. Instead, the school year ended on its customary note of finality and release, and a summer of repose ensued. The following school year also began in an uneventful, businesslike manner as Poye resumed his teaching responsibilities in Introductory Biology. Who could have known that all of this was preamble to a truly dark and dismal cloud come November when the people of the Theocratic Union of American States would elect the first Star Nation president who, once inaugurated, would go from licking his victorious chops to initiating his vehement agenda?

Bass Drum Henker was whooped into office with great fanfare. Those who were appalled by him shuddered, and another wave of refugees surged for the Canadian and Mexican borders. T.U.A.S. frontier guards threw back the desperate turncoats, who were promptly arrested for desertion on the order of a new president who had promised to not only reduce crime but eliminate it. The perfidious Americans who weren't willing to stay and put their shoulders to the wheel of his policies were viewed with contempt by President Henker, his enthusiastic minions, and his frenzied, quacking supporters in the general population.

When January came, I watched his inauguration on television with Poye and Clara. At 84, he was the oldest man ever elected to the office, and the thinnest, a mere stick figure with a sparse gray comb-over. When he spoke, he sneered. He lashed out at his opposition, his prognathous bottom teeth gnashing horribly. His heart had been studded with infarction after infarction, which led to the implantation, one after the other, of three donor organs. When the last one failed, the doctors feared cracking his withered chest again, so he was given an artificial device, a custom-tailored Tornado-3 — the latest in Sino-Russian technology — which an aide carried in an aluminum suitcase, the tubes and wires running up under Henker's jacket, the mechanical heart emitting an eerie, theremin-like whirr as it did its cardiopropulsive duty.

Henker's inauguration speech was vindictive and threatening. No representative of the government of the Theocratic Union of American States was permitted to speak any language other than English in public, on pain of dismissal and incarceration. Hiring preferences were to go to Christians, with disabled Christian veterans given head-of-the-line status and special license plates allowing them to park in front of fire hydrants. A brief video of Henker leading a morning prayer would henceforth be broadcast in all public schools, to afford the children, in his words, "a daily moral compass and reminder." The army would be dispatched to the Canadian and Mexican borders to aid Star Nation Security authorities in containing fleeing citizens. The size of the Coast Guard was quadrupled, with orders to lock down the Atlantic, Pacific, and Gulf coastlines, lest deserters seek sea routes of escape. The second amendment was renamed "The Prime Amendment," with firearms instruction commencing in the lowest grades. Citizens were encouraged to use deadly force to prevent or interrupt the commission of crimes, no matter how minor. "If you don't want to get shot," howled Henker, pointing into the television camera with an arthritic finger, "then don't break the law." The crowd went wild.

Then the affair proceeded to a call-and-response format, with Bass Drum making all of his initiatives seem like no-brainers.

"You do want security, don't you?" he bellowed, to which the crowd roared, "Yes!"

"You do believe that only Christian principles can keep this country on the right path, don't you?"

"Yes!"

"You do want to exercise your right to be armed and to openly carry those arms, don't you?"

"YES!"

"You don't want your elected officials to become mired in the distraction of talk about rising sea levels and climate warming, do you?"

This last syntax confused his supporters, who didn't know whether to shout "Yes!" or "No!" so they mumbled incoherently.

And it went on from there.

After whipping his audience to white heat, Henker saved his most robust volley for last. "The teaching of evolution will end. Period. It shall never be right to feed the young of this country such fantastic hogwash. Anyone teaching that humans descended from a lower order of animals will be fired and brought to trial. Do I make myself clear?"

"Clear!" screamed the crowd gathered before him, their faces mangled in hysteria.

While Poye and Clara continued to watch the debacle on the old black-and-white tube Clara had rescued from a dumpster, I snuck off to tell the Spong what was going on in the most powerful country on earth. I feared they would not be happy. Nevertheless, I stole into the narrow alleyway between Briody's and the Chinese laundry, got out the servo, set it on a garbage can, and established my connection.

"Greetings," said the four Elders in unison. "Spong has been looking forward to your report."

I told them about the new president and his initiatives, but I tried to sugar-coat the part about evolution.

Spong 1 raised its tentacles. "We don't understand," it said. "Our monitoring tells us that every other country on Earth accepts the idea of biological evolution, even though it neglects the issue of origins. And yet this one, which you have told Spong is the most advanced country, does not. This makes no sense to us."

I raised a finger to clarify my point. "I didn't say that it was the most advanced country. That honor would go to Finland. The Theocratic Union simply has the biggest arsenal. There's a difference. Socially and economically, it is more near the middle of the pack. A large number of its people live in poverty or are incarcerated."

Spong 2 spoke up. "Then these people have failed. Yet another reason to proceed with the Treatment."

"Hey," I said. "Don't blame us. You started it."

Spong 4: "Spong did not intend for humans to erupt. You took us by surprise."

"But it is your fault for not paying attention, for neglecting the planet," I countered, pleased with myself for being able to parry with such intellectual giants.

The Elders raised their eyeballs to one another. Then Spong 1 said, "That is true. If Spong had not been negligent, we could have nipped all of this in the bud, to use one of your expressions."

I decided to change the subject. "I'm worried about Poye," I said. "He met with his old professor, who seems to have inspired him to continue with the teaching of evolution."

"Spong is pleased with this," said Spong 3, "although we continue to wish that Poye would acknowledge a superior intelligence as having initiated life on Earth. To us, this represents a failure of education, and a paradox. Rate and Brother Eevin are uneducated men, yet they have somehow divined the correct answer in their work on Intelligent Design."

"Don't forget Dud Wilmot," I prompted. "He wrote the book."

"Yes, he is a genius," conceded Spong 1.

"He'd be pleased to hear that," I said.

"Maybe Poye should tell him," said Spong 4.

I shook my head. "I don't think Poye could bring himself to do that."

"Then he will never surmise the existence of Spong," said Spong 1, "whereas Rate, Brother Eevin, and Dud Wilmot are one step away from acknowledging Spong when they speak of a higher intelligence."

"I wouldn't hold my breath," I countered. "They're just dying to say 'God.' I don't think they could bring themselves to accept the idea that you guys, with all those tentacles and eyeballs, created humans, however inadvertently."

Spong 1 made the equivalent of a tsking sound from its orifice. "Then you disappoint Spong," it said. "It seems that you are losing your perspective because you doubt the wisdom of Spong."

Ouch. I was the world's leading expert on Perspective, yet here I was being impugned for lack of it by a bunch of gibbering invertebrates. "I still don't know what your endgame is for the people of Earth."

"If you had perspective you would," said Spong 1, and once again, I was stung.

"Look," I said, "we are in this together. Whether you like it or not, I am Earth's Perspective go-to guy, and I have faithfully delivered information to you about Poye and evolution and Intelligent Design. Do you really want to fire me at this point and look for somebody else?" I crossed my arms and waited for their response. It was time to let them sweat for a change.

The Spong intertwined tentacles and eyeballs and conferred. Then they disentangled, and Spong 1 spoke up. "Very well," it said. "You have a point.

Spong did not intend to offend you. You have done a very good job. It's just that we are disappointed not only in the fact of humans but also in what humans have become. From our vantage point, we see one of our gardens being despoiled. How can anyone deny this? It has forced other life forms to make desperate adjustments to survive."

All I could do was repeat myself. "As I said before, you created this mess."

"And we will correct it," countered Spong 1 darkly, looking at me with all eight of its eyeballs. Well, that was a staring contest I wasn't going to win, so after a few final, conciliatory words, I moved to sign off, but Spong 4 interrupted me. "How is Clara?"

The other three Elders rolled their eyes.

"She's fine," I said.

"Just as beautiful?" asked Spong 4.

"I wish I could tell her you said so," I ventured, not adding that Clara probably wouldn't appreciate a compliment from a squid.

"But you can't," declaimed Spong 1 before casting a sidelong glance at Spong 4.

"Of course," I said, and with that I left the Spong to what I was sure would be a lively conversation among themselves. After signing off, I stowed the servo, although, I admit, I sometimes wanted to throw it down a sewer drain.

TWENTY-TWO
AVALANCHE

Poye Trubb was arrested on the direct order of President Henker. It turned out that Dud Wilmot had made a handsome contribution to his presidential campaign and was therefore in a position to suggest that Poye would make a good whipping boy for old Bass Drum's anti-evolution policy. Besides, after Clara had routed Dud and the others in the basement of the Church of the Happy Clappers, he vowed revenge. Once Henker had achieved office and announced his war on the teaching of evolution, Dud knew that his moment had come. It was a simple thing, really. Just a phone call and an accusation, and within twenty-four hours the machinery was in motion.

Poye had been standing helpless before his class, which was chanting *Henker! Henker! Henker!* I watched in horror from my corner of the room as four men in dark blue jumpsuits and wearing the cross pendant entered. They glanced at Jared Hennemyer, who nodded — the signal that the students were being subjected to talk of evolution. The men surrounded Poye, who offered no resistance. He didn't say a word. They grabbed him by both arms and walked him out of the room as the students cheered. I jumped to my feet and launched myself at the team of enforcers, wielding my legal pad, the only weapon I had at the ready. But one of the men caught my arm in mid-swing, twisted it behind my back, and hauled me off with Poye.

If only the timing had been different. Poye had dedicated three weeks to the topic of evolution. When the arrest came he had only one lecture to go. Then he could have concluded the section in good conscience, congratulating himself for having stayed the course. He would have done so even without the encouragement of Professor Todelaw. Instead, Poye now harbored a nagging sense of incompletion, of loss. We were taken to Penobscot County Jail, where Poye was allowed to place a brief call to Clara. Then we were brought to a holding cell which contained four other inmates, three of whom were wearing the cross pendant. Poye's own pendant had been stripped from him by one of the arresting officers, who growled, "You have surrendered your privilege to wear this," whereby Poye immediately became a so-called Naught. Beyond this, it was not lost on me that, despite his earlier vow, Poye was now living in a closed space with people he would otherwise not choose to be with.

One of the other men in the cell wore a sad face pendant. He was the only one not scowling at Poye. He identified himself as WeeWee and was an old hippie, with a denim vest, a long, gray ponytail, and deeply incised lines in his face that looked as if they had been burned in with a soldering iron. "What'd you do, partner?" he asked Poye as the other three men showed passing interest.

Poye shifted on his bunk and smiled at the man, grateful for the attention. "I'm a teacher," he said.

WeeWee rolled out his lower lip and shook his head. "That's no crime."

"I taught evolution."

"Oh," said WeeWee as he scratched his beard. "Henker's big no-no."

One of the other men was leaning against a wall of the cell. He was a long drink of water with a Red Sox ball cap. He piped up, "You don't believe that stuff, do you?"

Poye had a smile for him too. "I guess I do."

The man pushed himself away from the wall. "So you believe that we came from apes?"

Poye shook his head. "It's not quite that simple," he said. "But there were natural processes."

And once again Poye fell victim to the fallacy that life on earth, and humans, in particular, could have somehow gotten started without input from a higher intelligence. I was beginning to grow impatient with him for not thinking outside the box on this one. But then again, that's not the kind of thinker Poye was. He was just reflecting what he had been taught by Professor Todelaw.

"Natural processes," mimicked the man. "Ha!" Then he spat on the floor of the cell.

One of the others — a stocky fellow who was sweating horribly and mopping his face with a red bandanna — spoke up. "You ever hear of Intelligent Design?"

Poye perked. "Why, yes. I have a book about it."

The stocky man seemed surprised at this response. "And...?"

"And I found it very interesting," said Poye.

The long drink of water sniffed. "'Interesting.' I hate that word."

Poye glanced back at WeeWee, who seemed sympathetic. But before the conversation could proceed any further, there was a commotion beyond the cell. A woman's voice. Harried. Demanding. All of us looked up as a door flew open and Clara precipitated like a powerful wind. She was in her oversized sweater and waving her arms as she approached the cell, with two police officers on her heels. "Bastards!" she cried, only I didn't know who exactly she was referring to. The other men in the cell? The policemen accompanying her? Those who had arrested Poye?

"Step back," said one of the officers as he took his key and opened the cell. "Out, Trubb," he ordered. Before leaving, Poye said goodbye to his cellmates, who were staring in wonder at Clara. "You belong to her?" said the long drink of water.

"A Naught for a Naught," remarked the stocky man.

Clara glared at him. For a moment I thought she might reach through the bars and grab him by the throat. But she hung fire. First things first. "C'mon, Poye. You too, Nestor."

After picking up Poye's cross pendant, we left the station, with Clara's hand hooked around Poye's arm as I took up the rear. "That's it?" he asked. "Aren't we supposed to sign papers or something? Pay bail?"

Clara stopped walking for a moment and looked at him. "After all these years," she said, "you still don't understand me and my ways, do you?"

Poye didn't ask any more questions. He allowed Clara to continue to escort him along. On the way home, we stopped at a grocery store so Clara could buy fajita veggies for the quesadillas she had planned for supper.

There was a surprise waiting when we arrived back at the apartment. There, sitting in the easy chair, was Professor Todelaw in his crisp, white, Good Humor man uniform, cap and all, with the coin changer clipped to his black leather belt. "Hello, Poye," he greeted brightly. "Hello, Nestor."

Poye was overjoyed. "Professor Todelaw! Sitting right here." He ran over and pumped the old man's hand with both of his. "How did you find me?"

"I didn't. Clara found me. She told me what the situation was and I dropped everything to come here. Business was bad anyway." Then he pointed to his sad face pendant.

Poye turned and looked at Clara, who was already clattering away at the stove. "Talk to your professor," she commanded as she unpackaged the vegetables. "I'll do the cooking."

Poye sat opposite Professor Todelaw, and I plopped down on the sofa. "I was arrested," Poye confessed.

Professor Todelaw put up a hand. "I know everything. Clara filled me in. You are the first martyr to the anti-evolution law. They're placing your so-called crime on the same plane as sedition."

"But why me?" pleaded Poye. "There must be others teaching Darwin."

"True," affirmed Professor Todelaw. "But there aren't others who have inflamed Dud Wilmot, who made eye-popping contributions to Henker's campaign. It was a perfect alignment of events and personalities. You're to be made an example of."

Poye became pensive. "So what happens now?"

Professor Todelaw sat back and regarded Poye. "You must know that your job is no more. Henker saw to that."

"So much for tenure-track," I said.

"There is no more tenure anywhere in the country, Nestor," said Professor Todelaw. "It's gone. Kaput. Part of the president's campaign against what he calls 'academic welfare'."

Poye's expression was pleading. "But how can the president tell a private college what to do?"

Professor Todelaw threw up his hands. "Because nobody cares about you and your college. Stop a person in the street and ask them what they would do if an unknown tenure-track professor at an out-of-the-way college in the Maine woods were fired. If it doesn't affect them, why should they care? Now, the union will fight back, but that's a long haul, and besides, we don't know how much longer unions will even exist. For now, Henker has done his dirty work and will deal with any potential consequences later. And don't forget his supporters. These are people who believe they've been dealt with unfairly in life and they want someone else to get hurt for a change. It doesn't matter who it is — immigrants, politicians, foreigners, or know-it-all college professors. Henker is their man and is willing to do the hurting."

"But I don't understand. Don't they profess love of country?"

Professor Todelaw threw Poye a pitying look. "They don't give a hang about the country. Why would they care about a country they believe has short-changed them? They just want a good show, and Henker is giving it to them."

It was now clear to me why Poye idolized Professor Todelaw. The old man had a clarity of vision and understanding, and a glib way of putting his thoughts into words. I scratched madly at my legal pad — and my beard — as I struggled to keep up.

It wasn't long before Clara dropped a platter of steaming quesadillas onto the table and called for us to come eat. Professor Todelaw and I dug in, slathering the steaming wedges with sour cream and guacamole. But Poye had no appetite. "Clara," he ventured, "why do you stick with me? I've been nothing but trouble."

Clara lit a Tiparillo, took a drag, and seemed to consider the question. "I guess you give me opportunities to fight," she said. "And I love to fight."

"The problem," I said between mouthfuls, "is that Poye isn't a fighter. He said so himself."

Clara looked at me with disgust. "Nestor," she said, "shut up and eat."

"We don't have many choices," said Professor Todelaw as he tamped his mouth with a napkin. "These quesadillas, by the way, are delicious."

Poye didn't understand. "I didn't think we had any choices at all. I'm going to trial, right?"

"Not right away, if you don't want to," said the professor with a mischievous twinkle in his eyes.

Poye's expression pleaded for clarification.

"We can always run," said the professor. "Make them chase us, find us."

Now Clara piped up. "Run where? I don't like to run."

The professor shrugged. "We head for Canada, of course. Perhaps, if we resist by running off, there will be a groundswell of grassroots support for Poye. Now that Henker has made a big stink about evolution, with his whipping boy on the run" — Professor Todelaw pointed at Poye with the stub of a quesadilla — "headlines will follow. Let's not make it easy for them."

"You keep saying 'we' and 'us'," said Poye.

The professor nodded enthusiastically. "Of course. I'm coming too. I don't want to miss a thing. As I said, business is bad. I have nothing to lose."

And we drew up our plans.

Twenty-Three
Nomadic

After dinner I snuck down to the alley, drew out the servo, and — *poof!* — there they were — my four Spong Elders, hovering before me in anxious anticipation. I made my report, telling them about Poye's arrest and the plan to become fugitives.

"There is something noble in this," said Spong 1. "On Spong we do not have nobility. If a Spong is accused of something negative, it presumes it is true and dissolves itself."

I shook my head. "That wouldn't work here," I said. "Too many opportunities for mayhem. People would be accusing each other of all sorts of things just to get rid of them. Here we have something called courts, where an accused person gets to defend himself in public. He often wins."

The Spong looked confused. "But if you are accused, you must be guilty. Why would you oppose the accusation?"

What was I going to do with these poor, naive saps? "Look," I said, "there are a lot of dishonest, self-serving people. Sometimes they accuse others just to hurt them, to seek revenge, seize their property, or to protect somebody else."

"This was not Spong's intention," said Spong 3.

"What are you talking about?"

"Spong did not intend to create a species that was so at odds with itself."

I called upon all my powers of Perspective to show them a bigger picture. "Hey," I said. "You're not listening. I said we have courts, where an accused person can fight back. We have a law that says a person accused of a crime has the right to face his accuser and demand evidence. If that evidence cannot be produced, the accused goes free. You need to understand what a wonderful thing this is. Before we had courts, there were kings. If a king said you were guilty of something he could have your head cut off, and there wasn't a thing you could do about it."

"So the king made the accusation," said Spong 2, "and then dissolved the accused. This seems fair."

I gulped. I had clearly made a poor reference. The Spong may have been geniuses, but they were too rooted in their social system to see any other way. I wanted to decry their rotten sense of Perspective, but I hung fire, lest they accuse me of being negative and dissolve me too. "In any case," I said, conveying my weariness with my benefactors, "Poye, Clara and Poye's old teacher, Professor Todelaw, have decided to flee. I will go with them, of course." I didn't add, *because if I don't, who will feed me?*

"Flee?" echoed the Spong in unison. "Flee where?"

"Canada, I think. It was Professor Todelaw's idea. He doesn't want Poye to surrender so readily. He thinks it unjust to persecute someone for teaching evolution."

"It is unjust," agreed Spong 1. "Even on Spong, it is permitted to speak freely. We have a saying: 'You have an orifice. So use it.'"

"We have something similar," I rejoined. "We call it the First Amendment. But our freedom to speak has been suffering as of late. People are frightened."

Spong 2: "They wouldn't be frightened if they had adhered to natural law and not lost..."

"Their Perspective?" I zinged.

"Yes," said Spong 2, darkly. It clearly didn't appreciate being upended.

I knew exactly what the Spong were talking about. Humans should have stuck to snuffling for food and sex, but they got ideas and started to make big things out of little things, somethings out of nothings. And evolution — which, although it was a great idea, was also a little thing because it was so elementary — got blown all out of proportion until it landed Poye in a terrible mess.

"We approve of Poye," said Spong 1.

"And Professor Todelaw," said Spong 2.

"And Clara," Spong 4 rushed to add. "Don't forget Clara."

I was taken by surprise, and deeply moved, when the quartet declared, in unison, "And we approve of you."

"Gosh, fellas," I reddened, looking down at my torn sneakers and wiggling my toes. "I'm speechless."

"We see all of you as worthy," said Spong 1.

"Worthy?" I echoed, recovering my composure.

"Yes. Worthy of being spared."

Four down, seven billion to go. I had my work cut out for me.

After signing off, I returned to the apartment and turned my attention to my friends. "Nestor, pack," ordered Clara as she snapped her valise shut with alarming finality. "Grab a coat. It's gonna be cold."

What could I do? I took a plastic garbage bag and stuffed it with a change of underwear, a polo shirt and a relatively clean pair of jeans. Then I threw on an old military-style parka. We clambered into the Rambler and drove off, headed east toward Canada and freedom. Clara was downright giddy, laughing like a schoolgirl and singing as she drove with one arm dangling out the window, with Poye riding shotgun. Professor Todelaw was in the back seat with me, delighted by Clara's attitude and manner. "I feel twenty years younger in your presence, good lady," he rejoiced and joined her in song. Only Poye remained anxious and pensive, his mien dark and constricted. Along the way, Professor Todelaw took off his sad face pendant. "We need to get rid of these," he said, tossing it out the window. "If we're going to be fugitives, we might as well go all the way."

I shrugged and followed suit, throwing my cross pendant into the woods. Poye wrapped his hand around his but hesitated. "Maybe it will come in handy," he said, but Clara made the decision for him. She grabbed the pendant and ripped it from his neck. Then she flung it out her window. "There," she said. "Now you're like us. Naughts on the run," reminding him that she had never worn a pendant and had never suffered for it. Of course, she had her peculiar "in" with the Minister of Pendantry whom she took care of but good.

And so we continued on our way, not knowing how we would cross the border, what we would find, or what the long-term game plan was.

TWENTY-FOUR
PURSUIT

Don't ask me how it happened, but a posse set out to track us down, and it was headed by Jared Hennemyer. He turned out to be living proof that, as the Wizard of Oz told Scarecrow, a brain is a very mediocre commodity. And so this short, chubby, inarticulate young man with the jet-black bangs, whose only aspiration had been to scrape dental plaque and instruct children in the proper use of floss, now found himself barking orders to a deputized contingent of the Star Nation Campus Compact. Thus, Jared and his posse gathered themselves for the hot pursuit, their armbands aglow with the cross of Christian soldiers, their pistols burning on their hips.

Posses are risky things because they depend on a riot mentality to accomplish their work. Otherwise bland, uninteresting, idle people are told that they matter, and to vindicate the suggestion that they matter, they display irrational enthusiasm. So it was with this posse, which, under Jared Hennemyer's leadership, was behaving as if it were on the trail of John Dillinger and not a mild-mannered college professor, a barmaid, a Good Humor man and me, a wreck of a philosopher wearing second-hand clothes.

In the meantime, we pushed on, the Rambler's cylinders pumping their little hearts out as the vehicle shuddered and wheezed ever eastward, the population thinning, the woods growing thicker, the vistas narrower. We had entered a part of Maine no longer defined so much by towns as by unincorporated outposts — wild areas that knew little government and would prefer to rid themselves of even the little they had. "This looks like Henker country," fretted Poye as he gazed out the passenger window at the setting sun.

Clara lit a Virginia Slim and took a deep drag. "Don't be so sure," she said. "I know these people. They're pretty freethinking. I wouldn't be surprised if we found friends here."

Clara turned on the radio to see what was on the air. It was then that we learned that not only the state of Maine but the entire country had been placed on high alert for the evolutionists on the run. Henker was hell-bent on vindicating his evolution eradication order by making an example of someone and, at Dud Wilmot's prodding, Poye fit the bill nicely. My friend, the soft-spoken, retiring college professor, was now the media item du jour. The radio reported that the photo of this nondescript-looking man was being flashed across TV, computer, and cell phone screens with the banner, HAVE YOU SEEN HIM?

"Well, there's your fifteen minutes of fame," I said as Clara clicked off the radio.

Poye fretted. "I just wanted to teach."

"All is not lost," counseled Professor Todelaw, finger raised.

We were halfway to the Canadian border when Clara identified a gentle plume of smoke rising above some pines. "There," she said as she slowed the Rambler and began to nose it down a dirt road, its suspension wheezing and oinking by turns as it ferreted out one pothole after the other. "It's late, and it's getting dark. Let's rest."

"I don't like this," said Poye, wringing his hands.

Professor Todelaw squinted in the dim light, hanging onto the seat back as the vehicle bounced along. "Where is your sense of adventure, Poye?"

"I am his sense of adventure," said Clara without taking her eyes from the road, and Poye threw her an appreciative look because she was right. His hooking up with Clara had been as unlikely as getting hit by a meteorite. He never knew what to expect from one day to the next. I could see how, in Poye's mind, this was the very essence of adventure.

The road opened onto a clearing which hosted a decrepit log cabin. Clara stopped the car. A mangy mutt snuffled around out front but otherwise didn't pay us any heed. The porch was cluttered with a ragged sofa, a rocking chair, an empty rabbit hutch, a pile of wood, and all manner of tools and odds and ends. The Rambler's headlights were playing over the scene when someone half-opened the rattly screen door. No more than a thin shadow, the figure looked us over but didn't move or say a word. Clara turned the vehicle off and quit the accusing lights. It was then, in the abrupt silence, that the figure revealed a rifle by its side. This didn't daunt Clara. She got out of the car and took a step toward the cabin. "Hosanna?" she probed.

The figure pushed the door wider, and now we could see that it was a man, a lean, weedy, scarecrow-looking man, with coveralls and a floppy, beaver-felt hat. His mouth was puckered deep within the nest of his unkempt beard. "Don't you 'hosanna' me," he said as he picked up his rifle but didn't point it. "I am armed. Why ain't you armed? You Canadians?"

Clara cackled, and the man's eyes widened. "Not yet," she said. "But maybe we're aiming to be." Then she turned and signaled to the rest of us. "Come on out," she said. "I got a good feeling about this one."

A good feeling? The man was armed, and we were alone with him deep in a remote hollow, the existence of which was probably unknown to any authority. "Where's your pendant?" he asked, hoisting the gun a little higher.

Clara was unafraid. "Where's yours?"

"Well," he said. "I guess that's fair, then."

"We need a place for the night," said Clara. "This is my man Poye, and that's Professor Todelaw. And back there, looking doubtful, that's Nestor."

The professor gave a slight bow, which made his coin changer ka-ching. "I am a Good Humor man," he said, perhaps in a bid to mollify the armed figure, if indeed he needed mollifying.

"Good Humor," the man echoed as he regarded the professor's white uniform. "What's that? Military?"

It didn't escape me that if this man didn't know what Good Humor was, he probably didn't know anything about Poye. I tested this theory by peeping, "Trubb."

The man drew back. "What language you speaking?"

I continued with my experiment. "Henker," I said, and the man raised his rifle toward me and stared down the sight. "Say that name again, and you can take it to the heavenly bank. Or to hell."

Professor Todelaw put up his hands and patted the air. "Good work, Nestor," he said. "We know everything we need to know." He turned to Clara. "Your instincts are sound. I think we have found a kindred spirit."

Flurries began to drift down from a low, solid cloud cover, reminding us that the night ahead would be a cold one. Clara reiterated her request for a place to lay our heads. The man assented and admitted us to his cabin. Once inside, Clara didn't have to ask whether he lived alone. There was no evidence of habitation by anybody other than someone who seemed to be a collector and never entertained guests. The space was a congeries of pelts, tools, wood, and assorted furniture in various states of utility. A pig-shaped woodstove pulsed in the far corner, throwing off a welcome warmth, the fire visible through its loose joints. The four of us sat down under a bare light bulb at the man's plank table. Our two parties looked each other over for a few moments. Clara broke the silence. "You got a beer?"

The man looked surprised at the request. After a moment's consideration, during which he buried one of his thin hands in his beard, he drew himself out of his chair. But he remained on suspicion's knife edge. He opened a squat refrigerator that apparently had a bad hinge because he had to support the door with his foot while he rummaged for a cold one. He eventually extracted it from behind a hunk of uncovered meat on a platter. He struggled to twist the cap off, but couldn't manage it. This seemed to embarrass him, because he turned his back to us, hunched over the beer, and continued to struggle.

"Give it here," said Clara with her hand extended, her fingers feathering her palm.

The man turned and harrumphed. Clara's comment seemed to amuse him. He handed her the bottle. She grabbed hold of the cap, and with a brisk twist had it off and chugged away while the man looked on in wonder. "I ain't never seen a woman like you," he said.

Clara wiped her mouth with the back of her hand. "You got that right," she said.

It didn't seem to occur to the man to offer the rest of us a beer, and I know I didn't feel comfortable requesting one. Poye wasn't a drinker, but Professor Todelaw was licking his lips, his eyes filled with desire. The man resumed his seat opposite us and stared at Poye. Then he addressed Clara. "You said he belongs to you?"

"That's right."

The man shook his head. "I think you could'a done better."

I could feel Clara's ire rising, but the man's gun stood by his side, so she hung fire. "He's done nicely," she said, and Poye glowed. And then, "What's your name?"

The man hesitated, as if identifying himself might be divulging too much. Finally, he clipped, "Shane." And then, "So you're on the run. Making for Canada?"

Clara put the beer down, and I could sense her automatic radar engage. "Could be," she said, which brought eyes on her from the rest of us.

"Could be yes or could be no," said Shane. "Which is it?"

"Maybe Mexico," said Clara, which really had our eyes pleading. Finally,

Poye peeped, "Mexico?"

Clara shot him a harsh glance, which wasn't lost on Shane, who was clearly taking notes. "You goin' the wrong way to Mexico," he said. "Unless you mean Mexico, Canada."

Clara clearly regretted having explained our circumstances to this man. She regarded us with a sort of low-key expression of alarm. Who knew how loose Shane's lips were? Or who he was connected to? After all, under Henker we lived in a nation of suspects. I looked about the cabin and didn't see a phone, so I concluded that we were pretty isolated all right, unless Shane had a cell phone stashed somewhere. But that damn gun stood between him and us. I concluded that Shane was alone because of the way he was — ornery and suspicious. It was his nature. There was no TV or radio in the room, so it was unlikely he knew anything about the manhunt. I was surprised that he even knew who Henker was.

Shane seemed to relent. "Well," he said, "I'm gonna make some food. I can share it with you."

"That's nice of you," volunteered Professor Todelaw. Shane stared at him as if he had never heard the word 'nice' uttered in his hovel. "It ain't nice," he finally said. "It's food."

Professor Todelaw stared at the man. Shane turned away and tended to his impossibly cluttered kitchen area. I could see that Clara's impulse to get up and do the cooking was strong, but she held it at bay. We watched as Shane retrieved the hunk of meat from the refrigerator, placed it on a butcher block next to the stove, and hacked away at it with a meat cleaver. His rifle continued to stand by his side as if magnetically attached to him.

The meal was simple but filling. Each of us received a chunk of the meat and some mashed turnip, and a fork but no knife. I had to hold the meat down with one hand while clawing away with the fork at the tough cut to break it up. "Sure is good," chirped Poye, attempting to lighten the mood.

Shane stopped chewing and looked at him. "Moose," he said.

I noticed that Clara was keeping one eye on Shane, who was watching Poye, while Professor Todelaw kept both of his eyes on Clara and I took copious notes on my legal pad. Everyone at the table seemed interconnected in this manner, and a low hum of tension permeated the scene. After the meal, Shane got up. He collected the plates and clattered them into the already full sink. Then he opened the woodstove to expose the dying embers and threw in another log before turning off the two bare light bulbs in the cabin. The only illumination now was the weak glow thrown out through the loose joints of the stove and the pale light from the full moon that poured through the grimy window. Shane moved toward a filthy cot against the far wall, dragging his rifle with him, its butt scraping along. "You folks got the floor," he said.

Clara was determined to make herself as comfortable as possible. Spotting a blanket slung over one of the chairs, she grabbed it and balled it up for a pillow. Poye cuddled up against her, resting his head against her breasts. Professor Todelaw and I sat up against the woodpile. And so night descended.

Except that Clara didn't sleep. I know because I didn't either, and I was watching her. She kept one eye open and focused on Shane. And then, sometime after midnight, with the stealth of a predator, she crept upon him. While Poye and Professor Todelaw transited the sleep of the dead, I looked on as Clara and Shane rolled on the cot like a couple of alley cats. I sensed that Shane had never been touched by a woman. Now he had one in full and was emitting mammalian grunts and incomprehensible syllables while Clara coaxed and prodded him and tongued his hairy earlobe. I strained to make out what he was muttering to her. Finally, the deed was done, and Clara slipped off the cot with the rifle as Shane, sighing with repletion, fell off to sleep. She quickly emptied the chamber and deposited the handful of shells in her coat pocket, after which she returned the weapon to its sleeping owner. Then she crept along the floor on her hands and knees and rejoined Poye. But she also caught sight of me looking at her. She squinted and nodded, then signaled for me to come over to her.

"I'm furious with myself for my poor judgment," she whispered, making fists. "I was wrong from the get-go."

"What do you mean?"

"I don't know how he did it, but he sent a signal. Maybe it was a puff of smoke from the chimney. That anti-Henker business was an act. He knew exactly who we were all along."

"No one's blaming you for anything, Clara. But what do we do now?"

I soon had my answer. Clara shook Poye and Professor Todelaw awake. "Get up," she commanded in a harsh whisper.

There was a wheezing of floorboards on the porch. I crawled to the front window and rubbed some of the grime away to make a peephole. Jared and his posse, in their broken-down van, had found the Rambler and were crouching just outside the door. The assault was about to begin. His men looked to him for direction. "Should we go in shooting?" one of them asked.

"No," said Jared. "We might hit Shane. I say we just burst right through the door and swarm them. We corral them and then tie them up and haul them off. It's perfect."

The others nodded. The only problem was that it wasn't perfect. Jared hadn't counted on a wild card — Clara. I scrambled back across the floor and told her what I had heard.

Shane looked like a dead man over on his cot, lying on his back with his hands crossed upon his chest. Then he stirred, and it was all one-way from there. We watched as he sat up and reflexively groped for his rifle. Then he caught sight of our eight eyes locked tight on him. We turned toward the clumsy shuffling on the porch. "I guess it's show time," he said as he got up, raised the rifle, and pointed it at Clara. "Guess I fooled you good."

"Pull the trigger," commanded Clara as she deftly fetched up one of the shells from her pocket and clasped it tightly in her fist.

"Clara!" cried Poye.

Shane looked amused. "You got guts, woman," he said. "But I got a gun."

Poye and Professor Todelaw huddled behind Clara while I remained crouched on the floor. "Don't egg him on!" pleaded Poye.

"Shoot!" challenged Clara. "If you don't, I will."

"Ha!" said Shane. "With what?"

Clara drew back and flung the shell point-blank at Shane. He dropped his rifle and threw both hands over his face. "My eye! My eye!" he screamed, falling back on the cot. In a flash, Clara grabbed the weapon. As if on cue, Jared and his men exploded through the door. Clara aimed straight for the serpent's head and, with her free hand, winged another shell, hitting Jared on the nose. Blood immediately began to course, which brought his five men up short as they stood around him, watching dumbly. "Blood!" screamed Jared accusingly as he held his hands out with the evidence of the deluge.

"Come on!" commanded Clara as she rushed past the paralyzed group with the rest of us in her wake, loading the rifle as she went. Once outside, she shot out three of the van's tires. Then she flung the exhausted weapon into the woods, and we took off in the Rambler. Only one word was spoken as we bumped down the approach road, and it was spoken by Professor Todelaw.

"Remarkable."

Poye, for his part, was taking his own pulse and measuring his breaths, while I wondered how on earth I would explain all this to the Spong.

TWENTY-FIVE
CANADA

Some fifty miles down the road we made a pee stop. I wandered off deep into the woods, set out the servo, and reluctantly summoned the Spong for a chit-chat. My fear was that this most recent event would only affirm their disapproval of our species, and yet I felt obligated to make my report.

As I anticipated, the Spong were not happy. "Violence everywhere," declaimed Spong 1, shaking its tentacles ruefully.

Spong 2 and 3 chimed in. "We don't see what any of this behavior has to do with snuffling for food and sex. Why can't humans behave like turtles or salamanders?"

Spong 4's thoughts were elsewhere. "How's Clara?"

The other three Spong moaned. "Please keep her DNA out of this," lamented Spong 1. "You're only making things more difficult."

"Boys," I interrupted. "Please." Somebody had to speak up and be the adult here.

"You are correct," said Spong 1. "Arguing is unknown on Spong." And then it raised a tentacle and scratched its orifice. "It seems that Spong has been contaminated through contact with you. We are picking up some of your bad habits. This cannot go on."

"Now wait a minute," I continued in my oppositional vein. "First you compare us unfavorably to salamanders, and then you claim that we are influencing you. If we are so advanced that we can alter Spong behavior, then maybe we're worth saving." I congratulated myself on what I thought was a fine bit of reasoning. It seemed to throw the Spong into a good deal of confusion. They ran all those eyeballs over each other as if hoping that, of the four of them, maybe one could come up with a decent response.

"What will Poye do now?" asked Spong 1. It was clear they wanted to change the subject. So be it. I had made my point.

"We're headed for the Canadian border."

"And how will that benefit Poye?" asked Spong 2. The others emitted a hum of agreement.

"Good question," I said. "The border is not easy to cross. The Canadians do not want fleeing Americans, and the Americans will try to arrest us. It's a real pickle."

"Spong senses," said Spong 1, "that this will not end well."

"Give us a chance," I counseled. "You're not short of time. You're short of patience."

I thought I was simply being game and was surprised when the Spong, in unison, said, "We agree."

The servo jumped, and the connection ended. I returned to my friends. Clara upbraided me. "That was a hell of a pee," she said.

"I had to find a private place. I can't pee if someone is watching."

Clara clucked her tongue. "There's nothing I haven't seen before."

We resumed our journey toward the border. Poye had regained his emotional equilibrium, and Professor Todelaw was soon asleep. After a short while, Clara stopped the Rambler about a tenth of a mile from the crossing. She wasn't sure how to proceed, how to get past the American border guard. None of us was wearing a pendant, and this in itself was grounds for arrest. "Do you think it was a bad idea to ditch the pendants?" I noised from the back seat. I had my answer in Clara's uncharacteristic silence.

"What do we do now?" asked Poye.

"I'm thinking," said Clara.

Professor Todelaw stirred. "I take it this is the border."

"Yes," said Clara. She let off the brakes and began to inch the Rambler ahead, in those wee hours of the morning, before there was any hint of light on the horizon. Finally, we could see the crossing, the flag of the Theocratic Union of American States — a gold cross with a circlet of stars — waving above the guard booth, illuminated by a spotlight. Clara pulled over and moved to get out. "Wait here," she said.

Poye was on edge, nibbling his lips compulsively. "What are you going to do?"

Clara threw her hair back and plumped up her breasts. "I'm going to use what's never failed me," she said.

Poye and I knew exactly what she meant, but the professor seemed mystified. Nevertheless, he looked on, rapt, as Clara got out of the Rambler and ambled toward the booth, moving slowly, sinuously. I hopped out as well. "I'm going to trail you," I said, amazed at my cheek. "Just in case."

"Suit yourself," said Clara. "But don't let the guard see you."

"My heart is racing," confided Professor Todelaw as he mopped his brow with a bandanna. Clara stopped and waited until a T.U.A.S. patrol passed. Then she moved forward again.

As she neared the booth, with me dogging her from the bordering bushes, the guard perked up. He was wearing a dark blue, almost black, uniform, and a sort of shako with a gold cross embroidered on the front. Around his neck was an illuminated cross pendant. He stepped out of the booth and laid a hand on the butt of his holstered pistol. He regarded Clara the way a scientist might be pleased with sighting an uncommon species of bird, his face alight with fascination. Finally, when Clara drew close, he said, "Hosanna."

"Hosanna," she replied, conjuring a smoky voice. "How are you?" The guard was little more than a boy, perhaps twenty-two or twenty-three. His face bore the pink flush of youth, and his uniform hung loosely on his lean frame.

"This border is closed," said the guard, but in a matter-of-fact way, with no hint of hostility.

"Even to me?" asked Clara, hands on hips, twisting about to display the full breadth of her wares.

The young man continued to look her over. "No one can pass," he said, darkly now. "Everyone knows this. Unless you have a special exit visa from the Transit Council. Canada is hostile territory."

Knowing Clara, she no doubt wanted to say "bullshit," but she stayed on task. She glanced around. "The place looks deserted." She took another step toward the guard. He studied her more closely, his eyes moving over her body, from face to feet, laser-like, as I held my breath, my palms awash in sweat. Clara was close enough to reach out and touch him, which is exactly what she did. But he recoiled, and Clara drew back. "Well," she said, "this is something new." I watched as she regrouped and lunged for him in an attempt to wrestle him into the booth to do what she needed to do. But when she acted, he pushed her away, yelling, "Let me go!" the way a child would.

"What's wrong with you?" demanded Clara. "You're all alone. You're a man, right? I'm giving it to you for free." She grabbed him with unusual desperation, but holding him was a tremendous effort. He squirmed like a spirited puppy. He whimpered, "Get away!" And then, "Let go! *Hag!*"

Clara dropped her arms and watched as the guard stepped back and drew his pistol. She lowered her gaze and rested it on the thing, which was unsteady in the boy's trembling hand. Her face bore a profound sadness as she turned and slowly walked back toward the Rambler, the guard shouting at her back, "Stop! I'll shoot!"

"No, you won't," said Clara without turning around, without emotion.

She was right. He didn't shoot. He didn't say another word. Clara and I got back into the car and found Poye and Professor Todelaw almost manic with worry. "What happened?" begged Poye. "Will we get across?"

Clara didn't say a word. Even if she had, she would have been upended when the Star Nation van pulled up and disgorged Jared and his boys, joined by Dud Wilmot this time. Jared's eyes had blackened, and his nose was swollen in comic fashion. "That's her!" he said, thrusting out an accusing finger. "She's the one who hit me in the nose with that bullet."

All four of us had the hangdog looks of gamblers who had played their last cards and lost the remainder of their assets. We stood, helpless, as Dud Wilmot, in his coveralls and striped choo-choo cap, shuffled up to us. Barely moving his lips, he said, "Well." And then, "I hate being called out in the middle of the night to deliver spare tires. I hate the cold. I hate the inconvenience."

They loaded us into the van and slammed the doors. Clara, talking to herself, as if in delirium, confided that maybe the gambit with the young border guard had been a fluke. "Maybe I could try Dud," she said. "There's a ditch not ten feet away. It would do nicely. Wouldn't it, Poye?"

Poye, Professor Todelaw and I smiled sympathetically. But I don't think any of the others sensed what I did, that Clara had encountered a feeling completely alien to her: rejection. The very thought of it must have been unbearable.

Utterly unbearable.

TWENTY-SIX
ARREST

We were conducted without protest to Washington County Jail. Jared drove while Dud Wilmot rode shotgun — literally: a twelve-gauge was angled malignantly between his legs. The other members of the posse were distributed about the van, all with their hands near their pistols. "Keep an eye on 'em, boys," rumbled Dud without turning around. "Don't let one of them fetch out your weapon and turn it on you."

It was, of course, absurd. Neither Poye nor I nor certainly Professor Todelaw knew how to handle a gun, and Clara had other methods to get her way — until recently, at least. That spurned woman sat there, staring into the night as the van bumped along and swayed around the bends in the deserted road. Poye kept glancing at her as if he were observing a stranger. Her face bore the most exquisite pain and was frozen into a grim rictus. Poye was inexpert in these situations and had no idea what to say because he didn't know what was wrong. So he continued to keep silent, and to occasionally glance at the woman who had been his friend, lover, and ally for more than five years.

Professor Todelaw watched as one of the posse members, a milk-faced kid with stringy hair, opened a lunch box packed with ice and retrieved an ice cream on a stick, which he began to munch. "Tsk," noised the professor, and the kid turned to him. "What?"

"That's not ice cream," said Professor Todelaw. "It's ice milk. There's a difference. I'm willing to bet you paid about twenty-five cents for that."

The kid took the pop from his mouth and huffed. "Right on," he said.

The professor looked vindicated. "Ice milk is a much cheaper product. At Good Humor we sell only ice *cream*. Do you want to know the difference?"

Everyone in the van seemed to be listening now. The kid nodded tentatively.

"When you freeze ice milk, the water separates out and crystallizes, and you get this gooey frozen glaze."

The kid looked at the pop and screwed up his face in disgust.

"Ice cream, however, retains its homogeneity. And when it slowly melts as you eat it, it remains, well, creamy. No crystal goo."

The boy regarded his half-eaten treat one last time and then tossed the pop at the partly open window but missed. It hit the side wall, and everyone in back of the van watched as it languidly slid toward the floor. "Sad," said the professor.

The only one maintaining disinterest was Clara. She continued to stare into space and seemed to be struggling to hold back tears. Poye finally rested his hand on hers. "Whatever it is," he whispered, "it will be all right."

Clara, without turning to him, said, "The river flows only one way."

Poye had no feel for metaphors, so he only nodded. "Of course it does," he said, and Clara whimpered.

When we arrived at the jail we were photographed and fingerprinted. Reporters swarmed and flashed the bejesus out of us with their cameras. We were escorted to two separate cells, one for Clara and the other for us three men. We were able to peer out at a television mounted high on the wall. It wasn't long before the story of our capture precipitated. It showed us being escorted into the jail, as well as an interview with Dud Wilmot, who clipped, "We got 'em," as if he had just whacked a particularly noisome mosquito. And then the frame jumped to Bass Drum Henker, standing on a platform behind a lectern with the presidential seal on the front. The suitcase with the life-sustaining Tornado-3 was on the floor beside him, whirring while his aid hovered over it, his belt studded with emergency tools.

"When I give my word, I keep my word," snarled Henker, his bottom teeth gnashing, his small eyeballs bouncing in their sunken sockets. "We must eliminate the infection of evolution once and for all, and this is a splendid start. This Poye Trubb is the vanguard of something intensely wicked. He is the head of the serpent. And you know what we do with the head of a serpent, don't you?" he asked. He made a slashing gesture across his throat with his finger while his aid, carried away by the moment, raised his eyes and hands in an "alleluia" gesture. Henker turned to look at him and, nodding, hissed, "Yessss."

Poye, for his part, watched President Henker with fascination as he talked about him on TV. "He mentioned my name," he said. "I'll bet this is the first time a president has ever said 'Poye Trubb' in public."

The door to the holding area opened, and three men walked in: Dud Wilmot, Rate and Brother Eevin. Poye brightened when he saw the two representatives from the Church of the Happy Clappers. "I'm sorry the circumstances are so uncomfortable," Rate said.

Dud huffed. "Not for us they ain't."

Brother Eevin threw the cement king a disapproving glance. "Brother Wilmot, a little compassion, please."

"They're going to be compassioned straight to court," said Dud, squinting at the prisoners with restrained jubilation.

Brother Eevin walked up and pushed his face between the bars. "We forgive you," he said. "But it would still benefit everybody if you would recant. Then this wouldn't go to trial." And here he turned to Dud. "And I wouldn't be surprised if you got your job back at Wytopitlock. Isn't that right, Brother Wilmot?"

The cement king looked incredulous. "I wouldn't bet on that horse," he clipped.

Poye had listened quietly. Then he spoke up. "Recant what?" he asked. "I didn't say anything that wasn't true. Do you want me to recant the truth?"

I wanted to reach out and give Poye a good clunk on the head, because, as I've said over and over, he had taught only part of the truth, because he had missed the big tamale: the creation of life by a superior intelligence. This is where Rate and Brother Eevin had a leg up on him. If Poye could only make that mental leap, then he would indeed be telling the truth, the whole truth, and nothing but the truth. And maybe the Spong would reconsider the Treatment.

"Well, then," concluded Brother Eevin as he stepped away from the bars. "I'm afraid Brother Wilmot is absolutely right. This will be settled in court." He placed his hand over his heart. "But it will give me no joy to see it proceed in this manner. No joy at all."

Poye watched as the three men retreated. Professor Todelaw was sitting on the edge of his bunk, shaking his head, as if disapproving of the antics of disobedient children. "It made me just want to reach out and give each of them a Toasted Almond," he said, swiping the air with a hand. "It never fails to do the trick. It cheers a lad right up. Brings him right around."

Poye listened to the professor and then glanced over at Clara, who was standing in a corner of her cell, looking as if she were a million miles away. "Maybe you have one for Clara," he said. He reached through the bars toward her and, welling with irrepressible tenderness, gestured as if stroking her back. She raised her head, focused her watery eyes on him, and registered a note of incredulity. Poye was appropriating her approach, her job, her modus operandi; in essence, he was performing a deft jujitsu. Five years with him and this was the first time he had initiated anything resembling affection. "I bet this would feel good if I could touch you," he said.

Clara felt herself melting under the mimed caress. "Please don't stop."

Poye intensified the gesture, then ventured to rotate his hand as if he were cupping one of her breasts. Whatever forces dispersed painful memories and elevated the mood and provoked optimism, they were alive in Clara now. "Why do you stay with me?" she asked, and the tone in her voice suggested she was desperate for an answer to this question.

Poye was taken off guard. It had always been he who had wondered why Clara chose to stay with him. But he seemed willing to consider the question on her terms. "You know, I have a theory," he said, searching for the right words. "I have always thought that there are two kinds of people in the world — finished and unfinished. You can't expect anything new from finished people. But unfinished people are always surprising us. I never know what to expect next from you — or from Nest or Professor Todelaw over there." As he said this, the professor perked up and touched the visor of his cap. "And that's what makes you so exciting to me," he concluded.

Clara was uncharacteristically speechless. Had she ever heard Poye talk like this? I know I hadn't. Perhaps she thought him incapable of such considerate reflection. She finally found her voice again. "Poye, you have just shown me that you're unfinished too."

Poye smiled, and I noted how attractive it made his unremarkable face look. This must not have been lost on Clara. "I don't care about that border guard," she said out of the blue. "He was only a boy." I'm sure she was right. He had probably never been kissed, much less seduced. Clara knew she was a fine glass of wine, so what could she expect from a guzzler of Pepsi and energy drinks? "Now that I think of it, why did I waste my precious time on that mean-mouthed child?" She reached out through the bars of her cell for Poye and made a gesture as if unbuttoning his shirt. "Clara," he said, blushing as he wrapped his arms around himself. "Professor Todelaw."

Clara glanced over at the professor, who had removed his cap and was shielding his eyes with it. "But you do want me to," she said.

"Of course," said Poye. "More than you know."

Clara reached out as if to gather Poye to herself. Then she made a robust squeezing motion. Poye, for his part, sighed as if he were melting in her arms. "You know," she said, "I think I'd make a good chiropractor. I think I've got a knack for it." The two continued to gesture longingly toward each other.

•   •   •   •   •

Since I hadn't peed during our pee stop, the pressure finally caught up with me. I took off a sneaker and rattled the bars until a guard idled over. I crossed my legs like a little boy and hopped up and down. The guard shook his head, opened the cell, and conducted me to a windowless bathroom. "No funny stuff," he said.

"What?" I said as I disappeared inside. "Am I going to break down the concrete wall with my bare hands?"

After emptying my bladder, I took out the servo and placed an emergency call to the Spong.

"He called her *what?* Shall Spong kill him?"

That was Spong 4. I had made the mistake of reporting the incident with the border guard. Spong 4's tentacles twisted into a knot of consternation which the others worked to untangle. "Spong apologizes for this display," said Spong 1 as it assisted in the effort.

"Well, now you know what love can do," I said.

Spong 1 darkened and turned to me. "Then love doesn't strike Spong as a good thing. Look what it's done to Spong 4. It is totally incapacitated. It has lost its judgment."

"Hey, welcome to humanity." (What I really wanted to say was, "'Superior Intelligence', my foot.")

The entanglement had given Spong 4 time to cool off. "What happens now?" it asked. "Spong 4 does not like the idea of Clara being in a cage."

"I think you've lost your" — *Zing!* — "Perspective," I said, and I could feel all four of them bristle. "This isn't about Clara. It's about Poye and his failure to resolve the origins question of evolution by acknowledging the possibility that a superior intelligence..."

"Spong," all four said in synchrony.

"Yes, ultimately," I conceded. "But let me finish. I was saying that he failed to accept that a superior intelligence got the ball of life rolling on Earth."

"Which is where Rate and Brother Eevin and Dud succeeded."

"Yes, as much as it pains me to admit it."

"So tell us again why Poye is being hectored by your government."

I took a deep breath. "Humans think they're special," I began, "and that they were created separately from everything else and have special rights that other living things don't have. They don't like to think of themselves as related to other creatures, much less descended from them. It's an old story. Back in 1925, another teacher was caught teaching evolution, and they dragged him to court as well. But in the end, he came out on top, and the law was overturned."

"Then why," asked Spong 2, "if everything was settled, are they doing this all over again with Poye?"

"Because," I said, impatient now with their slow grasp, "overturning a law is one thing, but getting people to think differently is another thing entirely. Especially in the Theocratic Union of American States, where people couldn't give a hoot in hell about history and laws. They're far more interested in the great everyday deals at Walmart."

That was too much for the Spong. Their eyes were spinning on their tentacles.

"Spong does not understand your language," said Spong 1. "Hoot? Hell? Deals? Walmart?"

"Let's just say people have poor memories."

"Another flaw in the species," said Spong 3. And then, "Tell us what happens next."

"Poye will go to trial," I said. "It will be a big deal because the government will want to make an example of him so no one else will ever dare teach evolution."

The Spong remained silent, until Spong 1 spoke. "Is there a chance that Poye could win? That he would be permitted to continue to teach evolution and come to understand the need for a superior intelligence as Rate and

Brother Eevin do? And then, perhaps, enlighten others?"

"No, no, no," I said. "It's just not going to happen. Not in this political climate."

"You are a pessimist," said Spong 4.

"Yeah," I said as I closed my eyes and embarked on a daydream. "I suppose I am. I'd make a good Spong, don't you think?"

Twenty-Seven
Presidential

Once back in my cell, I turned my attention to the TV again. According to the reports, the arrest of Poye Trubb had electrified the nation and cleaved the population in a lopsided manner. Most whooped to the executive blow President Bass Drum Henker had dealt the poison of evolution, while others despaired. Indecisiveness reigned among these latter souls, and the dramas played out all over the country, mostly in the form of a renewed stampede for the borders. One group attempted to head for Cuba, but many drowned in the streets of Miami, which were hip-deep in ocean waters rising in defiance of Star Nation denials. Others saw salvation in the wilds of the country's border with Canada but were disabused of this belief when Mounties helped the American forces repulse the fleeing refugees, for fear of being overrun. Another intrepid group in Minnesota cobbled together a hot air balloon using tarps and duct tape, but it caught fire and went down in the Lake of the Woods, where valiant samaritans attempted to rescue the aeronauts before being surrounded by T.U.A.S. Special Operations forces, who dragged the lot of them away.

As for those who viewed themselves as victors in the evolution war, they coalesced in the form of rallies and marches, swarming the streets and rousting out anyone they considered to be a sympathizer with godless Darwinism. How they identified these transgressors was a mystery. Did they have a certain look, or aspect, that marked them as opponents of Star Nation ideals? Or did they simply wear a non-cross pendant? Or no pendant at all? It didn't matter, because the juggernaut needed feeding, and in a pinch, anyone would do. As we watched the television from our cells, the news related the sad case of Flavis McKinney, a simple baker, who was dragged from his shop by a Star Nation mob because he failed to greet a customer with a robust "Hosanna!" As they hauled him off — even they didn't know where they were taking him — he screamed, "But I bear the cross!" as he clutched his pendant and pushed it in the faces of his waylayers, one of whom ripped it from his neck and barked, "You don't deserve to!"

Bass Drum Henker presided over the general madness, which he viewed as a cleansing and re-ordering. He had lit a fuse, which led to a detonation. The mania grew to where the ochlocracy began to decry not Darwinism, but *Poye*-ism. And they lusted for a vigilante style of justice.

Poye himself seemed oblivious to the cataclysm. He, Clara, Professor Todelaw and I occupied what seemed to be the inflamed nation's only oasis of calm. The jail was quiet, safe, and orderly. It was a redoubt of tranquility in the midst of rabid and unforgiving social and political environments. It was a place where a man could sit and think, knowing that he was beyond the reach of deranged mobs. At one point the guard on duty remarked that Poye's potential allies preferred to run rather than stand with him. "Where are your friends now?" he sneered as he peered through the bars at the sacrificial lamb.

Poye pondered this question. Then he raised his face to the guard. "Why, they're right here," he said, gesturing toward me, Clara and Professor Todelaw. To which the guard replied, "Hah!"

In the meantime, things were percolating behind the scenes. The next report showed Bass Drum Henker arriving in Maine under cover of darkness, unusually energized for a man of his years and state of health, his overcoat draped loosely on his frame as if on a wooden clothes-horse. Underneath the custom-tailored garb was a mere stick figure with a cavity once occupied by a flesh-and-blood heart. As he arose from his sleek, black limousine, he was greeted by a swarm of reporters and a welcoming committee which included Rate, Brother Eevin, Jared Hennemyer, Eulalie, and Dud Wilmot, who hadn't altered his appearance one iota for the occasion. He still wore his cement-dust coveralls with his choo-choo cap at a casual angle, twirling a toothpick in the corner of his mouth. Henker, accompanied by the aide carrying the Tornado-3, approached the cement king, his hand outstretched. The surrounding microphones caught the ensuing conversation. "Hello, Dud. Thanks for that last contribution. It put us over the top."

"Yessir," Dud slurred as he slipped his clubby paw into the president's withered hand.

Henker turned to the others and looked them over for a moment. "Yes," he finally said. "You'll do. You'll do just fine." Jared straightened up under the approbation, while Rate and Brother Eevin quietly glowed and Eulalie looked adoringly at her father. Then the group piled into the armored limo and roared off.

I desperately needed to report this development to the Spong, so I pulled my pee stunt again. Once in the bathroom, I took out the servo and conjured the Elders. When I told them the president had arrived and was conferring with Rate, Brother Eevin, and Dud, they made a momentous decision. "You must listen to what they are talking about and interpret it for us," said Spong 1. "Prepare to be separated from your body."

"What?"

"Don't worry. It won't hurt. Prepare yourself."

Not knowing how to prepare for such an event, I closed my eyes and wrapped my arms around myself. There was a subtle "whoosh," and when I opened my eyes — *bam!* — I was in the basement of the Church of the Happy Clappers. Bass Drum Henker and the others took seats at the round table, while the guardian of the Tornado-3 stood behind the president, glancing warily about, and a fit Secret Service agent in dark glasses stood watch at the entrance, his hands crossed in front of him. I hovered in the background like a cloud, absorbed in my weightlessness. I drifted over to Henker and waved a hand in front of his face, but he didn't flinch. Wonderful!

"Let's talk about this Poye Trubb," said Henker as he glanced from face to face. "I need to know what I'm dealing with when I stand him up as representative of all that is wrong with this country."

Dud Wilmot nodded. Brother Eevin piped up with, "We still hope to get him to recant."

The president regarded him with amusement. "I think it's too late for that, son," he said with a karate chop. "We're in this whole-hog now."

Rate took up Brother Eevin's slack. "But, respectfully, Mr. President, don't you think that if he publicly recants, it will demonstrate to others that if someone gets on the right path, salvation is possible?"

Henker pulled back and looked at Rate with intense disgust. "You clearly are ignorant of my needs," he said. "I called for action. The people now expect action." He squinted and leaned across the table, his lower lip pulled back to reveal his long, gray, lower incisors. "You're not trying to soft-soap me, are you, son?"

Rate pointed to himself and looked about for witnesses to his distress. And then he returned to the president. "Not me, of all people," he said in his own defense. "But I do have a duty to the virtue of Christian charity."

"Bah!" huffed Henker with a wave of his hand, and the whirring beat of the Tornado-3 intensified. The president glanced down, patted the suitcase, and said, "Easy there."

Brother Eevin rejoined the conversation. "There is a wild card," he said.

Henker grew impatient. "What do you mean by that? Give it to me straight. No picturesque talk."

Brother Eevin lowered his voice as if what he was about to say was indelicate. "A woman," he said.

"What?" barked Henker. "Woman? What woman? Tell me."

"A whore," murmured Dud Wilmot, seeming to take great pleasure in uttering the word.

Eulalie blushed and waved her hand. "Oh, dad."

The president's eyebrows arched. "Whore? Who's the whore?" He looked at Eulalie, the only woman in the room.

Dud rotated his head and regarded his daughter. "You weren't there, Peaches. She attacked me with a knife."

"Well..." noised Brother Eevin. "Not exactly. I..."

Dud drew in his breath and leveled his eyes at the cleric. "I said, she attacked me with a knife."

The president slapped the table. "I don't understand," he said, cocking his head about for someone to clue him in. "Woman? Whore? Knife? Attack?"

"She is Poye Trubb's concubine, evidently," said Brother Eevin. "When we had him here in an attempt to talk reason to him, this woman burst in, upset the proceedings, and spirited him away." As he said this, he fluttered his hand, emulating the flight of a bird.

President Henker looked pleased. "So you're telling me that he's a sinner as well as a felon, right? This will make my work easy." He rubbed his hands together with glee, making a dry, sandpapery, slipping sound. Then he returned to Eulalie, who looked uncomfortable as she twisted one finger after the other as if keeping track of a countdown. "And what about you, dear? Where do you fit in?"

Eulalie identified herself as the person who had hired Poye. After divulging this she rolled in her lips, bracing herself for the president's response.

"So," said Henker, looking not at all displeased. "What you're saying is that you gave him a chance and he squandered it."

"Yes," peeped Eulalie. "I had to fire him."

"Of course you did, my dear," said Henker, soothingly. "Of course you did. You gave him a chance, he blew it, and you fired him. I like that. You have spunk."

Eulalie's face brightened under this caress, but Dud interrupted the bonhomie. "What now?"

"We go see him," said President Henker.

"See him?" echoed Brother Eevin. "Isn't a jail an unseemly place for a president?"

"We could bring him here," suggested Rate, but Henker vetoed that idea.

"No," he said. "I want to see him in his natural habitat. We can march him out later. In front of the cameras." Then he took note of Jared Hennemyer. "What's your story, son?"

Jared had been sitting stock still during the proceedings, looking adoringly at the president, tickled to be marinating in not only his wisdom but his mere presence in the same room. He cleared his throat and attempted a relaxed pose, but it was no-go. Bass Drum Henker had totally unmanned him, and he stammered in his attempt to get up to speaking speed. "I-I'm the team leader for our Star N-Nation Campus Compact," he finally managed, choking on his own saliva.

Henker brought a thin finger to his chin and regarded the pudgy young man with his shirttail hanging out. "Hmm," he intoned. "Commendable, very commendable. We must have the youth on our side." Then he asked, "What happened to your nose?"

Jared's schnozzola was still swollen from Clara's assault, having turned purple in the interim. "I-I was shot," he said. "His woman shot me."

Henker clapped his hand down on the table. "Well, that's it," he said. "We go after the fox *and* his vixen."

And that was the last word. The group was flattered to be invited to ride in the presidential limousine again, and they sped off into the night while I was returned, posthaste, to my body in the jail bathroom. What a rush. I pulled out the servo and waited for the inevitable.

"You're not going to like this," I told the Spong.

The borders of their orifices rippled as they quivered with anticipation. "Tell us."

I related the involvement of the president and his intention to make a public example of Poye. Maybe I went a bit overboard when I likened this to the burning of witches, because the Spong darkened until they were sort of russet-colored. Spong 1 spoke first. "Even though Poye does not believe that life on Earth was the work of a superior intelligence, we do not see this as reason for others to persecute him."

"Ahh..." I said, "so you do have a sense of fairness."

All four of the Elders seemed taken aback by my comment. They directed their eyeballs toward each other in a thoughtful manner. Finally, Spong 3 said, "We are not acquainted with fairness, but would like to ask your opinion on something."

"Shoot."

"Shall Spong kill him?"

"Kill who?"

"The president."

I almost bit my tongue. "God, no," I said. "You can't kill a president. It's a huge no-no. It would unleash national chaos, and then conspiracy theories. Someone would suggest that it was the work of aliens. That's always an attention-grabber."

The Spong turned to each other and fell into a frenetic conversation. A multitude of disparate noises — squeaks, squawks, and quacks — emanated from their orifices. They sounded like four children learning to play the clarinet.

"Gentlemen," I interrupted. "Or whatever you are. Please tell me what you want me to do next. But let's put away this talk of assassination."

The Spong quieted and returned to me. "You once said that this was all Spong's fault," said Spong 1. "And you were right. All we wanted was a garden in this quadrant of the galaxy, a way-station to re-supply our nutritional needs during our journeys. And then human life erupted. We blame our scientists for this. The seed DNA must have been contaminated."

I shook my head. "No, no, no," I said. "It wasn't your fault. The law of averages was at work. First, there were plant cells, and then some of those plant cells sprouted tails. Then — *voilà!* — animals appeared and began to snuffle about for food and sex. It was bound to happen. That's how evolution works."

"But Poye and his friends are not happy," said Spong 2.

"Happiness?" I said with a carefree shrug. "It's oversold. Nobody's happy. Are you happy?"

The Spong, in unison, admitted that they were not.

"See? Case in point."

At that moment there was an aggressive pounding on the door. "Are you done in there? You got one minute, then I'm coming in."

I flushed the toilet for effect, pulled myself together, and returned to the cell.

Twenty-Eight
Visit

When Bass Drum Henker arrived at the jail, he didn't find four defiant perpetrators lunging through the bars, screaming out against injustice and threatening the world at large. Such would have filled him with great pleasure as he sought to make an example of Poye. Instead, what he was met with was a sedate quartet, except, perhaps, for Clara, who was pacing circles in her cell, her prodigious sexual energies having been pent up far too long. As for Poye, he was sitting quietly in a corner of our cell, his hands under his thighs, watching Clara and counting her laps. Professor Todelaw was sitting on his bunk, dispensing coins from his money changer and then filling it again, compulsively. When he noticed the president and his entourage he examined them with curiosity, nothing more.

Of course, I couldn't divulge what I had heard during my out-of-body transit to the Church of the Happy Clappers, for fear of affecting the course of events. Besides, who would believe such a thing? This retention of vital information filled me with tremendous anxiety and gave me a headache to boot.

President Henker approached Clara's cell, his aid holding the Tornado-3 close behind him. Placing his parchment face between the bars, he asked, "Do you know who I am?"

"It doesn't matter," said Clara as she flew to the door of the cell. "Come in here, and I'll make it worth your while."

Henker recoiled and looked pleadingly to Brother Eevin, who had reddened. The whirring from the suitcase quickened and Henker sought to compose himself. He turned to our cell but kept his distance. "Poye Trubb," he said.

Poye stood up and, standing slightly bent, said, "Mr. President!"

"Let me get a look at you," said Henker as he ran his eyes over the unremarkable man standing before him. "You don't look so threatening to me."

Poye inclined his head and drew a puzzled mien. "I didn't think I was threatening anyone."

"And neither did anybody else!" said Clara, who cast loving eyes at her man. "This is insane."

President Henker folded his hand around his cross pendant. "Godless evolutionists," he growled. "We will have the answer for you. And damned soon."

Rate and Brother Eevin were plainly discomfited by the president's vernacular, but they remained silent.

Henker continued. "Do you know why you're here?"

Poye looked like he had a strong desire to hear someone say it out loud, so he shook his head.

"You broke the law," said Henker, throwing up his hands. "You knew it was against the law to teach evolution, yet you persisted. And now you must pay." After a pause, he added, "We must respect the law, no?"

"Not if the law is unjust," piped up Professor Todelaw as he rose from his bunk, his coin-changer jingling.

Henker drew back, looked at our friend, and inquired, darkly, "Who are you?"

Professor Todelaw introduced himself as a professor emeritus of biology.

"Then why," asked Henker, "are you dressed like a Good Humor man?"

"All honest work is good."

"No, it's not," shot back Henker. "Not if it inconveniences society."

"Bah," said the professor with a dismissive wave of his hand. "You yourself are an inconvenience, yet you persist."

There was a knocking sound in the suitcase as the Tornado-3 jumped in its compartment. The professor's affront enraged Henker. "No one has ever spoken to me like this!"

"Then you're overdue," said Professor Todelaw.

Poye regarded his mentor with wonder, wishing, perhaps, that he had some of the old man's moxie. This was the Professor Todelaw he had described to me, the one who took no prisoners, had a furious sense of justice and, when the students had rallied in support of increased wages for the campus custodians, had leaned out his office window and shouted, "March on, my people!" And now he was going toe-to-toe with the President of the Theocratic Union of American States and prevailing.

The president reached for his sidearm. Rate, Brother Eevin, and Eulalie leaped to assist the aide in restraining the manic Henker, while Jared Hennemyer hovered uselessly in the background. "I'll shoot you myself, you bastard!" thundered Bass Drum as the frantic scufflers stumbled over the suitcase, the Tornado-3 whirring and whining as if fighting its own battle. All the while, Professor Todelaw watched from his side of the bars with the cool dispassion of the scientist that he was until Henker calmed and shook off the four pairs of restraining arms. All the while, Dud Wilmot was regarding the scene with contained amusement, moving his toothpick from one side of his mouth to the other. Henker smoothed out his overcoat in an effort to regain some sense of decorum. When he glanced up again, he caught Professor Todelaw's eyes. "What are you looking at?" he demanded.

The professor shrugged. "I don't know. What do the anthropologists say?"

The melee repeated itself, with Henker going for his gun again as his hapless aide and the others held him back. I was amazed that a man of Henker's years could possess such strength. The arms in those sleeves must have been as lean as broomsticks.

Once again Henker composed himself, but by then Professor Todelaw had shuffled back to his bunk, mumbling, "*Sic semper tyrannis.*"

"Eh? What did you say? Tell me!" demanded Henker, grabbing the bars of the cell, but Professor Todelaw waved him off. "It's inconsequential."

Henker could do little more than seethe, his narrow chest rising and falling with his rasping breaths. "You think you're so smart," he sneered. "But I'll show you who the superior intelligence is."

Ach, if he only knew!

Twenty-Nine
Transport

Poye was, at last, resigned. Turning to me, he confided, "Nest, I feel the freedom of a man who knows the die has been cast." The uncertainty was over — he would be put on trial. Well, I had already told the Spong what to expect, but Poye still enjoyed the bliss of wistfulness. "If only we were twelve again. I would give anything to shimmy down the drainpipe from my bedroom window and run off to Debec Pond with you."

"On a blistering summer night," I added, smiling. And then, "But Clara's right, my friend. The river flows only one way."

The four of us were transported to the Washington County Courthouse in a short bus with no windows. While Professor Todelaw sat lost in thought, and I wondered what exactly the Spong had in mind, Clara and Poye had found their ways to the floor, where Poye lay spooning against Clara's back. Unaccustomed to initiating anything of a romantic nature, Poye now found himself in the role of the doting lover. I felt a certain pride in him for his unselfconscious display of affection; but then, what did he have to lose? He ran his fingertips ever so delicately over Clara's body, following the broad curve of her hip toward her muscular thigh. He ran his hand over this too, with a studied expression, as if noting the palpable strength which resided there. And then, like many a wanderer lulled by the challenges of the boreal reaches of the Earth, he traveled north and soon found his hand cupping one of her breasts, which elicited from Clara the most profound hum or moan. "Pleasure or pain?" he whispered. When Clara laid her hand upon his, he had his answer. And then she said, "I have done nothing to deserve you."

Poye smiled into the back of his woman. *His* woman. He didn't want to parse her statement, and so he continued to lie there, and Clara continued to coo under his caresses, and Professor Todelaw tactfully continued to occupy his own thoughts, while I took avid notes on my legal pad, which I had been permitted to keep. And all the while the short bus bumped along the poorly maintained roads of Maine's Washington County, the driver on the lookout for moose. One unexpected encounter could alter the course of all our lives.

It didn't seem to me that this was the end of Poye, and I believed that he was capable of something great, or at least bigger than himself, something other than Clara — his better half, as it were. I now sensed a rising up within him, and Clara seemed to sense this too, so much so that I didn't perceive in her the slightest rancor or guile. She was content, for the moment, to lie with Poye and allow him to be good to her. "You know," she said, so quietly, "I don't think we ever talked about children."

Poye's eyes widened. And I must say that I was also taken by surprise. Clara had never shown any interest in children — hers or anybody else's. "I don't think I ever heard you say the word before," Poye remarked. For my part, I couldn't picture Clara as ever having *been* a child. She seemed to have precipitated into the world exactly as she was now: expansive, energetic, self-possessed and, of course, hypersexed. But I had no doubt about her fertile potential — she could have birthed a nation. Drawing from my deep philosophical well, I regarded Clara as the primal woman. Eve. Sarai. The original intent of God. It struck me how little I knew about her past. And I was sure Poye shared my ignorance in this regard. Where had she been born, and exactly when? What had her parents been like? Were they still alive? Any siblings? Tragedies? Or was she of another species, old when the earth was young, the distillation of raw survivalist and sexual impulses that are humankind's primary drivers? But it really didn't matter. These issues were academic, and if neither Poye nor I ever discovered the answers, it would make no difference. I could see that all he knew with any certainty was that he loved her. And that was enough.

Poye lay tight by Clara until she fell asleep. He looked up at Professor Todelaw, who seemed to be drifting off as well. "Professor," he whispered, and the old man stirred and looked at him with dim, gray eyes, curtained by drooping lids. "I'm sorry to have gotten you involved in all this."

Professor Todelaw smiled. "Sorry?" he echoed. "I should be thanking you. Controversy is my milieu. I saw this coming, this vomiting up of indignation toward evolution. The irony is that those who object to its being taught in the schools know nothing about it. They continue to believe that it means humans are descended from apes when quite the opposite seems to be true. Our persecutors are apes who descended from humans who once upon a time were more tolerant and understanding. More intellectually curious."

Poye looked on in admiration at the professor's ability to see things so clearly, even on the brink of sleep. "I wish I were as clear-sighted as you," he said, "but I've always been too willing to see the other person's side of things, to the point of too readily yielding my own." He was right about this. That's the way it was when Joe Christiani hit him in the head with a snowball in fourth grade. It struck him in an already very cold ear, and it stung terribly. As he stood there blubbering, Joe convinced him that if he hadn't been in the path of the snowball, he wouldn't have been hit. And so it was all really Poye's fault. At the time the logic seemed infallible, and it took a while for me to convince Poye of the actual truth of the matter. But that didn't alleviate his continuing tendency, his impulse, to believe that he deserved everything that befell him.

And that's how it was now, but in a manner that threatened to benefit him. "Nest, I can't help thinking about the anti-evolutionists and the Intelligent Design proponents. Is there the slightest possibility that my understanding of evolution is not so complete after all?"

I had to bite my tongue to keep from blurting out, "Yes! Yes! You're missing a piece. Let me introduce you to my friends, the Spong." But I summoned the last modicum of inner strength and hung fire for dear life, lest I become more than the biographer my patrons had commissioned.

"I've never really thought about origins," mused Poye, hand to chin. "How did life get here? How did it all start? How did humans come to be? Isn't that the mystery of mysteries?" He glanced at me and caught my broad, knowing smile. "What is it, Nest?"

"Oh, nothing," I sang, leaning back against the side of the van with my hands behind my head. "I'm just so goddamn proud of you."

Poye returned my smile. He cuddled deeper into Clara's warm, soft back as if clinging to life itself, as if girding himself against the creeping chill of this night, and all the nights to come.

Thirty
Re-Jailed

Bass Drum Henker had accomplished his mission. The nation cheered Poye's arrest and transport to the trial venue. The anti-evolutionists were organized, militant, and vocal. Star Nation marches, torches on high, continued in the cities and towns of the land. The marchers were resolute in their intention to make an example of Poye and rid the country of perfidious evolutionary sentiment — *Poyeism* — once and for all. Jared Hennemyer had been hand-picked by President Henker to act as the *Brigadier* in charge of the paramilitary units which invaded both college and high school classrooms to monitor the tone, tenor, and content of the instruction. The professoriate was cowed to the point of being crippled. Most complied with the directives of the President's Council on Right Thinking, which previously had allowed the mention of evolution so long as it was accompanied by an effusive narrative about how Intelligent Design, in contrast to Darwinism, accounted for life's origins. But now the directives had been amended to compel teachers to dictate that evolution was a discredited idea responsible for most if not all of the ills afflicting the Theocratic Union of American States, blessed be its name.

Poye and I were separated from our companions and isolated in a holding cell in the basement of the courthouse. We didn't know where Clara and Professor Todelaw had been taken. Perhaps they had been released, for what were they guilty of? I presumed I was being held for attempting to obstruct Poye's arrest.

Poye was sitting on his bunk, lost in thought. Clara was resident in his heart, but Jared Hennemyer was on his mind. Not in a rueful way. He was simply an element of wonder. "The idea, Nest, that all of this started because a student of extremely limited abilities objected to something he really knew nothing about."

In other words, Jared Hennemyer had made a big thing out of a little thing, a something out of a nothing. If the course on the history of dentifrice had not been closed due to full enrollment, compelling Jared to substitute Introductory Biology, none of this would ever have happened.

"Maybe there is some superior intelligence after all," said Poye, once again flirting with the truth of the matter. "Something like a guiding hand that planted us like grass seed. If so, should I feel special?"

I sat down next to my pensive friend. "One of your virtues, Poye, is that you've never thought of yourself as singular in any way — except for your luck in finding Clara. But neither have you ever felt like a victim, even when Joe Christiani relentlessly bullied you all those years."

Poye sighed. "How I wish Professor Todelaw were here so that I could bounce these ideas off him to see what sparks of wisdom came of it."

A door flew open and, as if conjured by Poye's ruminations, Jared Hennemyer marched in. He was grim-faced and wore a shako with a purple tassel, similar to the one worn by the border guard who had confronted Clara. He had on a brown shirt with a purple armband bearing a gold cross, and around his neck was an unusually large cross pendant the size of a Frisbee. If Jared's appearance was the first surprise, the second was even greater: he was accompanied by Joe Christiani, wearing a similar uniform a couple of sizes too small, his great bulk stretching the polyester to its limits. He smiled when he saw Poye. "So we meet again."

Poye beamed. "Hey, Joe," he said, rising from the bunk. "Yes, we keep running into each other."

Joe didn't appreciate Poye's equanimity. He smirked, "Only this time you're on the other side of the bars."

"So are you," said Poye.

Joe considered this for a moment. He reloaded for a return volley, but Jared Hennemyer raised his hand and the large, looming bully obediently relented.

"Do you know why you're here?" demanded Jared, his expression fixed and intent.

Poye didn't seem to grasp the question. "Can you tell me where Clara is? And Professor Todelaw?"

Jared Hennemyer doubled down. "You should be worrying about your own skin."

Poye examined him in detail, with intense fascination, as if peering through a microscope. "Why are you wearing that uniform?" he asked. "Are you in the military?"

Jared darkened. "Answer me!" he barked, and his voice broke.

Poye continued to look him over. "I would really like to know where my friends are."

Jared relented a tad. "They are free. The state has no interest in them."

"Thank you," said Poye. "I'm so happy. When can I see them?"

Jared firmed his lips and reddened at Poye's failure to cower. Then he eased off and tried another tack. Stepping toward the bars, he lowered his voice and pleaded, in the manner of a struggling student seeking extra credit, "Professor Trubb, don't you see that if you hadn't taught evolution, you wouldn't be in this situation? It's not too late. If you recant, they will let you go. I'll see to it."

It didn't escape me that what Jared Hennemyer was actually saying was that he wanted credit for the resolution of a situation that had riveted, and distracted, the nation. Who knew to what heights his career might rocket if he could single-handedly wrap things up? It could open an entire universe of political possibilities for him.

Poye, grasping the bars, became serious. "This really is no way to treat your professor," he said.

Jared Hennemyer stepped back. "You're not my professor. Now answer me. Will you recant so we can put all this behind us?"

"Recant what?" asked Poye. "If I were a shoemaker would you want me to deny the existence of leather?"

I smiled, as this struck me as something Professor Todelaw might say.

"Don't try to confuse me," said Jared Hennemyer. "Your professor's tricks won't work with me. I am immune to logic."

Poye, his lips slightly parted, gazed at the young man.

At that moment another Star Nation foot soldier came through the door, a pale, middle-aged man, the pant cuffs of his uniform dragging under his heels. He was leading a Doberman pinscher on a chain. The animal snarled at the ether as it struggled against the leash. Jared Hennemyer regarded the sleek black animal and smiled. "This is Brillo," he said as he reached out to pat the Doberman on the head, but the dog snapped its jaws with an audible click as Jared snatched his hand away.

"Nice doggy," said Poye as he regarded Brillo. "Most people talk about the breeds of dogs as different species, but it's not true. They are varieties of the same species. That's what Professor Todelaw said. There's nothing preventing somebody from crossing a Great Dane with a Chihuahua. Of course, the difficulty there is that..."

"Shut up," said Jared Hennemyer in agitated disgust. "Brillo has a bad habit of barking through the night. No one has been able to cure him of this."

Poye drew a finger to his mouth in thought. "Perhaps it's not too late for obedience training," he suggested.

Joe Christiani shook his head. "You don't understand," he smiled. "We're going to chain Brillo right here outside your cell."

"I will be mindful of that," said Poye for lack of anything else to say, all the while keeping his eyes on the dog, which was elevated on hind legs as he struggled against the chain which the other man was holding onto with both hands.

Jared Hennemyer grasped his Frisbee pendant. "Do you see this?" he said, lifting the pendant toward Poye. "This is what you should be mindful of."

In a flash Brillo howled and broke free, seizing the pendant in his great jaws. With a shake of his head, he ripped it from Jared Hennemyer's neck and began to leap about the room. The three uniformed men engaged in a chaos of pursuit while Poye and I watched from our side of the bars. Jared finally got hold of the pendant and managed to retrieve it from the clamp of the canine's jaws. But Brillo only traded one object for another and sank his teeth into Joe Christiani's ankle, growling with mammalian vigor as Joe screamed, "I'm bit! He's got me!" In the instant, five more Star Nation foot soldiers flooded in, separated Brillo from Joe, and helped the limping, whimpering adjutant through the door.

Jared, sweating and disheveled, his pendant dripping with Brillo's saliva, turned one last time to Poye. "Now what do you have to say?" he demanded.

Poye was nonplussed. "Joe never had much luck with dogs."

"You had your chance. See you in court," said Jared as he turned and exited the room.

Thirty-One
Trial

I stood leaning against the bars of our cell, looking out into the nothingness, while Poye lay on his bunk, staring up at the ceiling, brooding. I considered how hard-wired he was to Darwin, yet he didn't seem to be bothered that the great naturalist had never dwelt on just how living things had first appeared on Earth. Strange for someone familiar with *The Origin of Species* chapter and verse. I had read the book as well. My mind fast-forwarded to its last paragraph, the only place Darwin refers to the origin of life in general, attributing it to a "Creator" who "[breathed life] into a few forms or into one." This made me wonder — with a twinkle in my eye — whether the Spong had tapped Darwin on the shoulder and asked for honorable mention. Failing this, the old boy never knew how close he was to the truth of the matter.

Truth or no truth, since his solitary confinement Poye had heard nothing from Clara or Professor Todelaw, and this made his heart ache. "It's killing me, Nest," he mourned. "This not knowing where she is. How she is." His love for Clara intensified the longer he was separated from her. Beyond this, he *needed* her. And so he continued to brood.

A sheriff's deputy came through the door. He unlocked the cell and addressed me. "You, out," he said, pulling me by an arm and clanging the door shut again. I looked back at Poye, who turned his head to me and made a brushing away gesture. "Go on, Nest," he said. "See if you can find Clara and Professor Todelaw." And so I left my friend and stepped out into light and freedom, only to be confronted with a dramatically changed scene.

The grounds around the Washington County Courthouse were now a circus. There were TV crews from all over. The advent of a late-winter thaw had made it easier for the curious to flood in from every Maine village, offshore island, and forest redoubt to witness the prosecution of a man who had been portrayed as a major anti-American and minor anti-Christ; a man who, it was rumored, bore an oval scar on his chest from where his erstwhile cross pendant had seared itself into his skin in protest of his errant, godless ways. Vendors had set up their stands and were hawking Bibles, crosses, and relics of the saints, as well as lemonade, hot dogs, lobster rolls, and fried dough. Awning-draped Winnebagos jammed the parking lots and the town green. Their inhabitants, beers in hand, were sitting like pashas in their great idle bulk in front of guttering fire pits, delighted to be part of the general mayhem. Children romped, old women jawed, and weathered men in ball caps and checked flannel lumberjack shirts held shooting practice in a litter-strewn lot not far from the courthouse.

Slinking among the masses was a tall, expansive, imposing woman in a print dress who glanced about warily with her knit shawl drawn tightly about herself. She repeatedly swept her windblown red hair from her face. As she made her furtive movements, men approached her with glints of recognition in their eyes. But she pushed them away, saying, "Not now" or "The flesh is willing, but...," as she focused on her mission. Following her at a small distance was a man in a Good Humor uniform. He was being hectored by a horde of children demanding ice cream and then growing hostile when he confessed to not having any at hand. The two coalesced in the thick of the crowd gathered before the courthouse. I caught up with them, and the three of us embraced in a tight huddle. "Oh, Nestor!" exclaimed Clara. "Where's Poye? Is he okay?"

"He's calmer than we are," I said. "All he thinks about is you."

Clara put a hand to her mouth, closed her eyes, and nodded.

"We'll never get in," lamented Professor Todelaw, recalling the task at hand.

Clara was resolute. "We'll get in," she said. "I always get in."

"Let's separate," I suggested. "I'll see if I can find a soft spot."

I headed off on my own, milling about and straining against the crowd. As I approached the front of the courthouse, the two massive oak doors swung open, and I was swept into the maw with a surge of anxious bodies. Once inside, I scrambled into a seat directly behind the defense counsel's table, where I would be able to hear everything. The room was overheated and stuffy, so the gathered spent much of their time fanning themselves with newspapers, advertising flyers, and cheap Japanese fans from the dollar store.

The prosecutor was the district attorney himself, Horace Bleening, a well-known figure who was famous for his courtroom antics and willingness to say anything he needed to say to win a case, not even offering to apologize later. He was thin, bald, red-faced, and stooped on long legs, giving him the appearance of a grasshopper. Mr. Bleening was also a devoted congregant of the Church of the Happy Clappers and an associate of Dud Wilmot. When people asked how he was doing, his inevitable, smiling reply was, "I've got joy in my heart. How about you?"

As Bleening shuffled his papers and acknowledged the approbation of well-wishers — many of whom ventured to slap him on the back, a gesture he particularly detested — Poye was led in and brought to the table of defense counsel. He went largely unnoticed, for he was the quintessential face in the crowd, the prototypical everyman. Many of the people who had been whipped up to the point of mania at the mention of his name had no idea what he actually looked like, and so there was no eruption at his appearance in court. Someone in the jail had found a blue sports jacket for him to throw over the disheveled clothes he had been wearing for days, but he was unshaven, and his hair was matted, making him look like he had spent a weekend sleeping off a bender.

I jumped to my feet. "Poye!" I called out, grabbing my friend by the arm. He turned around and broke into a bright smile. "Nest!" he said. And then, "Where's Clara?"

"She'll be here," I promised. "I saw her outside with Professor Todelaw. She'll be along presently." Poye seemed to take heart from my assurance.

In the meantime, every seat in the gallery was taken up by the curious. Ordinary, humdrum lives had been given meaning by the opportunity to be present at what was being touted as "the trial of the century." Rumor had it that Bass Drum Henker himself might show up, and whenever a door opened all heads craned in anticipation of the great leader's appearance. Off in a back corner sat Brother Eevin, Rate, Eulalie Wilmot, and of course Dud in his coveralls.

Poye was so nondescript that even his counsel didn't recognize him. Like Bleening, the attorney was absorbed by his papers. Blair Toothman was also well known to the people of Maine because of his frequent op-eds in the newspapers decrying his own profession. Whenever anyone uttered the word "justice" in his presence, his knee-jerk response was, "Justice? What justice? It's all bullshit." Poye glanced up at the man who looked like a sixteen-year-old boy, with a mop of strawberry blond hair awash across his brow and a curious "fed up" look on his freckled face. Completing the picture was a small red bowtie clipped askew under a lethal-looking Adam's apple. When he finally glanced at Poye, he remarked, "Who are you?"

"I think I'm the accused."

Toothman gave Poye the once-over before asking, "And what do you think we will accomplish today?"

Poye, alone and out of place in the crowded, noisy courtroom, said, "Not much?"

Toothman looked surprised at this response. "Then you're a genius," he said. "Because nothing ever gets done in court. It's all rigmarole. Take it from me."

Poye attempted a smile. "Do you think we will win?" he asked.

"Win?" echoed Toothman in disbelief at Poye's naiveté. "There are no wins. There is no justice. American jurisprudence, like the defense budget, is a jobs program. We are here to support vested interests, nothing else." And then, "What do you expect me to do for you?"

Poye looked sheepish. He shrugged. "Get me back to Clara?" he suggested.

This earnest response unmanned the attorney, if only briefly. "Well, we'll see what we can do." And then he recouped ground. "But don't expect me to go head-to-head with Horace Bleening," he said, wagging a finger. "He plays hardball."

Poye didn't respond to his attorney's comment. He glanced about self-consciously at the people who were now pointing at him and whispering. He looked uncomfortable, maybe because everyone was carrying a weapon as per the constitutional directive. Even Horace Bleening had a sidearm strapped to his pant leg. Every so often he reached down and patted it.

I found myself constantly looking around, willing Clara and Professor Todelaw to appear. My exertions finally bore fruit as Clara squeezed into the courtroom, pulling the professor by the arm. The two of them miraculously found a wide space in a bench seat, just behind me. A middle-aged man wearing a plaid sports coat came over and charged, "Hey, I was sitting there."

"You were," asserted Clara. "If you want to fight me for it, I'm ready."

The man begged off, and Clara began to strain for a glimpse of Poye. Then her eyes met mine. We clasped hands and touched foreheads. When she looked up, she caught sight of Poye sitting bent and alone at the defense table. "Look at him," she said. "He's all folded up. He does need me after all."

To Professor Todelaw this was self-evident. "He's always needed you.

Even before he knew you."

Clara sniffed and dabbed an eye. "You know," she said, "I think I'd make a good lawyer. I like a good fight."

When the judge walked in the courtroom fell silent. Judge Rinc Sample was a heavy, expansive man of about sixty. When he inclined his head at the right angle, the overhead light glinted from his bald, waxed pate in a blinding fashion. The lenses of his horn-rimmed glasses seemed impossibly thick and heavy. He kept pushing the glasses back up his nose, where they just did not want to sit. "We have here a violation of the law," he intoned in a high-pitched voice that seemed inappropriate to his great bulk. "The teaching of a theory of creation that suggests the development of humans from a lower order of animals and disregards faith-based accounts of the same." As he uttered these words, he kept his head down, his eyes roving over the documents in front of him. His manner was distracted and unsettled, as if he were looking for something of little importance, like a paper clip, that he nevertheless was determined to find. And then, by way of coda, he looked up, pushed his glasses back up the bridge of his nose and, staring out over the room, said, "This is very grave."

Clara tapped me on the back. "I wish he'd smile," she said. "He looks so sour."

"It's over," murmured Blair Toothman, loud enough for me to hear. "We might as well plead guilty."

Poye leaned toward the attorney's ear. "But shouldn't you defend me?"

Toothman turned and regarded Poye with utter astonishment. "Defend?" he laughed. "The judge himself already thinks you're guilty."

"Still..." peeped Poye.

Judge Sample sighed and said, "All right, then," as if it were still important to go through the motions. He indicated Horace Bleening with a thick finger. "Okay, counselor. Make your statement."

Horace Bleening sprang up and struck an orator's pose, clasping one lapel. "Ladies and gentlemen," he began as he swept an arm before the jury. "I can tell from the look of you that you have grave concerns for our beloved country. I want you to know that I share your consternation. I'd also like you to think — make a mental list — of all the things that you are dissatisfied with. Your job, your truck, your house, your children. Now be honest: is there a single one of those things that can't be laid to godlessness?" Here Horace Bleening held up a hand. "No need to shout out your answer. I know what it is. The answer is 'no.' Furthermore, this godlessness has a name: Evolution. Darwinism. *Poye*-ism. I intend to show that this man" — and here Horace Bleening swept his arm about and aimed an accusing finger at Poye — "is the flesh and blood embodiment of this toxic philosophy that would have our children believe that they arose from a mire of slime rather than having had their souls breathed into them by a higher intelligence. We have a law to protect us against such claptrap. Mr. Trubb broke this law, and I aim to prove it."

The jury turned toward Poye with a look of utter contempt while those seated in the gallery murmured their approval of the prosecutor's speech. Judge Sample gestured toward the defense. "Mr. Toothman, it's your turn."

Blair Toothman rocked his head from side to side and rose to his feet in a manner suggesting that it was a great effort to do so. "If I thought an opening statement would make any difference, I'd spout one. Let's get on with the trial." Then he dropped back into his seat. Poye looked at him and blinked.

"All right, then," said Judge Sample. "Mr. Bleening, bring your first witness."

Jared Hennemyer was called to the stand. I turned and whispered to Clara and Professor Todelaw, "He's the source of all the trouble. It all started with him."

Jared was wearing a crisply pressed Star Nation Campus Compact uniform, the gold cross on his armband blazing forth as testament to his allegiance. Jared looked bewildered by all that was happening around him and gave a start when the court officer approached to administer the oath. Jared placed his hand on the Bible that was presented to him and agreed to tell the truth. Then he was approached by Horace Bleening, who focused on Jared with great intensity. After getting Jared to identify himself, he asked, "Now, Mr. Hennemyer, what was it about Professor Trubb's class that discomfited you so?"

Jared stared at the attorney. He swallowed audibly and said, "Discomfited?"

Horace Bleening's gaze didn't waver. "Yes. Made you feel uncomfortable."

"Oh. Well, he said that we came from apes."

Poye leaned over to Blair Toothman, tugged on his sleeve, and whispered, "I didn't say that."

"It doesn't matter," said Toothman wearily.

Poye drew on some deep reserve of strength and assertiveness to utter, "Yes, it does. He's not telling the truth."

Blair Toothman made a low moaning sound and drummed his fingers on the table. In the meantime, Horace Bleening pressed on, springing up and down on his thin grasshopper legs, as if preparing to leap into the air. "And how did that make you feel when he said that humans came from apes?"

"Terrible," said Jared with a pout.

"And why did it make you feel terrible?"

"Because it's a lie. And it's also illegal."

Horace Bleening turned from his witness and faced the court. "Yes," he said, throwing out his hands as if pleading for alms. "It's illegal. And that's all we're concerned with today. The law. It's important not to forget this." Then he resumed his seat.

Judge Sample asked Blair Toothman if he wanted to cross-examine the witness. The attorney stood and gave his response: "And ask him what? I can't make him feel less terrible. Oh, what's the use!" Having said that, he collapsed back into his seat.

The parade continued. Rate, Brother Eevin, Eulalie and Dud Wilmot, in that order, took the witness stand and wove fantastic stories from new cloth about Poye's efforts to unravel the fabric of Christian civilization by dint of his teaching a minor course at a third-rate college in a Maine backwater infested with bear, moose, and somber, bearded men whose highest aspiration was to be left alone. Brother Eevin pointed out that Poye could not bring himself to acknowledge the hand of a higher intelligence in creation. When Dud Wilmot took the stand he resumed this thread, troubling himself to raise his eyes heavenward in supplication as he declaimed, "If there is no higher power up there, strike me dead." The entire courtroom looked up as if expecting a tongue of fire to lash down upon the cement king's head. But it didn't, and they took this as proof of the rightness and truth of Dud Wilmot's heartfelt conviction. Finally, as a finale to his armada of witnesses, Horace Bleening indicated a side door. There ensued a wave of laughter as a guard brought in a large, rocking chimpanzee by the hand and seated it on the witness stand, where it clapped and grimaced. "Given the fact that animals cannot speak," said the prosecutor to the bench, "it is logical to conclude that they cannot tell a lie. Therefore I beg the court to waive the oath for this witness."

Judge Sample already looked time-pressed as he repeatedly checked his watch. He rolled his eyes and waved a hand at the attorney, who strode to the witness stand. "This is Bingo," Horace Bleening said by way of introduction. And then, leaning with both hands on the bar in front of the stand, he addressed the primate. "Bingo," he said, "please point out your nearest relative in this room."

The chimp bobbed its head and clapped its hands, bearing its teeth in a mock comic manner. People in the gallery hung their heads and averted their eyes, fearful of being fingered by the ape and having their ancestry thrown into question. Mr. Bleening turned toward the defense table and put out a hand, inviting cross-examination, but Blair Toothman shook his head.

Poye tugged on his attorney's sleeve. "Can't you cross-examine this witness?" he suggested, but delicately.

The defense attorney threw Poye a pitying look. "You want me to talk to a monkey? What about my self-respect?" He turned to Horace Bleening. "No questions, of course."

"The witness is excused," said the prosecutor, who signaled to the guard to remove the chimp. "Let the record show that this witness was unable to identify any *Homo sapiens* as being related to it." With that, the gallery exploded in a roar of laughter, and relief.

I turned and looked at Professor Todelaw, who was grinding his teeth and making fists in his lap. "This is an outrage," he said. "I have to do something." He stared headlong at Clara, boring through her with eyes ignited by the passion of conviction. Then, turning, he struggled to his feet and made his way to the defense table. Judge Sample pounded his gavel. "It's all right, your honor," Professor Todelaw said. "This is a change of counsel at the request of the defendant."

Blair Toothman's mouth was agape. "You're excused," said the professor. "If you don't leave, I'll call someone who can make you leave." With this, he turned to Clara, who nodded her approval.

At this point, one would be entitled to ask what on earth the status of my vaunted Perspective was. Need I point out that the courtroom was a chaos of *anti*-Perspective? I was despondent. Everything I stood for was moot. Disinterested attorneys, harried judges, lying witnesses — and a chimpanzee! How could Perspective get a foothold, much less flourish, in such a place? And poor Poye. He seemed to have grown so small, so inconsequential. The only hope, then, for restoring anything resembling Perspective was Professor Todelaw. In the meantime, the servo was going crazy in my pocket. I hadn't checked in with the Spong in the longest time. They were no doubt wondering what was going on. The truth is, I didn't have the nerve to tell them, for fear of what they might do. Losing my job as Earth's final biographer had become the least of my worries. All I could think of now was Mars.

Back in the courtroom, Professor Todelaw had taken a seat at the defense table and was conferring with Poye. But then events took a turn. The chamber doors swung open, and there stood Bass Drum Henker, rail thin and stilt-like in a neatly-pressed navy blue suit and red tie, a shining, battery-powered gold cross blinking in his lapel, his grim-faced aide at his side holding the aluminum suitcase with its precious mechanical heart. The silence of the gallery upon seeing the head of state was so complete that the only audible sound was the whirring of the Tornado-3. Professor Todelaw looked the president over and remarked, to no one in particular, "This clearly prejudices the case against my client."

Henker walked into the courtroom, his aide in his wake, and took the seat vacated by Professor Todelaw — right next to Clara, who threw him an indignant look. "Good day," said the president curtly as he scissored in next to her. "How do you like your boy now?"

For her part, Clara looked betwixt and between, as if wondering whether she should use her wiles on the man or simply finish him off with her fists. She watched as he casually unbuttoned his jacket to reveal a revolver resting neatly in a shoulder holster.

"Continue," said the president, who leaned forward with anticipation.

Professor Todelaw's money changer ka-chinged as he stood. "I have one witness," he said. "Poye Trubb." The courtroom erupted in boos. The professor, undaunted, turned to his adoring protégé. "Go ahead, Poye, take the stand. This is your moment."

Poye rose, and the courtroom became a riot of catcalls. He was hectored all the way to the witness stand, where he was sworn in. When he recited, "So help me God," someone called out, "Not even God can help you now!"

Professor Todelaw, resplendent in his Good Humor uniform, moved to the front of the courtroom and fingered his money changer as he struck a relaxed pose with his thumbs hooked in his belt. "Now, Professor Trubb," he began, "just what is it that you taught Mr. Hennemyer and his classmates that got them all stirred up like this?"

Poye's expression was one of deep consideration. "I think they were upset about evolution."

"Is that so?" continued Professor Todelaw. "What exactly did you tell them about evolution?"

Horace Bleening sprang to his feet. "Objection," he said. "To describe evolutionary theory is to teach it. This is forbidden by law."

Professor Todelaw shook his head, feigning deep disappointment in the prosecutor. "Your Honor," he said, "Poye Trubb will be teaching nothing, as he is no longer a teacher. And, need I point out, this is not a classroom."

Judge Sample acquiesced and motioned for Professor Todelaw to continue. "Sorry for the interruption, Poye," said the professor. "Go on, now. Answer the question."

Poye blinked a few times and then, looking straight at the man to whom he owed so much, continued. "Evolution tells us that all living things are related and that, as the environment changes, they must also change."

Professor Todelaw nodded. "And what if they don't change?"

Poye's answer was immediate and matter-of-fact. "They die."

"That's it?"

"That's it."

"So you didn't break the law?"

"Not that I know."

Professor Todelaw turned toward the jury. "I see no injury here," he said. "The environment changes and creatures have to keep up with the changes or else they perish. If the grass dies and all the food is now in the trees, the short-necked giraffes starve, but the taller giraffes have a distinct advantage. When they breed, they have tall offspring. I don't see how anyone can deny this unless you believe that your children don't look like you." This sent a rumble of confusion through the gallery. Professor Todelaw let it simmer for a few moments. Then he gestured toward the prosecution before resuming his seat.

Horace Bleening had been listening with a condescending smile, pressing the eraser tip of a pencil against his temple. He eased himself to his feet and walked around to the front of his table, bobbing rhythmically on his grasshopper legs. "Tell me, Mr. Trubb, how did all these, er, creatures get here to start with?"

Poye rolled out his lower lip. "I don't know," he said.

"Do you think they just appeared like dew on the morning grass?"

"No."

"But you must have some idea."

"I'm sure it was some sort of process."

"And who started this process going?"

"I can't say."

"Isn't it logical to conclude that things don't appear from nowhere?"

Poye couldn't deny it. "Yes."

"So they must have come from somewhere."

"I suppose."

"But you refuse to acknowledge the most logical conclusion."

Poye stared at the man.

"Let me help you. The logical conclusion is that there is some higher intelligence that kicked things off. Isn't that the logical conclusion?"

Poye turned his gaze to Clara as if to say, "I'm sorry about all this."

Clara, for her part, was beset, grabbing my arm in her desperation. She had become a woman who, uncharacteristically, seemed utterly powerless. The conqueror of men was now at a loss. I knew that if she erupted, she could overturn the proceedings and do substantial bodily damage to anyone who tried to stop her, but how would that benefit Poye? All she could do now was sit there in her frustration, clutching my arm.

"I'm waiting for an answer," pressed Horace Bleening. The gallery leaned forward, and Judge Sample leaned down from the bench. As the walls closed in on Poye, he forced a smile of compliance. And then, measuring his words, he asked the prosecutor, "Are you suggesting that creation was the work of aliens?"

The servo in my pocket all but exploded. I had no choice, then. I carefully but firmly unknotted Clara's arm from mine and excused myself. Descending to the bathroom in the basement, I established my link.

I could feel the indignation ooze from the Spong like lava from a volcano — hot, intense, and inexorable. "Where have you been?" demanded Spong 1, which sentiment was echoed by the other Elders.

"Sorry," I apologized. "So much has happened here that I didn't know where to begin. A kind of approach-avoidance, I guess you could say."

"Status report," demanded Spong 2.

"Not so good," I said. "As anticipated, Poye is on trial. He's on the witness stand right now. They asked him who started the ball of life rolling on earth and he suggested — get this — that it might be aliens."

The demeanor of all four Elders of Spong changed in that instant. Their tentacles rose, and they seemed lighter, disburdened, their eyes brighter. "This is good," said Spong 1. "The truth has dawned on him. The missing piece. Now he, Rate, Brother Eevin, and Dud Wilmot are occupying the same realm of understanding. They are clearly Earth's superior minds and must be rewarded. They will be spared."

"Don't forget Clara."

The other three Spong turned to number 4. Spong 1 spoke up. "Clara is not relevant to Spong's plan."

Spong 4 was resolute. "Of course she is. You forget that a female is necessary for this species to propagate."

Spong 1 darkened. "Please don't try to force your will on the collective. It is not Spong."

There followed a few moments of uneasy silence, after which Spong 4 turned all eight of its eyes on the others. "If you do not include her I will kill myself."

This threw the Spong into tremendous disarray, not least because of the unprecedented use of the pronoun "I." I was riveted to the scene, not knowing which one to watch or what to say. All I desired was for the action to continue.

Spong 1 spoke. "Using suicide as coercion is unknown on Spong," it cautioned. And then it turned to me. "Is it not so on Earth?"

The only thing that came to mind was John Donne, and so I recited, "Every man's death diminishes me..."

"There is a first time for everything," said Spong 4, averting its eyes and disregarding my poetic citation.

"You embarrass Spong," said Spong 2.

"And you shame Spong," returned Spong 4. "All Spong asks is that Clara be included in the plan." Then it cast its eyes down. And it wept. Large, blue, gelatinous tears that oozed like honey from all eight of its eyes. "You see, I love her."

The other three Spong rolled all twenty-four of their eyes in synchrony.

"Wait, wait," I said, impatiently. "What's all this about a plan? Do I sense some sympathy for the humans that you otherwise consider an infection?"

"Spong has decided that the members of any species who can divine, or nearly divine, the truth of their own creation may have significant potential," said Spong 1. Then Spong 3 chimed in, "Mars had been similarly infected. They thought they were the be-all and end-all of existence and not a single one of them so much as considered the possibility of a superior intelligence. And so..."

I shrugged. "It seems to me that your track record for creating life is pretty poor. Shoddy and unpredictable."

"You're wrong," said Spong 2. "Spong has had many successes. The Acamar system, for example. Completely botanical. It has some wondrous plants, including a species that roams overland in search of alcohol."

"And don't forget the Gorgonea Tertia system," chimed in Spong 3.

"Oh, yes," said Spong 2. "A rousing success. One of the plants, the Gimma-Gimma, is truly wondrous. It releases an acid that permeates the atmosphere and prevents the evolution of animal life."

I recoiled. "What's so wondrous about that?"

"It has a delicious seed pod," said Spong 2. "It takes the dexterity of multiple tentacles to open it, but once one succeeds" — and here it placed the tip of a tentacle to its orifice and made a smacking sound — "Scrumptious. You should try it."

"Yeah, well, maybe another time. But let's get back to Earth. We have a courtroom drama playing out. I'm worried about Poye."

"Don't worry about him," said Spong 1. "It doesn't matter."

"What?" I said, incredulous. "After all this, you're telling me it doesn't matter?"

Spong 1 waved a tentacle at me in a calming gesture. "What we are saying is that the outcome of the trial doesn't matter. To use a metaphor, would you worry about your personal appearance if you were about to fall off a cliff?"

I relented. "How bad is it?"

All the Elders raised their tentacles in unison. "It's not bad at all," said Spong 2. "In fact, it's wonderful. We don't give many second chances."

"Second chances?" I echoed. If I didn't know better, I'd say the Spong tittered, or chuckled. "You'll see," they said.

"And what about me?" I begged, justifiably concerned for my own skin.

"You worry too much," said Spong 1, and with that, the connection was lost and the servo returned to rest.

Back in the courtroom, Horace Bleening was springing gently on his legs, as if marking time. Poye's comment had upended him. The erstwhile college professor had unintentionally pigeonholed the Intelligent Design camp into clarifying what it meant by "higher intelligence."

Professor Todelaw seized the moment and rose to his feet. "The witness has asked counsel a very good question. It would please defense to have an answer."

Horace Bleening seemed to sway. He licked his lips indecisively. But Bass Drum Henker pounced. He got up and strode to the bench, with his suitcase-toting aide hurrying to keep up. This rendered an incredulous Judge Sample dumb. He held his gavel aloft, his eyes wide. After all, this was the President of the Theocratic Union of American States. Henker turned to face the courtroom. His panic-faced aide clutched the suitcase to his chest. "This procedure is a mockery!" cried the president, who turned fiercely on Horace Bleening. "You oaf," he said. "The witness is not supposed to be examining you." At which Clara stood up, raised a fist, and chimed in, "It certainly is a mockery!"

For a moment Henker hung fire, not knowing whether this was ally or enemy. The Tornado-3 whirred apace as the aide stroked the suitcase to calm it. Finally, the president shouted, "Sit down, woman!" and brought his arm down in a chopping gesture, like an executioner pulling the release on a guillotine.

Poor Henker. He didn't know that Clara didn't like being commanded. She gazed about the courtroom and assessed the situation as she got back that old-time feeling of control. This was no different than being the queen of Briody's, where every eye was on her, where she was the toast of the room, the woman who could satisfy every man's desire. But now the only desire she acknowledged was her own. A rage welled up in her that took on its own identity and egged her on to dramatic action, as if an imp were saying, "Do it! Get rid of him, and people will thank you." Whatever force was controlling her, it brought her eyes to rest on a man sitting to her right. He was wearing a sidearm, which Clara, in an instant, seized.

She stood there, pointing the pistol indiscriminately forward as the gathered made a mad dash for cover. She looked at Poye, who was wearing a look of absolute love and longing. He had become liquid, his desire flowing out from him and toward the object of his irrepressible affection. Clara returned her gaze to Bass Drum Henker, who threw her a condescending smile. He allowed his jacket to swing open, putting his own sidearm in plain view.

The president stood there, legs apart, hands plied out before him, limp at the wrists like the loaded paws of a large predator. The room was now silent, the only ambient sound the whirring of the Tornado-3, the suitcase once again resting on the floor, Henker's aide having taken shelter behind the judge's bench.

"I've heard terrible things about you," said Clara.

Henker huffed. "Oh? What have you heard?"

Clara didn't mince words. She ground them out in a measured fashion. "That you're a heartless bully."

Henker smiled. Cool. Calm. Collected. He pursed his thin, dry lips. "Prove it."

Waiting...waiting...and then —

Pow! A slug in the chest. Clara stood there, holding the smoking pistol.

"Ha!" triumphed Henker as he staggered. "No heart!" Then he reached for his own weapon.

Clara recalculated. Before Henker could draw she pivoted and discharged one lovely shot into the suitcase. The Tornado-3 wound down in a pathetic manner, like an old-time Victrola, and Henker collapsed to the floor, where he reposed in a twisted heap. His face, relieved of its ugly mask of hatred, was now composed and clarified in death.

Perspective had, at last, rallied and triumphed. The anti-Poye hysteria had been a viper from which Clara had removed the venom. In the process, she had also won the unanimous approbation of the Spong.

Thirty-Two
Mars

An umbrella of light — not unfamiliar — swept down from the heavens and, almost lovingly, scooped up Poye, Clara, Professor Todelaw, Dud Wilmot, Brother Eevin, Rate and me. Poor Eulalie had apparently not made the cut. We found ourselves lying side by side, like babes in a nursery, afforded a comfort, peace, and security that rendered us mute. There was a sense of movement and direction. I ventured to reach out to feel for the boundary of whatever it was that contained us, but I touched nothing. Poye lay to Clara's right, Professor Todelaw to her left. All of us were staring up into an endless whiteness. It was Clara who broke the silence when she asked, "Where are we?" To which Poye replied, "I don't know." And on we sailed.

We had, in truth, been removed from one Perspective and placed into another. And just in the nick of time. I guess I can tell you now that the Spong, those master galactic gardeners who had seeded Eden so long ago, had said, in effect, "Damn, we've got humans." And then they applied their Treatment. In other words, they sprayed.

But they showed that they were not incapable of some modicum of mercy toward promising animal species. The Happy Clappers among us had not conceived of Spong, but they had acknowledged Intelligent Design. And Poye, belatedly, had proven himself malleable on the subject. All of this was close enough. Now it was only a baby step to the real truth of human inception.

When our motion stopped, I found myself standing alone, in twilight, separated from the others. I took out the servo, concentrated on it, and watched it do its little Watusi. The Spong appeared. "This will be our last communication with you," they said in unison.

Casting my eyes upon the Spong, I asked the question that had to be asked. "What will become of me?"

I wouldn't have thought them capable of it, but Spong 1 bent its orifice into the arc of what looked like a smile. "You understand Spong. We are counting on you to enlighten the others."

And then, Spong 2: "We've decided to give Mars another chance. Spong chemists have completed the re-seeding. We'll take care of Earth and the long de-toxification process there, but someone else has to tend the Martian garden. Any species that can come so close to knowing the truth of Spong is certainly capable of hoeing Martian soil."

"So this is it."

"Join them."

I handed over all my notes, like an offering. The Spong accepted them with gratitude. Then there was a snapping sound, followed by a sharp, resonant ping, like a bullet ricocheting off a rock. I watched as the Spong evaporated into whatever it was they evaporated into. I had the strongest impulse to call out, *"Spong! Come back!"*

That was my last thought as I relinquished contact with my Spong overseers and my commission as Earth's final biographer. I felt a sort of shift, or shove, and found myself standing in red sand, in a red landscape, in a cup-shaped bowl, or crater, ringed with red mountains. Overhead, a butterscotch sky with dusty wisps of red. And then, gazing straight ahead, I saw them — Poye, Clara and the others, huddled in a grotto, where water was flowing in a narrow, curling rivulet. I went over to them. We all sat in a circle while I related my experience as Earth's final biographer, my knowledge of the Spong, and where we all fit in. The information seemed to mesmerize them. Poye spoke up. "How long were you taking notes about me?"

"Since shortly after you met Clara," I said. "One of us had to be the biographer. I was just following orders."

Poye nodded and smiled.

"This was not what we had in mind," said Brother Eevin.

Rate chimed in. "What are we supposed to do now?"

"Look at the bright side," volunteered Professor Todelaw. "You were absolutely correct about Intelligent Design."

"And I was wrong," said Poye, at which Clara drew close to him and enlaced her arm in his.

"Not wrong," said Professor Todelaw. "Just unaware. How could you have perceived such a thing?"

"We did," said Brother Eevin, raising a finger.

"Yeah," brooded Dud Wilmot. "And look where it got us."

"Hey, hey," I admonished. "Buck up. We're the survivors. The select. And we've been given a world."

"I don't see why we couldn't have stayed on Earth," said Dud, grinding his teeth.

"Because," I said, perhaps a bit too glibly, "the detoxification will take time. Then the Spong will return it to what it was meant to be. As one of the Happy Clappers, you should know this. You called it Eden. But without Adam and Eve."

Rate, Brother Eevin, and Professor Todelaw nodded their understanding.

Poye, Clara and I got up and slipped away while Professor Todelaw remained behind to comfort the others and assist them in making the most of the hand they had been dealt. As we walked, Poye voiced his thoughts to Clara. "I spent years living in fear of losing you to some worthier man. That fear has now vanished."

I continued to accompany them as they walked hand-in-hand in the new world. "I'm surprised to find air on Mars," said Poye.

"The Spong have provided everything," I said. "I think we will do well here," I added, trying to put a bright gloss on our situation.

"I'm the only woman," said Clara. She stopped and peered into Poye's eyes. "You know what that means," she said, "if we're going to survive as humans."

"Yes."

Clara reached out and brushed the hair from his forehead. "So nothing has really changed," she said. "You put up with it for five years, but you stayed."

"Yes," Poye said again.

The air just ahead of us blurred and wavered, as if becoming liquid. All three of us stared and waited. Finally, it appeared. Bigger than a man, with eight tentacles, each bearing an eyeball, and a curious orifice in what appeared to be its forehead. Poye and Clara were not afraid. In fact, Poye was seized with intense curiosity, while Clara threw out her bosom and flung her red tresses back in a seductive manner as if challenging the entity to confront human womanhood in all its glory.

"I am Spong," it announced as it raised its tentacles, its eyeballs alight.

"Tell me about love."

Clara smiled. "You're in luck."

I excused myself and headed back to see how the others were doing. Poye caught up with me, and I realized that he knew, instinctively, that when Clara was done, she would return to him. As always.

END

ABOUT THE AUTHOR

Robert Klose teaches at the University of Maine at Augusta. He is a regular contributor of essays to *The Christian Science Monitor*. His books have won a 2016 Ben Franklin Literary Award and a USA BookNews Award.

NOTE FROM THE AUTHOR

Word-of-mouth is crucial for any author to succeed. If you enjoyed the book, please leave a review online—anywhere you are able. Even if it's just a sentence or two. It would make all the difference and would be very much appreciated.

Thanks!
Robert

Thank you so much for reading one of our **Sci-Fi** novels.

If you enjoyed our book, please check out our recommended title for your next great read!

Culture-Z by Karl Andrew Marszalowicz

In the year 2190, mankind has made great strides forward in the worlds of technology, science, and greed. However, when all three get together one last time, this oblivious generation may not exist much longer.

View other Black Rose Writing titles at www.blackrosewriting.com/books and use promo code **PRINT** to receive a **20% discount** when purchasing.

Made in the USA
Middletown, DE
08 February 2021

33384579R00113